APOCALYPSE WEIRD

C.D. WATSON

Bone Diggers Press
www.bonediggerspress.com

First edition © 2020 C.D. Watson. All Rights Reserved.

Cover design © Bayou Cover Designs.

Published by Bone Diggers Press, Clayton, Georgia.

ISBN 978-1-943465-56-9

TABLE OF CONTENTS

Introduction

In late 2019, the virus now known as COVID-19 (for short) was wreaking havoc in Wuhan, China.

By the end of March 2020, the world was in a panic.

It sounds like the start of an apocalypse, doesn't it? And in a way, it is. Life in the United States came to a screeching halt. People voluntarily sheltered in their homes, then were forced to by government mandated stay-at-home orders. Millions of people lost their jobs as whole segments of what had, just a few days before, been a thriving economy collapsed. Rumors ran wild on the internet, particularly on social media, and mass hysteria gripped the nation as news outlets reported the daily rise in case numbers and deaths.

Now, some six months or so after the March lockdowns began, the populace has been placed under mask mandates; forced to remain socially distant from their neighbors and folks on the street, sometimes on threat of state violence via law enforcement personnel; and otherwise sunk into a bizarre, proto-Orwellian world in which our cellphones track our movements for contact tracing research.

For me, the moment when it became apparent that society had reached the point of no return for top-down social control was when I saw a large sign reading, "Mask up. Life is waiting."

Six months after the lockdowns began, we now live in a world in which people are shamed and, occasionally, ridiculed for not wearing a mask in public. Masking is now a form of virtue signaling, right up there with simpering platitudes spouted by those living in the self-righteous moral vacuum of the politically regressive, on both sides of the aisle.

I never intended to compile a collection of apocalyptic and post-apocalyptic short stories, but in the face of this sudden and pervasive shift in our culture, how could I not?

These stories are not, however, intended as a commentary on the way we've reacted, in part and in whole, to the COVID-19 pandemic. I have done that elsewhere.

They are instead a reminder that life goes on. Perhaps not life as we knew it. Perhaps not even a life we would enjoy. But life, in some form, persists.

This is what life does.

The stories collected herein are an eclectic bunch if ever there was one, ranging the gamut from serious to slightly comedic, and from plausible scenarios to completely improbable ones.

Most are centered on survival in one form or another, from the more traditional post-apocalyptic survival fiction found in "The Moments Ending in Day" to the surreal form of survival achieved in "The Infinite Bright."

The former is a post-apocalyptic road trip taken by a mother and her son, narrated from his perspective. It's one of the longer stories in this collection. There are zombies, but not exactly as we know them from television and film. You just can't have a good apocalypse collection without one zombie story.

The latter is a thought experiment that I shan't elaborate on as I don't want to spoil the surprise. Read it. You'll like it, and perhaps it will inspire reflection on the exact nature of reality.

Other stories are drawn from different inspirations. "Silver Birds," like "The Infinite Bright," involves airplanes. As I spent quite a bit of time watching airplanes take off and land while writing the stories contained herein, that's only natural.

"The Wandering Man" was written in one evening while doing exactly that. The idea came to me while I was heading south from my home in the mountains of North Carolina to the Greenville-Spartanburg (South Carolina) International Airport to sneak in some plane spotting. When I got there, I sat in the seat of my vehicle and fleshed the idea out into a story. In it, a cowboy-esque sorcerer travels the desert searching for a girl spoken of in a prophecy. There are hellholes and demons and hints of an army of skeletal soldiers.

Like I said: Some of the stories are improbable. That shouldn't detract from your enjoyment.

On the other end of the spectrum is "Love in a Winter Garden," which does, indeed, have a love story or two (or more, depending on how you count them), but not exactly the kind you think of when you hear the phrase "love story." It's set a few generations after a nuclear holocaust, when humanity is on the brink of extinction. While I did take some liberties with the setting and background, much of it is based on the actual science of what would happen to the environment after a full-on nuclear war.

Along those lines, "The Kinder, More Gentle End of the World as We Know It" is set just after the Chinese detonate nuclear weapons above the US. The resulting high-altitude explosions create electromagnetic pulses which wiped out the US's electrical grid. That just sets the stage. The story itself is an exploration of what we value most.

The final two stories are, like many of the others, stories about family, motherhood in particular. In "Good Eats," a mother faces the challenge of feeding herself and her child after most of the plant life is wiped out. That was an interesting story to write and the first in this collection to be conceived.

"Under Our Skin" is set in a very different story world, though it still takes place on Earth. Extraterrestrials released spores into the upper atmosphere, which infected humans, changing them into a creature the narrator struggles to understand on multiple levels.

Two women, two tales of motherhood, told from the perspective of those trying to make the best of a world they don't quite recognize. These are stories of hope, even "Good Eats." Life persists, not just persists, but thrives, and with it, the hope that's moved humankind from the savannahs to cities to outer space.

If anything defines *Apocalypse Weird*, it's that.

The Moments Ending in Day

The Camry's tires hummed against the asphalt. Dad's car, about the only thing left of him but ash. Momma did it, three weeks ago when he got too bad to handle. Too sick. It was a mercy, she said, taking care of him like that. No lingering, no suffering, not like with the cancer, where a body's dying bled the life out of the rest of the family, too.

He would've wanted it that way, she said, quick and painless. I think mostly *she* wanted it that way. It was easier to take the pain yourself than watch somebody you loved suffer. She would've never said it, though, especially not like that. Her way of protecting me, I guess. Her way of apologizing for what she done to him.

We drove through Rosman near sunrise, skirting around the barricades and warning signs and the burned-out husks of tanks, and took Highway 178 south. That'd been on the radio, when the National Guard abandoned the last few holdouts in the mountains. We were two days behind them, maybe three, headed toward the coast, toward Charleston and the hope of refuge, of a cure.

Well, Momma hoped for a cure. For my sake, she said, like her life didn't mean nothing.

Where would I be without Momma? Trapped in Asheville with the trust-fund crazies, maybe took sick like Daddy?

She pulled her sweater sleeve down over her hand and coughed against it, turning her face into the window. It was a dry cough, like something was tickling her throat. Not the precursor of the sickness, of *it*, the thing that'd taken Daddy, taken him, chewed him up, swallowed him down. Consumed him. Consumption.

Come to think on it, that's what they should've called the plague instead of just, you know, *the plague*. Only consumption was already taken, and it'd hit so hard, so furious and fast, scientists didn't know what to do, let alone did they have time to search for a more creative name.

I was pretty sure consumption was already taken anyhow, if my dimming memory of eighth grade history was right. It wouldn't be a good name anyhow, 'cause the plague didn't just consume a body. It spit 'em back out again, vomiting life back into them, or a sort of life.

Momma coughed again, that wheezing cough.

I took my eyes off the road long enough to sneak a peek at her. "You ok, Momma?"

"I'm fine, baby."

"You're all hunched up over there. Need me to cut on the heater?"

A ghost of a smile touched her lips. She closed her eyes and leaned her head against the window. "Boy," she said. "That's like asking a furnace if it needs more coal. It's going on ninety outside and the cock just crowed."

"Well, you look like you're freezing."

"I'm fine, baby."

"You saying you're fine don't make it so," I muttered, only I hoped my muttering was low enough to miss her hearing.

"Baby."

My shoulders tensed. She was gonna light into me, I just knew it. Me and my smart mouth. What was I thinking, testing her like that?

"You remember that time we went to the Outer Banks?" she said.

"When I was, what, about eight?"

"About that. Just me and you, humming along I-40, about like now only a different road. You remember that?"

I did, so well. The memory was a magical interlude in my head, a bright, shining moment captured in technicolor laughter. Momma in the front seat, her arms bare to the sun, her red hair shining like a halo. Me in the back, strapped into the booster seat I hadn't quite outgrown. Music playing on the radio.

I cocked my head, searching through memory, and finally caught the tune. The electronic riff of guitar and bass, the bluesy grit of a master overlaying it all.

Yeah, that was a good time, just me and her and Hendrix.

"I remember," I said.

"Your daddy had to work."

I remembered that, too, but all I said was, "Yeah."

Somebody honked, way back, and a skunk skittered across the road, and down that narrow strip we went for what seemed like an age and a half before she spoke again.

"He wanted to come, though." She lifted her sweater-covered hand to her mouth again, coughed, and curled her hand around the bright red spots staining the cloth. "He wanted to come real bad."

My hands tightened on the steering wheel until my knuckles were nearly white. Blood wasn't a good sign, not a good sign at all. We'd heard rumors of a vaccine back at the last rest stop, a vaccine and maybe that cure Momma was so anxious about, if we could just get to a doctor. But where was the nearest one? Were they all down south along the coast now, or were any still floating around up here, hoping to help the refugees?

"He was worried about us being on the road alone," she said, startling me out of my thinking. "Said we should stick to the interstate as much as we could and not talk to strangers and such. Can you imagine, not talking to strangers on a vacation?"

I said as how I couldn't, seeing as how that was half the point of going somewhere, so you could talk to somebody you ain't seen ever dadgum day your whole life through, and she laughed and laughed. The radio sputtered out a burst of static, then a song came through loud and clear, courtesy of somebody holed up most likely. Me and her shared a grin, and off in the distance, the sun finally popped all the way up over the mountaintops.

I WAS the slowest driver. We passed into South Carolina going a steady thirty-five, pulling over to let faster cars pass and so Momma could stretch her bones. Made it to Pickens around lunchtime and stopped again just past the barricades, on a stretch of road with enough room to pull over, but nowhere near town and the folks patrolling the streets with rifles at the ready.

Daddy would've been mad at us for taking the smaller roads, if he'd been here to say it. Not backroads, exactly, but not the interstate either. We could've taken a straight shot from Asheville to Charleston down I-26, only the interstate was so crowded and Momma was worried we'd never get nowhere. These roads were still crowded, mind you, but nothing like the bigger ones to the east.

Long as we were careful, you know? Long as we kept an eye out for scoundrels and scavengers.

And the plague ridden. Them, too.

But those weren't the worst of it. Oh, no. The fires burning had nothing to do with the plague victims. They were slow, at least at first while their brains or nerves or whatever mutated from sickly human to living corpse, slow and easy to pick off, if you got to 'em quick enough.

No, the fires didn't burn because of them. The plague had spread beyond humans. That's where the danger was.

I shuddered and shoved that thought right out of my head. That's what Daddy's shotgun was for. I unsheathed it from the holster Momma had jerry-rigged to the back of the center console, checked to make sure it was loaded, just to be on the safe side, then I slid out of the Camry into the muggy South Carolina heat.

Momma got out, too, a little slower, and groaned as her joints popped.

I grinned at her across the hood. "Old woman."

She sniffed, but the corners of her mouth twitched into a half smile. "I'll show you what an old woman I am when I chase you down with a hickory for sassing me."

I snorted out a laugh. Momma had never raised a hand to me. Didn't see her doing it now.

A couple of trucks passed us, slowing to gawk maybe. Folks were more careful of each other now, more watchful. Most still tried to help where they could. This was still the South. People still tried to be kind and help their neighbors, even if their neighbors were total strangers riding in a vehicle alongside you.

Momma put her hands to the small of her back and leaned backward, stretching, and I scanned our surroundings, searching for trouble. We couldn't take long. Travel was slow anyhow. The less time we spent on the road, the quicker we'd get where we were going, the sooner Momma could visit a doctor.

A car passed us, and another, then a familiar engine throbbed as the driver downshifted and a faded red dually pulled in behind us and stopped.

Momma looked at me across the Camry's roof and her mouth twitched into another faint smile. "Red Vern."

I shrugged. "Maybe he's got a crush on you."

I think she might've laughed if times had been different. Maybe if Daddy hadn't took sick like he done, she would've thought my teasing was funny. Lord knew we could use a laugh.

Vern cut the engine off and slid out of the truck followed by three young'uns, all toting guns. Mia, the oldest, was a year younger than me. She had hair the color of sourwood honey braided down her narrow back and eyes the same color as an October sky.

She could also knock a running squirrel off a tree branch from forty feet away with the revolver tucked into a holster slung low around her hips. The first time I met her, at a makeshift campsite outside Asheville, she whipped it out and pointed it straight between the eyes of a boy who was getting a mite too fresh with her. Her own eyes had been flat and empty as I'd ever seen, more like ice than a cloudless sky. I was dead certain she would've shot that guy if Red Vern hadn't said, real quiet, "Mia."

Quick as a flash, she'd swung the revolver, pointing it over the boy's shoulder, and squeezed the trigger. Before the report's echo faded, there was a crash of branches and a light thump. I never knew squirrel made such good eating, and we never saw hide nor tail of that boy again.

Vern's youngest two were ten-year-old twins, Dylan and Daisy, each carrying a twenty-two rifle. They weren't as good a shot as Mia, but they were pretty darn close.

The twins were spitting images of Mia. Nobody ever said what happened to their momma, or even if Red Vern was their daddy or uncle or grandfather or what. They sure didn't look nothing like him. Nobody asked questions like that anymore. It was enough that he hadn't left them to fend for themselves, and he sure never raised a finger to hurt any of them.

Red Vern glanced around as he ambled toward us, scanning our surroundings, looking for trouble the same way we had, only with the same flat-eyed gaze Mia used. He was rangy and lean and sun browned, like he spent his days outside working. A farmer, maybe, if farmers looked like they could single-handedly take down an enclave of cave-dwelling terrorists armed to the teeth with more weapons than sense.

He jerked his chin at Momma. "Y'all ok?"

Momma's smile widened and she leaned against the Camry's door, already worn out from the stop. "Sure, Vern. Just stretching our legs."

"Don't stretch 'em too long, Bella. Smoke's on the wind."

And where there was smoke, there was a fire. I bit back a curse and spat it onto the graveled verge. How'd I missed the stench of burning varmints?

Mia came to a stop beside Momma and touched her fingers to Momma's elbow. "I could use a bathroom buddy," she said, real soft, and Momma nodded and turned and walked to the tree line with her.

Soon as they were out of earshot, Red Vern adjusted his hat, a battered red baseball cap emblazoned with the logo of a regional farmer's supply chain store. Momma had taken one look at that cap and dubbed him Red Vern, and no matter how much I hated nicknames, the name stuck.

"You two shouldn't wander off like that," he said.

Irritation surged through me and I gritted my teeth. Nothing like a well-meaning adult to knock a teenager down a peg. "She needed to stop."

"Next time, wait until we can cover you before getting out of the car."

What if you're not there? I wanted to ask, but I wasn't a fool.

Safety in numbers. That became clear about an hour into the plague when the news reports started streaming videos of plague victims and, not much later, the varmints.

And I was still just a kid. I wanted to protect Momma all on my own. If I'd been near the shot Mia was, or even the twins, I would've put up a fuss. But I wasn't a great shot, even with a shotgun, and Momma was still shy enough that she didn't like peeing with me nearby.

So I swallowed down my irritation and said, "Yes, sir."

Red Vern's eyes gleamed for a minute and he almost smiled. Then the women folk appeared on the edge of the woods and his expression flattened. "Y'all follow us. Keep close."

I looked to Momma, and she arched the fine lines of her eyebrows, still a strong strawberry blonde, though gray shot through her red hair.

"Vern wants us to follow him," I said.

Her gaze shifted between me and him, and after a minute, she nodded. "Mighty kind of you, Vern."

He nodded, adjusted that faded red cap. "Mia's got a good hand behind the wheel, if you need a break."

"I got it," I said, a little harsher than I'd intended, but dang it all, a feller could only stand so much. Sure, I was only fourteen, but this was our car and my Momma and I needed to do something. I wasn't helpless, even if my nose wasn't as sharp as Vern's and I fumbled with the shotgun from time to time.

I hadn't been born with a gun in my hand like Mia and the twins. Fact was, outside of shooting bb guns at scout camp, the first time I laid a hand on a real gun was the day Daddy took sick and Momma decided it was time to hightail it out of the city.

Momma arched her eyebrows at me, shaming me, and I muttered, "I really got it, Momma," and slid into the driver's seat.

I didn't have to see her shaking her head to know she was doing it. "Thank you, Vern. If you don't mind stopping in about an hour so we can eat and stretch the kinks out, I'd appreciate it."

Red Vern's murmured response was too low for me to hear, but since Momma got in the car and asked me to wait for him to lead, I figured it out.

Maybe it wasn't so much that he had a crush on Momma as that he recognized fellow human beings in need.

Momma strapped on her seatbelt. I cranked the Camry, draped both hands on top of the steering wheel, and craned my neck around, watching for Red Vern to pull out.

"Did I ever tell you about the day I met your daddy?" she said of a sudden.

Red Vern honked as the dually pulled onto the highway and passed us. I turned on my blinker out of habit and eased off the shoulder onto the highway behind him, then said, "No, ma'am."

"It was a day like this. Hot and muggy, big fluffy clouds in the sky."

"Cumulonimbus," I said as some fifth-grade memory lurched into the forefront of my brain.

"Them, yes." She settled into her seat and closed her eyes. "He wasn't the most handsome man, but he had the sweetest way about him. Charmed me right out of a dance at the county fair."

"Is that so?"

"Yes, it was. He was mighty prideful, too, right up to the end."

She fell silent, and my hands tightened on the steering wheel. In the end, Daddy hadn't been my father no more, and he sure hadn't been the charming man Momma met on a sunny autumn day nearly twenty years back.

MOMMA fell asleep not ten minutes out. Worn out from the pit stop, I reckoned. Red Vern pulled over around supper time, while the sun was still strong in the sky, and we took turns eating. Me and Mia were on the first watch together while the rest hunkered down on a worn blanket in the sparse shade thrown by the dually. No talking, just a lot of watching the shadows from our perches on the roofs of the vehicles.

Had to be careful not to touch bare skin to the metal, though. The sun had heated it to a nice crisp by that time. Heat waves rolled so strong off the roofs, you could see them rising into the air. By the time Red Vern and the twins took the watch, sweat dripped off my face into my t-shirt and Mia's skin was pink and glistening.

Me and her ate, then we divided up and took group bathroom breaks near the trees lining the road, women first, then us men, and we were off again, a pitifully small caravan.

The rest of the day went just like that. Drive for a bit, stop and stretch, maybe eat a bite, then back on the road. We passed half a dozen smoldering fires at least, one a military Humvee. National Guard, probably.

Once, from a distance, I saw a pack of varmints tear into something. We'd passed through Anderson by then and seen all kinds of folks, normal and plague bound and everything in between. Folks looting and rioting, throwing burning bottles at varmints and each other. Piles of bodies smoldering. Not varmints neither.

Hadn't made no never mind to Red Vern then, but not long after I spotted them varmints, the dually slowed down and Mia crawled out of her window and sat on the door with her fingers gripping the roof, balancing half in and half out of the dually.

I pulled up beside them, rolled down my own window, and matched Red Vern's speed. "What's up?"

"Pops says to keep going," she hollered. "If they follow us, keep your windows up and let me and the twins pick 'em off."

I gave her a thumbs up, rolled the window up, and wished the Camry's aging air conditioner was an even match for the day's heat.

Momma slept most of the time, but every once in a while, she'd rouse long enough to talk.

"I ever tell you about that time your MawMaw caught a squirrel in the woodpile? Wrung its neck with her bare hands. Not before it bit her though. Lucky she didn't get rabies."

Then another time, "Your hair was as red as mine the day you were born. Fell out when you were, oh, six months, I reckon. Grew back in so thick and black, your daddy said we must've had a grizzly bear hiding in the family tree."

And just as the sun slipped behind the horizon, "Your daddy loved crossword puzzles. Every Sunday with the one in *The New York Times*, before I could even read the front page. Used to make me so mad." She coughed hard into her sleeve, then added, real quiet, "I sure do miss that."

Not long after, we passed a sign for Greenwood. Red Vern pulled off the road into the empty parking lot of a strip mall, a long, single building made of bland brick with a metal roof. Five stores, one with busted out windows, the other four boarded up. Somebody had scrawled red paint over the plywood, proclaiming the end of days.

We gathered there, the six of us, while the engines popped and hissed in the cooling air. Red Vern and Mia exchanged a glance, then she nodded real solemn like, jogged back to the dually, and vaulted herself up and over the tailgate. Back she came holding a tire iron, chiseled end out. Red Vern took it and popped the boards away from the door of the hair salon, cracked the lock open, and ducked inside.

I turned around and kept my eyes on the roadside, watching for what, I didn't know. Didn't want to think about it too close. Mia did the same, leaving Momma and the twins to watch for Red Vern. A gunshot sounded inside. My heart jumped into my throat, and we all whipped around, right as another shot rang out.

"Oh, no," Momma said.

I swallowed down my heart and the automatic burst of fear. This was no time to be afraid. "Better go help him."

Mia put her hand out, stopping just shy of touching me. "No, he'll call out if he needs us."

"What if he's hurt?" I said, but just then, the salon's door swung open and Red Vern strode out.

"Beg pardon, Bella," he said. "Mia, stand guard. Ian, you're with me."

I glanced at Momma, waited until she nodded an ok, then let the shotgun dangle at my side and followed Red Vern inside.

The salon was cool and dry after the day's muggy heat, and smelled faintly of perfume and chemicals. It was open from front to back, with a seating area to the left, just inside the door. To the right sat a desk with an appointment book spread across the top next to a landline telephone. Beyond that, styling stations lined the side walls, with a big open space down the middle leading toward an open door built dead center into the back wall.

Red Vern's boot heels rang against the sparkly white linoleum as he walked down the middle of the salon. "Got two in the back. Help me drag 'em outside, then we can let the rest in. Mia can help clean up the mess while your momma and the twins start unloading."

I wasn't sure whether to be thrilled that he'd found a place for us to hunker down that night, or sick to my stomach at the thought of what he wanted me to do. I'd only ever seen the one plague victim up close. Never even been to a funeral, in the beginning, when those were still a thing. Momma never would let me, and she sure hadn't let me clean up after that one plague victim.

Seeing as how it was my own daddy, I was grateful.

My throat dried out as we neared the back, and I swallowed. Red Vern opened the door in the back wall, and another smell drifted out, something like a cross between raw hamburger meat and rotted animal. The sickly sweet chemical scent from the main part of the salon only made it worse. My innards started a slow roll in my midsection and saliva coated the inside of my mouth.

Please, God. Don't let me puke.

Red Vern led me into a small room. As soon as I got inside, my gaze landed on the two bodies huddled together on the floor, a woman and a little boy who was maybe six years old, each with a raw hole in the center of their forehead. The boy had chunks of flesh torn out of his neck and arms and legs. I was willing to bet if I raised his shirt, he'd be missing some of his torso, too.

Bile shot up my throat into my mouth, and I bent over, hands to knees, and retched. He was wearing a striped shirt, white with thin blue lines. I had one just like it at home, only bigger. Momma got it at The Gap. Not my style, but she'd bought it, so I wore it.

And so had that little boy.

My eyes started watering, from trying not to puke or what, I didn't know, and I wasn't too keen on figuring it out. I forced myself upright, caught Red Vern's gaze on me, and managed to choke out, "Get the door," without emptying my stomach onto the floor, to mix there with that boy's blood.

Red Vern didn't say a word, just stepped over the bodies and opened the door. A warm wind eddied inside, clearing out some of the stink. I was afraid of taking a deep breath. My stomach was still churning and I knew I was close to throwing up, but I was grateful for the relief anyhow.

Red Vern slapped a pair of yellow cleaning gloves in my hands and I pulled them on, snapping the rubber into place around my wrists. We dragged the bodies out, the momma first, then the boy. Their skin was like plastic through the gloves. I tried not to think about it. I tried real hard not to, just drifted into that empty place in my head that I'd found after Daddy died and the reality of how much the world had changed sank in.

After, Red Vern showed me to the bathroom and told me to wash up. He shut the door when he left, and my stomach gave out. I sank down on my knees in front of the open toilet as puke spewed from my gullet up my throat and out my mouth and nose, stinging my insides raw. I retched and heaved and cried, though I hadn't meant to, but by golly, when you're down on your knees in front of the porcelain throne puking your guts out, the tears are gonna roll.

Seemed like I was down there forever, spilling everything inside of me into that toilet. Finally, my stomach stopped cramping and bile stopped shooting up my throat. I spat the last of it into the toilet through the snot dripping down my upper lip. Grabbed a wad of toilet paper and cleaned my face, blew my nose. Wiped sick off the gloves and tugged them off, then pushed myself into a shaky stand and happened to catch a glimpse of myself in the framed mirror hanging over the free-standing sink.

My skin was white and pasty, and my hair, more bronze than red, stuck up in sweat-soaked spikes atop my head. Freckles stood out in between the twin red patches gracing my cheekbones, and my eyes were red and watery.

And I still had snot dripping out my nose. At least I hadn't puked on my clothes, though.

I heaved a shuddering sigh and let my gaze fall to the sink. The day had wrung the energy out of me about like MawMaw and that squirrel. I was so bone tired my muscles tingled. If I'd been any-where near a shower, I would've crawled into it, cut the water on as hot as I could stand it, and maybe fallen asleep while it sluiced the sweat off my skin.

No shower, but when I flipped the handles, water poured out of the sink's faucet, and a memory of Daddy's voice whispered in my mind.

Thank God for small mercies.

Yeah, I thought, and for some reason, it tickled me. Yeah, thank God there was water, even though my Daddy and that little boy and that woman were dead along with a whole lot of other people. Thank God for soap and running water.

I don't know when my laughter turned to tears, but when I looked in the mirror again, my cheeks were as wet as my laughter was dry.

BY THE TIME I finished cleaning up and left the bathroom, Momma and the twins had set out sleeping bags for the lot of us and Mia was done cleaning. Turns out, that room where Red Vern found the plague victims was the break room. It had a microwave, a small refrigerator, and a coffee pot, though I could've sworn a round two-seater table and chairs had been in there, too, earlier. It was a lot easier to notice stuff when you weren't worried about throwing up and shaming yourself in front of a near stranger, that's for sure.

Mia dug through the cabinets and found some coffee while me and Red Vern and the twins brought in necessities and re-parked the cars with the tail ends close to the door, blocking it from view. There was still electricity here, another small blessing, one that hadn't hit me when I got hot running water in the bathroom.

Somebody had stored frozen dinners in the fridge, and I let my mind shy away from exactly who that somebody might've been. We ate those instead of digging into our own supplies, though Red Vern had already made us bring in food from the vehicles before that. Varmints could smell what we ate, sure as they could smell us. Better to be on the safe side, same as if we were camping in the wild. You didn't leave food out where a bear could get at it. That was a good way to bring trouble down around your head. Even I knew that.

Once supper was done, we took turns washing up and drew straws, everybody except Momma. Red Vern assigned watch based on what we drew, with him taking the first shift at the door. The rest of us threw sleeping bags across the wide linoleum floor between the beauty stations lining the side walls, and I fell asleep before my head even hit the cushion of my curled up arm.

About ten minutes later, felt like, Red Vern's hand shook me awake. "Your turn now, son," he said, and I nodded and yawned and forced myself off the meager comfort of the sleeping bag.

I figured he'd go on to sleep, but no. He disappeared into the break room, came back out with a mug of fresh coffee, and handed it to me, there at the door. I sipped it, grateful for the caffeine, my gaze on the stars crowding into the night, beyond the darkened streetlamps at the edge of the parking lot.

Seemed like there were more up there than usual, winking at me from their perches in the heavens. Maybe it was just the darkness of the night making it seem that way. There were fewer lights now. No power in some places, no people in others. It made for a lot of dark when the sun went down.

Red Vern propped a shoulder against the wall and stared out the door. "You thought about how you're gonna handle it when she turns?" he said, low and quiet.

I stiffened with the mug's lip against my own. "We're hoping for a cure down Charleston way."

"And if there ain't one?"

Very carefully, I pulled the mug away from my mouth and shrugged, shifting the makeshift sling holding the shotgun onto my shoulder. Truth was, I'd done everything I could not to think about that possibility, about what would happen to Momma if there weren't no doctors along the way, if there wasn't a cure. It was too much like thinking on Daddy, and I couldn't do that without remembering the way Momma lifted that pistol, her hands shaking on the grip as she pointed the business end at his head.

My throat went dry and my stomach started cramping around

that frozen dinner. "There'll be one," I said, my voice cracking and wobbling, and I wished to God he'd never brought it up.

"Son," he said

I whipped my head around and hissed, "You ain't my daddy. My daddy's dead and gone, and I don't need you telling me what to do now."

Red Vern twisted his head around and looked at me, his expression flat, and shame flooded me, pushing through the anger until I was all twisted up inside. Before I could say sorry, he spoke again.

"Ian."

His voice was gentle, kind. I knew I didn't deserve it, but I was so grateful he didn't yell, I just nodded.

"Your Momma may not make it to Charleston," he continued.

I flinched, sloshing warm coffee across my hand.

"I saw the blood on her sleeve and I've heard her coughing. She doesn't have long."

"I know," I said softly, though I hadn't meant to say anything.

Something rustled behind us, then Momma's sweet voice drifted across the salon. "Plenty of time for that tomorrow, Vern."

He turned around and stared into the salon, then clapped an awkward hand to my shoulder and melted away from the door.

Dutifully, I turned my attention to the view beyond the glass door. The stars blurred as I sipped the suddenly tasteless coffee, and the night became a backdrop for the memory of how Daddy looked when Momma pulled that trigger.

THE NEXT MORNING, Mia opted to ride with me and Momma. Momma claimed to be too tired for the front and took the back seat instead. Where she could lie down, she said. Sure enough, before we even hit the edge of the parking lot, her gentle snores drifted through the Camry's interior.

"I don't think she slept much last night," Mia said.

I kept my eyes trained on the road and the dually leading us away from Greenwood on Highway 72, which Red Vern had deemed safer than continuing through the city on Highway 178. "She's never been one to sleep sound."

"This thing is hard on everybody." Mia was silent for so long, I thought she'd gone to sleep, too. Then she shifted on the passenger's seat and her fingers twitched against her jean-clad thighs, and she said, real low, "I think she was upset about what Pops said to you last night, when your shift started."

I pressed my lips together hard. "You heard that."

"Yeah. Sorry. I didn't mean to, but when Pops woke you up, it woke me up, too." She shrugged one shoulder and shifted her gaze to the side window. "I hate that you have to watch her die like that."

"She ain't dying," I gritted out.

It was such a whopper, I glanced in the rearview mirror to make sure Momma wasn't coming after me to wash my lying mouth out with a bar of soap. No, she was still asleep back there, but there was some traffic coming up behind us a little too quick for my comfort.

"Mia," I said, and jerked my thumb over my shoulder.

She turned around in her seat, took one look out the back window, and muttered a mild curse. "Just some fool rednecks, hot doggin' it on the highway."

I glanced into the rearview mirror again. "You sure?"

The dually's brake lights flared once, twice, and Red Vern slowed and inched toward the shoulder. I followed suit, edging up behind him much closer than Momma normally allowed. The lead car flew past us in the left lane. No worries on hitting oncoming traffic. Not a soul was bound for the mountains, none that we'd seen in the past two days anyhow. A second car flashed past, a snazzy Charger with racing stripes smeared down the shiny black sides, and more slowly, a third car, an older white Accord passed us.

Mia pulled the revolver out of its holster. "Something's back there."

I glance in the rearview mirror, searching for another car. Momma sat up right then, blocking my view. She rubbed the sleeve of a fresh sweater over her eyes, yawned, and I was torn between asking her to lie back down and saying, "Hello, sleepyhead."

Mia beat me to the punch. "I think there's a pack of varmints on the road behind us, Miz Bella. Dogs, maybe ten or fifteen. Best you stay down 'til we take care of it."

Momma twisted around and glanced back. In the rearview mirror, she seemed calm, like varmints to our rear weren't no big deal. "I'll take my chances."

"Momma," I said, then I heard it, the yip of dogs chasing prey. My heart froze in my chest and my foot eased off the gas pedal, slowing us even more. The dually began to pull away from us, but I wasn't really thinking on that. I was thinking on what a human body looked like after a varmint got ahold of it.

Mia punched me in the shoulder, hard. "Don't slow down, dummy."

I glanced down at the speedometer and about let a cussword slip. We weren't even going thirty, and those yips were getting loud faster than I liked to think on.

I jammed my foot against the gas pedal, and the Camry jumped forward, its transmission whining under the strain. Mia pulled the hammer back on the revolver and started to crank her window down. I looked past her, saw the hairless top of a varmint's head just above the edge of the door, and did cuss then.

"Ian," Momma said. "Ain't no call for that kind of language."

I met her gaze in the rearview mirror and muttered, "Sorry, Momma."

She nodded once, real sharp, then she did the funniest thing. I only caught part of it, 'cause I was driving, but later, much later when the sharpness of this day faded into memory, I pieced it together.

Momma carried a little pen knife in her dress pocket, or in her pants, or whatever she was wearing that day. Nothing big enough to hurt anybody, just a little something to help out when she ran into trouble. Say, a screw needed fixing and she didn't have a screwdriver handy, or she needed to slice off some fishing line. Something like that.

She pulled that pen knife out of her sweater pocket, flipped the business end up, and dug into her thumb. A bright red drop of blood welled up, and before me or Mia could say word one, Momma cranked the window down and held her hand out to that varmint.

Mia screamed and reached back, and I swerved off the road and cussed some more. Lord help me, Momma was gonna wash my mouth out for sure at the next stop. That varmint slowed down and leapt up to her hand, its toothy maw wide and slobbering, a swollen black tongue protruding into the Southern heat.

Then it dropped back and stopped. Momma drew her hand in and wiped it off on the edge of her sweater. Real calm, she said, "Like calls to like."

Mia turned around without another word, laid the revolver in her lap, and strapped herself in.

Me, I just kept on driving, my hands so numb, it's a wonder I kept ahold of the steering wheel.

THAT NIGHT, we set up camp near the Savannah River, in a parking lot close to a group of other refugees headed toward the coast. Red Vern assigned watch on the downlow and we ate, taking turns at it like we had the night before.

Momma hadn't said a word for so long, I wondered if her

tongue had dried up in her mouth.

But no, come watch time, she settled down beside me where I knelt on the still-hot asphalt, while Red Vern exchanged gossip and whatnot with a group come down from Tennessee.

"You were little when my grandfather died," she said, her voice soft as the wind whispering across us. "Grampy Miller. He was one of the best men I ever knew."

I shifted the shotgun in my hands and peered into the night. Truth was, a knot of anger had been building inside my gut all day long, ever since she stuck her hand out that window, and I wasn't ready to let it go yet.

"Mama said I followed him around from the time I took my first step." She smiled and rolled her head back, looking up at the stars, I reckoned. "His little shadow. I loved him so much, and I learned a lot from him."

My eyelids slid shut and I inhaled a deep breath. "I ain't in the mood for one of your stories, Momma."

"Now, Grampy Miller loved three things in this world," she said mildly, like she hadn't heard the thin edge of anger coating my voice. "His family, his God, and his hunting dog, not necessarily in that order. He babied that dog. Raised it from a pup after its siblings spurned it. What was that dog called? My goodness, I can't remember, only that it was the runt of the litter."

"Lots of dogs in the family," I said, my anger bitter on my tongue. I spat it out, but there it was still, getting bigger and bigger with every word she uttered. "Just like there's lots of dogs now, like the one that could've bit your fool hand off this morning."

"Runty!" she said, laughing. "I can't believe I forgot that!"

I lurched to my feet and stared down at her. "Would you shut up about that stupid dog?" I hissed. "It's dead and gone along with everything else in this God forsaken world. Can't you get your head around that, Momma? Don't you know what you were risking today?"

Her head fell forward and her shoulders slumped, and for a second, regret cut through the anger. I shouldn'ta sassed her like that. Mad or no, she was still my momma and I still loved her. She deserved respect whether I wanted to give it or not.

She sighed and looked up at me, still calm as the lake on a warm summer's day. "Life is risk, baby. Everything we do carries a price tag, everything, and everything has consequences."

I don't know why, but the anger drifted out of me like it'd never been. Maybe it was her words. Maybe it was the way she said 'em. I don't know, only that of a sudden, I wasn't mad at her no more.

"Grampy Miller didn't teach me that," she continued. "What he taught me was that life is built on an endless series of small moments, the little things that keep us going, the things we take for granted, then forget about as soon as they've passed. Watching the sun rise while you're walking to the barn to milk the cows. Gathering eggs and eating breakfast together before the day starts, and training up a dog that would've died if it had been left in the wild."

I swallowed, hard. "Momma."

"Oh hush, Ian. I'm not finished." She held her hand out to me. "Here, help me up."

"Yes'm."

I took her fragile hand in mine, felt the fineness of her bones, the thinness of her skin, and gently pulled her to a stand. Next to me, she was tiny, a sparrow up against a blue jay. Seemed like she'd shrunk half a foot at least since we'd left Daddy there, splayed out on the carpet of our living room floor. The good carpet, a nice tan color, just installed to replace the moldy old shag carpeting that had come with the house.

She squeezed my hand, drawing me away from the blood and gore into the present. "Every day is special, every moment. If you only live for the big things, the birthdays and celebrations and whatnots, getting your driver's license and graduating from high school and such. If you only live for that, you're missing out on most of your life."

"I ain't missing nothing, Momma," I said, gentle as I could.

"You're missing my meaning, Ian." She shook her head, squeezed my hand again. "You're my Runty, the being I love most in this world. I'd do anything for you. You hear me, boy?"

I nodded and murmured "yes'm," and she nodded right sharp and wandered back to the main group where Red Vern was listening away.

On the edge of the parking lot, just out of reach of the lights, yellow eyes peered at us from the shadows. The shotgun wouldn't reach that far, so I dropped it, let it dangle at my side from the sling, and picked up the rifle I'd borrowed from Dylan. The eyes eased back into the night before I could do anything more, but the back of my neck prickled during the whole rest of my shift.

MIA DROVE the dually the next day, giving Red Vern a rest. Me and Momma followed along in the Camry, skirting the larger cities, passing through smaller towns when we couldn't avoid them, too. We were looping through South Carolina, steadily easing toward the coast, going a little faster now when traffic and the roads allowed, though Red Vern sure made us stop often enough. Searching for supplies and gas at out of the way convenience stores with rocking chairs out front and night crawlers stored in white, Styrofoam cups next to beer and cokes.

The sun rose and fell, like it always had, and the world around us disintegrated into smoke and fire.

We'd picked up two other families by then, the folks from Tennessee and another car full of college kids come down from Clemson. We didn't really pick them up. They just tailed along, stopping when we stopped, camping near where we did, only farther away. Red Vern said it wasn't safe for us to congregate, that if we stayed a little ways apart, the two groups could protect each other better.

I think he just hated being that close to strangers, which begged the question as to why he'd picked up me and Momma. Maybe he just had a weakness for strays.

Momma kept on with her stories, sharing tales about her folks and growing up and a few more about Daddy. Her cough weren't no worse and it weren't no better. I didn't spot blood on her sweater but once or twice, and fool that I was, I took it as a good sign. If she could just hold on 'til we hit Charleston, she'd be ok.

We heard the rumors, of course, from other folks we met. The National Guard had set up camp along the coast. Doctors were holed up there, treating the sick when they could. The government had built a barrier between the refugee camps and the varmints, protecting what was left of humanity.

As we drew closer to the coast, the clouds grew into giant airships floating in huge armadas across the blue and a hint of marsh water lingered in the day's heat. It rained a couple of times, mostly quick afternoon thunderstorms that washed the air clear of the black smoke rising in wavering columns off of roadside heaps.

Once, we passed a school, a massive complex of brick and glass. Mia was riding with me and Momma that day, and I told her as how I was glad not to have to go back again. She shrugged and said, "Pops homeschools us."

That made a whole bunch of sense to me, once I thought about it.

A pack of varmints followed us. I caught glimpses of them in the rearview mirror a time or two, and Daisy got a good scare one night during her turn at watch, outside a town whose name I never got.

We were in a small shopping mall again, one with more glass than walls across the front. Three of the things took down a plague-ridden herd of deer in the shadows just outside the ring of light thrown by a working streetlamp. Daisy yelped, startling us all out of sleep, then came four steady shots, one right after the other.

Pfitt.

Pfitt.

Pfitt.

Pfitt.

I was sacked out just behind her, so I got a good look at what happened, once I woke up good. The varmints' heads burst and that deer, too, spraying red blood and gore into the streetlight. I thought it was Daisy at first, but she was flat down on this side of the door still, inside.

That's when I learned what Red Vern did before he was a farmer.

He hustled us out of there faster than I could spit, that's for sure. After that, we slept in the vehicles if we couldn't find a good place to hole up and other folks to camp near. There just wasn't enough of us to go around.

Big green signs appeared along the roadside, pointing us to Charleston, reminding us of the distance from here to there, and just as quickly disappeared. Momma coughed quietly, Red Vern led the way, and in the distance, varmints tore into the flesh of them that was unlucky enough to get caught out in the open.

THE CAMRY gave out between Orangeburg and Bowman, so close to Charleston, I could just about smell the ocean. It'd run just fine until then, just fine as far back as I could remember. That morning, after our first break, I noticed it was running a little hot. It was just me and Momma. Mia and the twins were with Red Vern in the dually, leading his little band of strays toward the promised land. We were sandwiched between them and the other two cars following close behind.

I had just enough time to tell Momma that the Camry was running hot when steam started billowing out around the hood.

"Shit," I said, and hit the hazards.

"Language," Momma said, but she said it real mild. She pointed to a smooth place along the shoulder, her sweater pulled down over the heel of her hand, her fingers holding it in place over a spot of dried blood. "Pull over there."

I slowed down and eased onto the shoulder, holding tight to the steering wheel as the tires bumped off the asphalt onto the grass verge. Ahead, the dually slowed and pulled over, and the two trailing cars pulled up even with him. Red Vern got out just as I was cutting the engine and bent over to talk to the folks from Tennessee, then both cars sped up slowly and moved ahead, leaving us there.

My heart was a twisted knot in my chest, pattering faster than it ever had. If the Camry was a goner, so were we. Without a car, we couldn't get to Charleston, couldn't outrun the varmints, couldn't shelter or carry supplies. We were in a world of hurt, and I didn't need nobody telling me so to know it.

Momma's hand fell down on mine, rubbing the white knuckles of my right hand. "Your daddy bought this car brand new. He was the first to test drive it, the first to take it off the lot. It's been a good car."

I turned my head and just looked at her for a minute. "You ever gonna run out of stories?"

"Don't plan on it."

I laughed then, short and sharp, and she just grinned at me, her face lit up from the inside like lights on a Christmas tree.

It was one of those moments she'd told me about, one of the pauses between big things like leaving Daddy splayed out on the living room floor and whatever lay ahead of us along the coast. I knew it the same way I knew we were screwed if we couldn't fix the Camry, but right then, it didn't matter. All I knew was the light in her eyes and the laughter filling the car's interior 'til there was no room left for nothing else.

Red Vern tapped on the windshield, and the moment shattered into a million pieces and faded into dust. Momma squeezed my hand and let go, and I popped the hood and got out, already regretting the loss.

It took Red Vern all of three minutes to diagnose the trouble. "Water pump's busted," he said, his voice gritty and grim. He backed away from the Camry rubbing his hands on a grease rag. "Dylan, Daisy, you know what to do. Mia, take Bella for a quick walk. Ian, you're with me."

Momma exchanged a faint smile with me, then she and Mia walked ahead, passing by the dually while Dylan and Daisy popped the Camry's trunk and began heaving out cartons of water and supplies.

Red Vern left the hood propped open. "So folks can get the good parts, if they need them, but won't make the mistake of trying to drive it."

He led me across the road, out of earshot of the others, and stared off into the woods lining that side. Tall pine trees, evenly spaced behind power lines strung up between poles. He stuffed the rag in a back pocket, rubbed the nape of his neck, and heaved a sigh.

He hadn't gotten a lot of sleep these past few days. The lack was beginning to show around his eyes, though his back was as stiff and straight as the trees planted off the roadway.

"We've got room in the dually," he said abruptly. "Your momma can ride up front with me. You and the kids can take the back. I'm telling you this to give you a choice."

I glanced away, hiding the bitter set of my mouth. "Looks to me like we ain't got a choice."

"We can drop you off at the nearest shelter, you want."

"You really think we're gonna find a shelter that ain't been burned out?"

He was quiet for a minute, then real soft said, "No."

I opened my mouth on a retort, closed it again with a snap. "It ain't up to me."

"I can't make you go with us."

"But Momma can."

He didn't have to say what we were both thinking, that sure, me and her could take our chances here or in the next town. She might look healthy, but she wasn't. She was sick. Dying. If we didn't go with Red Vern and his crew, she might not last to find a doctor.

And if she took a turn for the worse before then, I couldn't handle her on my own.

I spat the bitterness into the dust. "Yeah, whatever."

"Son," he said, then added, just as quiet, "Ian."

I swung my head around and gazed up at him, this stoic man with his lanky build and flat eyes. "Yes, sir?"

He looked at me for a long time, just looked, like he was sizing me up or something. Then he shook his head once and clapped me on the shoulder. "How much ammunition do you have left for that shotgun?"

I was betting he knew exactly how much ammo was left for it, down to the last shell, but I swallowed down that retort and told him, straight out.

"It'll do," he said. "You think you could handle a van or an SUV?"

My mouth twisted down. "I ain't never drove nothing but the Camry, sir. Don't even got my learner's permit yet."

He nodded, almost like he was expecting me to answer that

way, then he turned and walked back to the vehicles.

I trailed along behind him like a whipped puppy trying to figure out where it had gone wrong.

I SAT in the back, sandwiched between Mia and Dylan with Daisy on my lap so her brother and sister could watch the roadsides. It would've shamed me to be relegated to such a spot if Mia's arm didn't brush mine when she shifted on the seat beside me.

Every time our skin touched, my insides lit up like a bonfire and just as quick cooled down. All I had to do was remember the way Mia picked that squirrel out of a tree. It was a potent reminder of exactly how well she could take care of herself.

Me and Daisy took turns reading to the others, when the radio buzzed with static and the outside world was too much to bear. They were in the middle of one of the Harry Potter books. I'd watched the movies, but only read the first book, so I knew what was going on, sort of, but in a good way. A surprising way, because so many details had been left out of the movies.

That's how we spent the rest of the day. Reading, watching the roadsides, taking breaks when Red Vern thought it was safe, and trying real hard to ignore the varmints chasing after us, the plague victims stumbling out of churches and homes, the looters and the rioters and the just plain bad folk that'd happened to survive long enough to make trouble.

We caught up to the other two cars an hour before nightfall. By then, Daisy was doing the watching and Dylan was on my lap, and we were, to the last of us, ready to get out and set up camp so we could stretch our legs.

Red Vern could go faster without us tagging along behind the dually, slowing him down. Well, not us really. Me, the inexperienced driver white knuckling the steering wheel anytime the speedometer went over thirty-six.

If the plague hadn't come along, I would've gotten my permit in a couple of weeks, when my birthday rolled around. It was pretty much a moot point now.

Momma leaned forward and put her hand on the dash as the dually approached the other half of our caravan. I thought at first it was because she was so excited to see them. Momma was a social bird. So Dad always said.

Then the dually passed the cars and I got a good look at the scenery.

"Crap," I muttered, and stuffed Dylan between me and Mia so I could haul Daisy away from the window. Her face was pasty white and her eyes as big as saucers. When I picked her up, she went without uttering a peep.

I glanced up and met Red Vern's gaze in the rearview mirror, then turned and caught Mia looking at me. Yeah, that's what I'd thought. I reached up and squeezed Momma's arm, then opened the door and slid out, shotgun already in hand, leaving Dylan and Daisy to huddle together in the middle of the back seat.

The dually's engine chugged smoothly where it sat idling. I almost left the door open, maybe would've if it had been empty.

There were seven of them, the ones that we'd made friends with, as much as anybody could be friends nowadays. And it wasn't varmints that got them or the critters would still have been gnawing flesh off the bones.

Red Vern went first, a rifle held up and ready to fire. Where he'd got it from, I hadn't a clue. He'd stepped out of the dually with it in his hand.

Me and Mia spread out behind him, both of us keeping a close eye on what was left of our friends. They were already dead, by the looks of it. A couple twitched like they were trying to wake up, so they'd been dead for at least an hour.

They'd be slow for a while, which gave us plenty of time to take care of them.

And by *take care* I meant put 'em down so they couldn't rise again and take a bite out of the next stupid person to stumble along.

What worried me was that they were lying there in various states of trying to run, looked like, but whatever they'd tried to run from was nowhere to be found.

My gaze grazed the brick and wood-sided houses lining the road, to the trees beyond, to the cars scattered here and there up and down the road. Smoke drifted on the wind. From the smell, I guessed somebody'd caught a good herd of varmints and put them down, or tried.

The hairs on the back of my neck prickled. Absentmindedly, I rubbed a palm across my nape, trying to scrub away the unease. Another scent mingled with that one, not the stench of diesel from the dually's engine or the ocean or the land, which smelled so different from the mountains back home. Something else, like rot and ruin and...

A head popped up in one of the cars. I caught a glimpse of a haggard face pulled into a snarl, heard the low growl of an animal. Red Vern swung the rifle toward it, and a shot went off before I could bring the shotgun up and fire. Glass shattered and the head popped back and disappeared in a burst of brown fluid and rotten flesh. Before the shot's echo had faded, varmints came running around the nearest house, a whole pack of them led by a slobbering dog-like critter that looked as big as a fully grown black bear.

"Back in the truck!" Red Vern shouted.

I didn't need to be told twice. We were maybe forty yards from the front of that pack and a good fifteen or twenty feet from the dually. I turned around so fast, my feet slid out from under me, then I shoved off the ground and ran full out, as close behind Mia as I could get. She went around the dually, no idea why, and I reached the nearest door and crawled in at the same time as Red Vern ahead of me.

I slammed the door as the varmints' yips turned to the sounds of teeth ripping into flesh. Momma was half turned in her seat, staring out the side windows. I started to turn around and look, too, but she reached out and said, "No, don't look."

Her voice was strangled and soft, and that was what stopped me. I didn't want to see another person I knew die, even if they were already dead. I especially didn't want to see somebody I'd known torn apart by a pack of varmints.

Red Vern eased the dually forward to the chorus of angry yips and bodies hitting the dually. Maybe it was good we hadn't had to use bullets, though I vowed then and there to use one on myself if it came down to a choice between getting bit by a plague victim or eating a lead slug.

FROM THEN ON, me and Mia took the outside spots in the back seat. I wasn't the best shot, but I was old enough to...well, I was older. Seemed to me kids like Daisy and Dylan shouldn't have to see what'd happened when we found those people. Our friends, allies really.

That night, Red Vern spotted a free-standing mom-and-pop that looked like it was intact. He scouted it, made sure it was cleaned out and secure while Momma sat in the dually and the rest of us stood guard.

When we went in, looked to me like the place hadn't been abandoned long. The power was still on, and Mia found a generator out back with gas still in the tank. She would've siphoned it off, but Red Vern said no, leave it for the next people to come through, so they'd have some fresh food.

We ate good that night out of the restaurant's stores. Cleaned up after ourselves, which was the mannerly thing to do. The sunlight was near about gone by then, but we'd already unpacked the dually. All that was left was divvying up watch and laying out the sleeping bags.

Mia took first watch, stationed by the front door and windows, though the dually was backed up to block off the door. Red Vern disappeared out the back. Up to the roof was my guess, but I didn't ask no questions. Didn't have to. The memory of those varmints' heads splashing open was still fresh in my mind.

I'd settled down between Momma and the front door, a curled up arm as my pillow. Should've been tired after the day we'd had and getting a belly full of good food, some of it from my own momma's hand. Every time my eyelids slid shut, though, my fool brain cooked up something for me to think over, so I just laid there listening to the others fall asleep.

Finally, I couldn't take it no more. I stood up and stretched, joined Mia where she sat on a booth's table next to one of the windows. Made sure to scuff my feet so she'd know I was coming.

She didn't seem like somebody a fellow wanted to sneak up on.

"You want some coffee?" I said, soft and low.

She half turned toward me, barely visible in the moonlight glinting off the dually. "I'm ok right now. Thanks."

I shrugged and shuffled closer, leaned a shoulder against the wall between the door and one of the plate glass windows lining the front, right behind a booth. "How much longer you reckon it'll be?"

"'Til Charleston? A couple of days maybe. Depends on what the roads are like."

"I wish it was quicker."

"If wishes were horses."

"Yeah, yeah."

She shot me a quick grin, then turned her gaze to the world outside the door. The parking lot was bathed in moonlight. The road wound along its other side, and beyond that, just visible, a field of yellowing corn stood sentinel, like hundreds of leafy soldiers lined up in long rows. If things had been different, we might've waded into the field and pulled some corn down, shucked it right there, and dropped it into a pot of boiling water.

I shuddered and leaned my head against the wall, stifling a yawn. Nobody in their right mind would walk into that field while varmints were about.

"I've lived with Pops my whole life, just about," Mia said.

"Yeah?"

"My mom left me with him when I was a baby. He's my uncle. My mom's brother. She was..." A corner of her mouth turned down. "Strung out. High on something, probably. She was whenever I saw her."

My hands twitched against my sides. I wanted to reach out and squeeze her shoulder, maybe comfort her, but what did I know about that? I crossed my arms over my chest instead and said, "That sucks."

Mia shrugged one shoulder. "He took good care of me, then when the twins came along..."

"He took good care of them, too."

"Yeah."

That silence stretched out between us again. My brain was getting fuzzy and my eyelids were drooping again, but I was reluctant to leave her there, alone at the front with thoughts of her mom rattling around in her head.

"She came back a couple of weeks ago," Mia said, out of the blue.

I frowned. "How'd she get through the streets with the plague hitting everybody?"

"I don't know." Mia's voice had gone soft and rough, strained, like she was holding back a lot. She glanced over her shoulder, at the twins maybe, then leaned closer to me and lowered her voice even more. "She was already sick. We didn't know it, though. Didn't know much of nothing. That was before the news got out about what was going on, so maybe it was longer back, you know?"

Yeah, I did know. Dad caught sick around the same time, from a guy at work. We'd had to sit in lockdown while the government's scientists tried to figure out what was what. By the time news leaked out, it was already too late.

I didn't particularly like thinking on that, but it struck a funny chord in my gut. "She didn't make it, did she," I said slowly.

Mia shook her head and squeezed her eyelids shut tight.

"I'm sorry."

"It happens. Happened to your dad, didn't it?"

"Yeah, but still."

"Pops saved me. She died while I was sitting with her, reared up before I realized what'd happened. He heard me scream and came running and I—"

I reached out and wrapped my hand around her upper arm, holding her gently. If she wanted to take my hand off, so be it. I couldn't stand not touching her another second. "Me, too. Momma took care of Daddy right in front of me."

"So you know, huh." She turned to me, her eyes wide and glistening. "You know what it's like to watch somebody die and come back and die again."

"Yeah," I said, but the word came out choked and wet.

Mia's hand lifted and grasped my elbow, and we stood there for a long moment mourning the ones we'd lost. She blinked and two tears streaked down her cheeks, one after the other, then she sniffed, let go of me, and slid back, training her gaze on the parking lot.

I tucked my hands back under my pits again, feeling so awkward of a sudden it was all I could do to stand still. "Is that why y'all left, came down here?"

She shook her head. "The neighborhood was overrun. We couldn't fend off the, well, you know."

The plague ridden. Varmints. "Yeah."

"Couldn't do it on our own, so Pops locked everything up tight. Said we'd search until we found people we could bring back to help clear it out. People with integrity who wouldn't rob us blind."

They'd found us instead, a sick woman and a useless teenager. I sighed and pushed away from the wall. "You want some coffee now?"

She shook her head, sending her long braid flying across her back. "You'd better get some sleep. Pops will be back soon to switch out the watch."

I nodded, oddly stung by the dismissal, and turned away. I wasn't halfway back to my sleeping bag when she called my name.

"Ian?"

"Yeah?"

"Thanks."

I had no idea why she was thanking me, so I fell back on manners. "Anytime."

My brain took the hint and let me go to sleep, and the rest of the night passed quiet as the moon crossing the sky.

MOMMA WAS subdued the next morning. She dozed in the front seat, curled up against the door. Her skin had turned the color of old paste overnight, like every drop of blood had drained out of her. Even her hair seemed to've faded from bright strawberry to a dull, light gray.

I was sitting behind her, Mia behind her uncle in the driver's seat, the twins between us. Daisy had her head on my upper arm. She was out cold. Reckon she hadn't been getting much sleep lately.

I didn't think any of us had.

Would that change when we reached Charleston and the refugee camp? Would we finally be able to rest then?

The dually was quiet above the thrum of tires against the asphalt. Dylan had given up on the latest book, another Harry Potter, after a chapter of reading out loud. The morning sun shone through the window, warming me and Momma, casting the others in shadow.

I tried to stay awake, honest I did. The landscape beyond the road flattened between houses. Long fields stretched toward the horizon, filled with corn or peanuts or grass intended for hay. Traffic was heavier here, abandoned cars more numerous. Flies gathered in black clouds above the dead, human and animal alike, and the stench drifted out of the vents into the cab.

Somebody had done the dead a kindness with a bullet to the head, either putting them down or keeping them there. Wish that somebody had piled the bodies up and burned them, just to be on the safe side. I'd rather smell smoke than rotting flesh any day.

Ahead, the interstate loomed.

We'd talked about that last night before supper, when Red Vern set the watch shifts. If we got onto I-26, chances were good we'd be stuck there. The plan was to either cross over the interstate and keep to the back roads or find a way to avoid it all together.

We were fifteen or so miles from the outskirts of Charleston now, so close hope filled me from top to bottom. No signs for the camp yet, though there were plenty of signs the National Guard had passed through. We'd passed a slew of military vehicles. I didn't know what all they were, aside from the tanks. They were, to a one, abandoned and burned out, but that didn't stop hope from bubbling up inside me.

Then we hit the checkpoint.

A group of people dressed in camouflage, helmets, and what

Mia called tactical vests were guarding a barricade made of orange and white sawhorses topped with barbed wire. Soldiers, maybe, but when I asked, Red Vern just grunted, which wasn't much of an answer at all.

He hit the brakes, slowing us to a crawl behind a line of some dozen cars. The car at the front had three or four people surrounding it, each carrying long barrel guns. The armed men and women stepped back, someone pulled one of the sawhorses aside, and the car went on its way, slowly winding through a maze of barriers.

The next car pulled up and stopped, and I tuned out. What did we have to hide except Momma being sick? She was still on this side of the living, wasn't she? And besides. We were carrying her to a doctor for help. Nothing to fear there.

Still, a tiny stone of worry lodged itself in my gut, deflating the hope.

We eased forward one car length at a time. Daisy was awake now. She sat up in the seat, gripping the one in front of us with her gaze glued to the scene ahead. I kept watch out the window, like I was supposed to, and Mia did the same across from me.

Momma roused and stretched. "How long was I out?"

Her voice was thin and weak enough that I frowned at her through the seat separating us.

"Most of the morning," Red Vern said. "We're almost in Charleston."

Momma hummed under her breath, which could've meant anything. "I haven't been to Charleston since I was a kid."

"Took the kids a couple of summers ago." The dually eased forward and stopped, then he continued. "Nice city. Good for a visit."

I glanced across at Mia, but she was studying the land on the other side of the truck. The cab fell silent again. For some reason, the silence felt wrong. Incomplete. Some impulse nudged me, and I reached forward and squeezed Momma's shoulder.

"Tell me what it was like when you visited here," I said.

"I thought you didn't like my stories."

I heard the smile in her voice. It would've shamed me another day. Maybe it did a little then, too. "Tell me anyhow."

She shifted in the seat, sighed, rested her head against the window. "I was eight, I think. Maybe nine. Mama wanted to see the ocean, and Papa never could deny her a blessed thing."

The story unwound around us, holding us together for that brief moment while we waited our turn at the checkpoint. Even Dylan was listening, and he wasn't much for stories, aside from ones writ down in books. The line ahead of us dwindled, Momma told us of Ferris wheels and sand in her toes and some foolishness her Mama had gotten them into on a lark.

A car door slammed shut, startling me out of the half dream Momma's story had lulled me into. I looked up ahead, watching soldiers or whatever those people were surround a dark blue sedan. Someone shouted. I could just make out a frantic, "Open the door!" That was about it.

Then somebody stepped forward and yanked the car door open, the back one behind the driver's side. Somebody else reached in and hauled a German Shepherd out by its collar and dragged it away from the car, yipping.

"No, not my baby!" a woman screamed. "Don't take him! He's fine he's not infected I swear he's ok please don't take him he's all I have left!"

Every word was punctuated by another yip. The hair on the back of my neck rose and dread settled down low in my gut. It sounded just like a varmint, just like one of them things that'd been following us, just like—

The man that had opened the door raised his rifle, aimed it at the dog. A shot rang out and the dog collapsed on the road, and the woman screamed and screamed and screamed.

We were four cars back now. Four cars and they'd be to us.

Slowly, I reached up and pulled Daisy away from the view. Dylan had already slid back in the seat. He was staring straight ahead, his eyes wide and unseeing. Mia put a hand on his leg, patting it gently, and I tucked Daisy against my chest, hiding her face in my shirt over the rapid patter of my heartbeat.

Shit. If they'd do that to a healthy dog, what would they do to Momma?

Red Vern cut the engine and slid out of the dually, his hands raised shoulder high. He waited there as one of the soldier people walked up. They talked for a minute, too low for us to hear, then Red Vern nodded and got back in the dually.

"It's only the pets they're after," he said as he slammed the door shut. "They don't know what Charleston is like. Haven't had word in a couple of days."

I let out a breath I hadn't known I was holding. Only the pets. Thank God.

We made it through the checkpoint without a fuss. Momma didn't even warrant so much as a second glance from the folks inspecting us. I couldn't look at the dog they'd shot, and I didn't let Daisy look either.

Momma didn't speak another word until Red Vern found us a place to eat lunch.

WE ROTATED OUT guard duty in the parking lot of an overgrown convenience store, me and Mia first, like always. The air was so hot and humid, I could scarce draw a breath. Sweat coated my skin and evaporated, leaving a coarse layer of salt behind. Would there be showers in Charleston? Could we have a proper cleaning for once?

I almost laughed. Momma had always had to prod me into the bathroom for my nightly bath. Now I would've given my front teeth for one.

Soon as Dylan and Daisy were finished eating, they relieved us. I sank down onto the old quilt Momma had spread across the pavement, in the dually's shadow, and let her hand me a sandwich. PB & J. It could've been liver and onions on one of them fancy mushrooms and I wouldn't have cared.

Mia touched my shoulder and jerked her chin at Red Vern, who was standing on the edge of the parking lot with his back to us. He had a hand-rolled cigarette held between his finger and thumb, puffing it in short inhales. She took her sandwich and walked over to him, eating as she went.

I dug into my own sandwich, too hungry for much talk beyond please and thank you.

Momma coughed into her sleeve, pressed shaky fingertips to her forehead. Beads of sweat had popped up on her skin, though she was still so pale I wondered if she'd lost a pint of blood.

"I need to tell you something," she said, her voice so quiet I almost didn't hear her.

I chewed and swallowed real quick and set the sandwich on the paper plate she'd handed it to me on. "You still upset about the checkpoint?"

"It's not that. I—" She glanced at Red Vern, coughed again into her sleeve. "Did I ever tell you how me and Vern met?"

I choked down a laugh edging on hysterical. "We met him together, remember? At that camp outside Asheville?"

She shook her head once. "No, baby. We went to school together, way back. I was in the same class as his sister. Mia and the twins' mama."

My gaze followed hers to where Red Vern and Mia stood talking quietly. "Mia told me about her mom. How she was strung out on drugs and left her with Vern."

"He told me, that night we met him. At the camp."

Her body seemed to seize up, and she coughed hard into her sleeve for a long time, so hard, I thought she was going to spit out a lung any second. I caught Red Vern turning toward us out of the corner of my eye and waved him off, then reached for Momma to steady her.

The minute my hands touched her arms, I about regretted not calling him over instead. She was burning up. Even through her sweater, I could feel the scorching hot heat of her skin.

My eyelids slid shut. Dear sweet God. A fever now? Not good, so not good. What the hell were we going to do? We hadn't found a doctor yet, hadn't even reached a hospital or anything, hadn't—

Momma's coughing ended on a long gasp. "We were in high school—"

"It's ok, Momma. You can tell me later."

"No time, son. The plague's got me and you need to know."

I rubbed my hands up and down her arms, trying to chase the fever out, I guess. "Don't you say that. We got plenty of time, you hear?"

"Her name was Violet. Vern's baby sister."

"Momma, please."

"She was a beauty. Mia's the spitting image." Momma drew in a strangled breath. It sounded like a file scraping across metal. "She was a little wild. Not so bad that she had a reputation, just fun loving. One day, these boys cornered her and they...roughed her up a little."

I squeezed my eyes shut and felt a tear slip out and roll down my cheek. "Momma, don't."

"Vern found out, tracked 'em down. Beat 'em to a bloody pulp." She sighed out a laugh, got strangled on it, and coughed once, hard. Her sleeve came away soaked with blood. "They got what they deserved for what they did to Vi. Sure as hell, nobody else would've lifted a finger to them."

Gravel skittered beside us, and I looked up. Red Vern was looming over us, his expression hard and unreadable.

"Is it true?" I asked him, though I hadn't meant to. Hadn't even thought the question before it popped out of my fool mouth.

"Every word." He knelt beside us and pried my fingers off Momma's arms, gently unbuttoned her sweater and tugged it off, like a parent undressing a newborn. "I was seventeen and stupid. Thought I could avenge Vi's honor if I whooped those boys that'd hurt her. The judge was going to sentence me as an adult, but Bella's daddy stepped in. He and the judge played poker together every Thursday night. Good friends. Get me another sweater for her."

It took a minute for my mind to make the leap between his story and his request. Soon as it did, I popped up and dug until I found a clean sweater, then handed it to him and sat down again. By then, Mia was with us, and the twins were watching, too. If ever there was a story Momma needed to tell, it was this one.

Which kindly begged the question as to why she hadn't told me before.

Red Vern finished tugging the clean sweater on her and let me take Momma. She leaned against me, trembling so hard, it was all I could do to hold onto her. He wadded the sweater up and looked at me, just looked.

Finally, I couldn't take it no more. "What happened?"

"The judge gave me a choice. Enlist or do time. I chose the Marines." The hard line of his mouth wavered into a grim smile. "I don't regret a single day."

I nodded, though I still had questions, like... "So that's why she calls you Red Vern, because you beat them boys up?"

"My hands were red with their blood by the time I finished with them."

The words were quiet. That didn't make them empty. "I thought it was because of the hat."

He looked at me for a minute, then slowly, a deep rumble started in his chest and worked its way out his mouth, and he laughed so hard, I thought he was going to fall over.

I would've laughed, too, if I could've found something funny in what I said. Try as I might, I couldn't find a thing.

Vern clapped a hand to my shoulder, then heaved himself into a stand. "C'mon, son. Daylight's a wasting, and Bella don't have long."

We burned the sweater before we left, leaving it to smoke in the middle of the parking lot.

Momma sat in back between me and Mia, her head on my lap. I prayed the whole rest of the afternoon that we'd make it to Charleston in time, even as a tiny voice in the back of my mind whispered that it was already too late.

THE SUN arched high overhead, crossing the sky on its long journey to the other horizon. Vern pushed the dually, going as fast as he dared, I think, through the cluttered roads. We saw a suspension bridge in the distance, rising high like the bleached bones of a bird's wings. Then we saw the plywood signs with the word "detour" spray painted in dripping, orange letters.

After that came the logjam, and the people milling about, and wispy tendrils of smoke rising off of what had, not long ago, been the port city of Charleston.

"Those aren't people," Mia said.

Vern hit the brakes, threw the dually into reverse, and backed up.

Momma started convulsing then. I looked down and shouted, "Momma!" Foam was boiling out of her mouth between slack lips and her eyes rolled back in her head. The veins in her neck bulged black against the pale tenderness of her skin. I grabbed her shoulders, holding her down, and Mia grabbed her legs, more to keep from getting kicked than anything.

"We have to pull over!" I screamed. "We have to get help!"

"Not yet," Vern said.

I met his gaze in the rearview mirror, and knew my face was ugly and twisted and scared. "She's going to die if we don't stop soon."

"She was dying anyway," Mia said.

If I'd been able, I would've slapped her for saying it.

Even as some part of me resonated with the truth.

Momma had been dead before we'd even left Asheville.

She'd been dead before she shot Daddy, dead before we met Vern and his nieces and nephew. Dead before she'd put me in the Camry and told me to head toward Rosman, get off I-40 as soon as you can, baby, just keep driving, it'll be ok.

But it wasn't ok. Nothing was ok, not her, not me, not the whole mess of a world we were living in.

And I was mad about it, so mad I could've spit, so mad I wanted to scream until God heard me and did something to help us. So mad I wanted to wake her up and smack her for catching the plague and dying on me. So mad she was leaving me alone in a world I didn't understand, with people I barely knew.

Why did this have to happen to me? Why did it have to happen to her?

Mia's hand came down on mine. "I don't know, Ian. Why does anything happen the way it does?"

I glanced at her, tried to focus through the haze of tears gathering in my eyes. Dylan and Daisy were turned around in the front seat, watching me warily, and of a sudden, I was so ashamed I could've died right there on the spot.

What was I thinking, carrying on like that in front of them? They'd been through enough, seen enough to last them a lifetime. They didn't need to see me fall apart on top of that.

I swiped an arm across my face, smearing tears and snot everywhere, and didn't care. Momma had fallen still with her face turned toward me. Her eyes were open and so milky, you couldn't tell what color the irises had been.

The air shuddered out of her chest, and she stilled, and I knew she was gone.

My head cleared so suddenly, it would've surprised me if I hadn't been numb. "We need to pull over now, Vern. We need to..."

The words bottled up inside me. I just couldn't say it yet. I just couldn't.

"Miz Bella's dead," Mia said for me, and I realized her hand was still holding mine.

I couldn't look at her yet, but I couldn't let her think I wasn't grateful. "Thanks."

"Anytime."

I don't know how long we drove. Long enough to get away from the crowds of plague victims littering the roads. Long enough to see what was left of the National Guard where they'd made their last stand on the outskirts of the city. Long enough to backtrack to some farmland where Momma would have a nice view when we laid her to rest.

I lost track. Small wonder, huh?

Vern helped me pull Momma out of the car and lay her out on the roadside, near a forest and a field planted with browning corn. Momma would've liked that. She'd always loved her trees. There were some varmints there, on the edge, waiting for us, but I paid them no never mind. Mia and the twins were standing watch, their guns aimed at the pack waiting for us to finish.

Vern handed me a revolver, the twin of the one Mia carried. "I can do it, if you want."

I sniffed and swiped my nose, took the revolver and checked it the way Mia had shown me during one long stretch of road. "I'm her son, her only family. It should be me."

He nodded and stepped back, and I took aim, holding the revolver as steady as I could.

And I remembered. I remembered her hair shining like fire in the sunlight. I remembered her laughter ringing from the front seat, like a chorus of bells, on one of those road trips we used to take together. I remembered her soft kiss on my forehead, and her hands tucking me in at night, and a thousand other moments making up the days since she'd pushed me into the world.

I remembered every moment I could as I stood there staring down at her. Each memory filled my heart until it was a raw, throbbing wound in my chest, and I let the ache consume me, let it drown me in the beauty Momma had been, and the sorrow she was now.

Her eyes popped open and focused on me, and her mouth snarled around an animal growl.

I steadied my hand and pulled the trigger, and watched all those moments seep out of her into the cushion of grass beneath her head. Then I handed the revolver to Vern and walked away, letting him finish the job with a lit match and the tinder the twins had gathered from the dying corn.

Under Our Skin

Her face appeared in the window every time I opened the curtains. It was like she sensed when I would be there, or maybe she just knew my habits.

"Subject demonstrates a remarkable memory for routine," I murmured, and turned to the next window.

She followed, shuffling along the porch on grimy, bare feet, a rag doll tucked against her chest.

I ignored the doll. Carrying it didn't make her human.

For a long time after the Fall, I'd left the curtains closed, hoping she'd go away, hoping never to see that tiny face through the glass again. When that hadn't worked, I'd tried yelling at her, throwing things. Rocks, books, empty bottles, and, once, a toy. Whatever was at hand, that's what I hurled at her as I raged against a world so cruel it consumed the innocent.

Nothing had driven her off. She was always there, waiting,

wearing the face of a little girl like a mask.

At least she didn't attack anymore when I left the house for supply runs.

I snagged a protein bar off the kitchen counter on my way to the basement, then thumped down concrete steps to my workroom. It was a spare space carved out of the manmade underground cavern, a twelve by twelve corner smelling of dirt and fabric softener and the curious musty scent basements exude even when mildew isn't a problem. I'd shoved as much equipment into that space as I could manage to find in the past six months, and had learned not to wince at the thought of the amount of electricity it used.

Mo had helped. Not with the electricity. With the equipment. When the first spores were released into the atmosphere, he was at Grand Central, the lab we shared at a private testing facility outside Atlanta. He'd managed to tough it out until the first wave passed and contact was re-established, then spearheaded research into exactly what the spore was, how it worked, and, more importantly, how we could kill it.

We'd been friends before, but after? Mo was the one who pulled me through. He was the one I'd turned to when Melly was infected and my husband died. Mo was the one who counseled me through six months of grief and the pain of losing my entire family in one fell swoop.

The spore had taken the children, and the children had taken the adults. My husband hadn't had a chance.

My appetite disappeared down the same dark hole that had almost taken me. I dropped the protein bar next to the keyboard, sat down at my desk in front of the monitor array, and logged in.

Mo's pockmarked face appeared on the central screen. "How you doin', darlin' Diane?"

I relaxed into the chair and, for the first time in days, smiled. "Same as ever, Mo. How's Grand Central?"

"More central than grand," he retorted. "I never shoulda let the government in on this."

"Hey, I'm the anarchist here, Mo. Get your own label in the hierarchy. You can't have mine."

"Har. How's the young'un?"

My humor died a quiet death. I turned away from the central monitor on the pretense of lighting up my workstation.

Mo sighed. "Still hanging out on the porch, huh?"

"Good thing," I quipped, aiming for a light tone, "as she's the only research subject I have."

By the time I finished turning on every bell and whistle on my desk, the silence had dragged on entirely too long. I met Mo's steady gaze through the camera imbedded in the top of the central monitor. His eyes were dark brown and red-rimmed and held a tad too much compassion for my comfort.

"Leave off," I said.

"I didn't say anything."

"You didn't have to. Any progress on your end?"

"The spore's alien in origin," he said, so deadpan I would've done a double take if I hadn't already known where the stuff came from.

"Funny guy," I murmured, then settled in for a nice, long chat about the daily reports we'd sent to each other since our last video chat a week ago.

SHE WAS SITTING in a child-sized rocker when I stepped onto the front porch decked out in a white contamination suit. Hood up, booties on. No respirator. Those had gone the way of the dodo not long after the Fall. We'd burned through them too fast and there weren't enough people left to man the factories to make more. I used goggles and a mask instead, and prayed like hell that it was enough every single time I stepped outside.

I extended a new toy toward her, a floppy eared bunny Mo had tucked into last week's supply box, and kept the collection kit down. She hated the collection kit.

Yet here she was, waiting for me to use it on her.

I shook my head at the contradiction and slowly knelt in front of her, set the bunny down at her feet when her gaze passed over it and latched onto me. The vines growing out of her spine had twisted along her ribs like thin, brown limbs. They weren't vines, really, not in the botanical sense. Honestly, we weren't sure exactly what they were yet, only that they were attached to the symbiote curled around the host's spinal column and that the symbiote grew from the spore.

Six months and we knew little more now than we had then.

"Ok, you," I said. "Time for your weekly checkup."

Her mouth opened wide, displaying tiny baby teeth and a tongue laced with the brown and green spots of the infected. I slipped a swab out of the kit by feel, had it in and out of her mouth in record time, and dropped it into a labeled tube before her jaw slammed shut and those sharp teeth clicked together.

Practice makes perfect.

Next, I measured one of the downy, moss-like tendrils covering her head, where a glossy cap of chestnut curls had once been, then clipped a tiny sample. That was never a problem. Like human hair, the tendrils were little more than dead protein, albeit protein unlike anything we had here on Earth. She never cried out in pain when I clipped the tendrils, never jerked her head away, never screeched at me or tried to bite me...

I was stalling. Damn it.

But she was way ahead of me. Her tiny hands had curled into stiff fists against the rag doll as she shrank away from me into the dubious refuge offered by the colorfully painted rocking chair.

This was always the hardest part.

I tucked the tendril sample into a collection tube, picked up the measuring tape again, and inhaled slowly and deeply. Those vines around her torso had to be measured. How else could we monitor their growth against the baseline?

I reached toward her, slowly enough not to startle her, my gaze unfocused so I could catch any sudden movement. She gazed back, wary, I think, though it was hard to tell.

She wasn't human anymore. Maybe whatever she'd become had no feelings, not the way humans did. Maybe we shouldn't anthropomorphize them. I'd always hated when people did that to their pets, assigning feelings as if they were children.

And yet, I couldn't quite bring myself to call her an it.

I winced and gently tugged a vine away from her ribs, stifled another wince as the others shifted across her dress. Quickly, I measured its length and memorized the numbers. She'd only had to destroy my notebook once for me to learn that trick.

No change.

My hands shifted to the vines wrapped around her ribs, and her lips pulled back in a snarl.

Shit. Maybe I could still get one more measure—

Her hand lashed out, fingers extended, and her claw-like fingernails raked down my arm, snagging on the contamination suit. I scrambled back on all fours, an awkward crab walk lacking any semblance of grace. The porch's wooden slats were uneven under my feet and palms, some swollen, some chipping away from rot where the paint had flaked off. I could almost hear Matt chastising me for letting the house go as I slammed shoulders first into the railing.

This house is Melly's legacy, he said in my mind, his voice low and soft and perfectly rational. *We have to take care of it for her, the way your parents and grandparents took care of it for you.*

Well, screw that. If he'd wanted it taken care of, he shouldn't have tried to separate Melly from the spore's growth.

My breath heaved in and out of my lungs, alternately sucking the paper mask tight to my mouth and blowing it out again, and my heart pounded so hard, my vision jerked with every heartbeat. She'd fallen out of the rocking chair and now crouched behind it, staring at me through the back slats with what I would've sworn was a wounded expression. Betrayed, even.

That made two of us.

I glanced down at my arm, frowned at the brown streaks marring the white fabric. Was that a tear there, just above my wrist?

Shit.

Slowly, my gaze never leaving hers, I maneuvered onto my hands and knees, then stood and walked slowly toward the kit. Picked it up, opened the door, slipped through it into the decontamination room I'd rigged up not long after the Fall.

Once inside, I shut the door on her. Not that she'd try to come in. She'd stopped trying after that first day, after Matt...

Well, after that.

I flipped a plastic sheet down over the door, taped it into place, then started the long process of doing what I could to keep the house spoor-free for one more day.

I FOUND a small rip in the contamination suit, likely where one of her thorn-like fingernails had dug in a little too hard. I stared at it for a long time, my mind so empty I couldn't even process what I was seeing.

Finally, I discarded the suit in the decontamination room's trashcan and checked my skin. No swelling, no bruising, no welts. No worry, no panic, no fear.

I walked out of the decontamination room and upstairs into the shower.

I scrubbed and scrubbed, but no matter how hard I washed my skin, I didn't feel clean.

THE HOT WATER gave out before I did. When it was too icy to tolerate, I got out, toweled off, threw on some clean sweats. Focusing on the routine helped, on the procedure, the minutiae. That was easier than thinking about what had happened, about potential consequences.

Calm was a dispassionate blanket wrapped around me, insulating me from possibilities.

I padded downstairs barefoot, ignoring the chill of tile and linoleum and wood and concrete, and skyped Mo. His face appeared on the central monitor, his bushy eyebrows arched high. He had jowls now, a small sag under his jaw. Was that a touch of gray in the tightly kinked curls at his temples?

No, Mo wasn't old. Mo was my rock, my mentor, the shoulder I cried on. Rocks didn't age. They couldn't.

"Jesus, Diane," he said. "What's wrong?"

"Nothing. I—" I inhaled a deep breath. "Probably nothing."

"Then why are you crying?"

I touched waterlogged fingertips to my cheeks and discovered moisture. "She was a little upset today."

"Oh, Jesus," Mo breathed. "What happened?"

I ran through the incident, my voice clinically cold, detached even, but inside, a trembling began, first in my heart, then my lungs. It spread outward, rushing through me like wildfire until I was both hot and cold at once and my hands shook against the edge of my desk.

I tucked them into my lap, hiding them in the loose folds of my sweatpants, and let my words trail off.

The silence stretched between us for a moment as Mo stared

at me and I tried hard not to stare back.

Finally, he said, "I'll mark it in the log. We'll test you when you make your next supply run."

I opened my mouth to tell him not to bother. I'd know by then if the spore had taken root, and if it had, testing was moot. There was no cure, only a slow, rotting death.

No, there was no need to say that. We both knew it all too well. I closed my mouth and nodded, then shut down the call and turned to the collection kit. Work waited for no woman, no matter how rattled she was.

LATER, I ATE the protein bar (I'd forgotten all about eating until my stomach protested with a series of sharp rumbles) as I walked upstairs through the kitchen, then up another flight of stairs to the bedrooms on the second floor.

Melly's room was exactly the way she'd left it. Her bed was unmade, revealing the delicately pink flowered sheets she'd picked out herself. Four years old and making her own decisions. I huffed out a laugh and leaned a shoulder against the doorframe, with my back to the hall separating her room from ours. Matt had picked out her furniture, all wooden curves painted bright white with touches of gold accents. For his little princess.

Every time he said that, I cut my eyes at him. Why did little girls always have to be princesses?

His response? Because they held their daddy's hearts.

My own heart squeezed tight in my chest. I polished off the protein bar and stepped carefully over a life-sized doll Melly had tipped over on her way out the door that last morning. A book rested on her nightstand under the fairytale lamp I'd found at a local fundraiser. Behind it, a picture of Matt holding Melly high as they twirled around rested in an ornate silver frame.

I traced my fingers over their images and swallowed down the sorrow rising within me. "Oh, Matt. Why did you have to go after her?"

Why did you have to let her go? he said in my mind.

The words wounded me, however imaginary they were. Matt had never said them to me. There hadn't been time. As soon as we'd realized what was happening outside, even before the morning news could report it...

We could see it swirling down, you know? We could see it through the kitchen windows, drifting in gentle waves as the pods were dropped into the upper atmosphere and burst open as they hurtled through the air toward the earth, burning. Meteorites, we'd thought, but no, there were the spores dropping onto the grass, sprouting around Melly's swing set as we watched.

And there was Melly in the back yard, her arms spread wide, her head held back, that adorable grin on her face as she twirled 'round and 'round.

Matt dropped his coffee cup. It hit the floor at the exact same moment he opened the back door, and shattered, spewing dark, hot liquid across my bare feet.

I don't know what instinct prompted me to walk over and shut the door behind him, but I did. I shut the door and I stood there and watched as the spore slipped down my precious daughter's throat and took root as it had in the grass. I watched as it tore through her, molding her to its will from the inside out, contorting her tiny body into seizures.

I watched as Matt raced across the grass shouting her name, and I watched as she jerked and twisted and became a thing wearing my daughter's face. I watched, mute and immobile, as Matt reached her and bent down and put his hands on her waist, and as she—

I set the picture down with a snap and closed off the memory. The past was just that. I couldn't change what had happened, only try to clean up the mess we'd made of it. Wasn't that what we were doing now as we tested and researched and studied? Weren't we trying to fix that mess?

I turned and walked out of Melly's room, avoiding the doll laying on the floor.

THE SKIN above my wrist seemed perfectly fine the next morning. I scrubbed it again anyway, doused it with peroxide and rubbing alcohol, one after the other. Not that it would do any good, but it made me feel better.

I knew without looking what day it was. First of the month. Time for the power company's crew to come by, check the meter, and clear out any spore-produced vegetation. Damn stuff was worse than kudzu. If you didn't keep it in check, it covered everything in sight.

Which begged the question as to why her vines never grew.

I suited up. Suit, hoodie, mask. She was hiding behind the rocker, and for a minute, I wondered if she'd spent the entire night there, huddled against it.

No, of course not. She had to eat...something. What, we didn't know. I'd voted for following her and the other children around. Mo had pulled rank on me and vetoed that idea using a few surprisingly colorful words.

We just didn't have enough people left. Enough adults.

Right on cue, a once-white pickup truck with the power company logo emblazoned on the doors pulled into the driveway and parked well away from the front porch where she and I stood. I lifted a hand and waved.

The woman in the truck's passenger seat slid out and waved back. She was smiling behind her mask and goggles, and would've come closer if the thing that used to be Melly hadn't hissed at her.

I sighed and stepped between her and the crew, right up to the edge of the porch. "It's ok, Lynn," I hollered, hoping my voice carried across the yard through the muffling mask. "We had a little incident yesterday. I'll make sure she stays out of your way."

Lynn slammed the door and leaned against it. "Be easier if you took her inside, Di."

"Can't. Protocol."

"Effin' protocol."

I laughed. "What would we do without it?"

"Shame you can't take your own kid inside, though."

I stiffened and my smile froze on my face as the driver's side door opened and a hulking man slid out and toward the truck's bed, where the crew's equipment was stored. Not my kid. She hadn't been my kid since the spore took her.

"Especially Melly," Lynn continued. "She was such a sweet little thing, just like a girl should be. Sugar and spice and everything nice."

An image of spore-bound Melly leaping onto her father flooded my mind, and my gut churned. No, not Melly. Couldn't be Melly. She never would've hurt her father that way. Lynn was so right about that. Sugar and spice, that was Melly. Daddy's little princess.

But this thing, this *it* possessing Melly's body, she wasn't sweet. Anything but. Hadn't she fought me tooth and nail? Hadn't she ripped our family apart as surely as I had, when I'd stood there watching her devour Matt?

She wasn't Melly anymore. I couldn't call her that. I couldn't call her by the name she'd carried when she was my daughter. I couldn't—

Something wrapped around my calf and squeezed. Startled, I looked down. She was standing beside me, nearly plastered against my side, her rib vines sliding across my leg. Her face was tilted up to mine, and for a moment, I forgot what she was. I forgot what she'd done, what I'd done. For a moment, she was my sweet, innocent little girl, clinging to me. Comforting me, or maybe taking comfort in me, the way she used to before the Fall.

The truck's tailgate slammed down, breaking the moment, and the present flooded back.

"I'll keep her up here," I said, though my voice was so rough and soft I wasn't sure Lynn could hear me.

The vines squeezed my leg again, and when I looked down, her mouth was moving and a soft murmur drifted out of her throat.

"Mmm," she said. "Mmm mmm."

Slowly, deliberately, I hardened my heart against the possibility that she was trying to say "Mama."

WE'D NEVER SETTLED on what to call the children consumed by the spore, though we could ascertain several attributes. Their physical growth stopped the moment they were infected. One researcher theorized that their energy instead supported the symbiote's growth. It was as good a theory as any, though we'd never been able to prove it.

You had to be able to run tests on the symbiote for that. No one ever got close enough. The vines were a protection, a living shield surrounding both host and parasite. One poor soul had tried snipping off a piece of vine from a living source. She hadn't lasted three minutes. Mo aired the video every once in a while, just to remind us what we were dealing with.

We knew the children communicated with each other, but not through speech, or if through the spoken word, no one ever saw it. I'd never heard of a single host speaking once they were infected by the spore.

I'd also never heard of one of the spore-bound voluntarily approaching a human and sheltering against one. Plenty of others seemed to sense their researchers' routines and tolerated them with varying degrees of patience, but that was different. We'd discussed the possibility of the symbiotes studying us just as we were studying them. That was a rational reason for the former children's cooperation during testing, much more rational than believing the children were still alive in their skin shells, or that they had any control over what was happening to them.

After the crew finished their slash-and-burn treatment of the yard, I disentangled myself from her vines and went inside, my head buzzing. Why had she reached out to me? Was this a turning point? Or was it something else entirely and I wasn't objective enough to understand?

As soon as I could, I recorded the entire incident in my log. Read through it twice, tweaking, refining, then pushed back from my desk, suddenly so hungry I could eat a horse.

Upstairs, I opened the fridge, found three dried limes, a cup of milk curdled in the bottom of a plastic quart jug, half a dozen slices of processed cheese, and a limp stalk of celery.

For crying out loud. When was the last time I'd gotten fresh food on a supply run?

Right. That would be never. Mo kept offering it to me. I preferred the protein bars. Quick, easy, nutritious. No fuss, no muss.

I slammed the refrigerator door shut, opened the freezer, and laughed. There, stacked neatly in vacuum-sealed bags, was six months' worth of frozen meat and fish. Bless Matt. I'd forgotten all about his penchant for overbuying.

When was the last time I'd even wanted real food?

I snagged a packet of frozen hamburger patties, tucked it under my arm, and, ignoring the cold seeping into my skin through my sweatshirt, scratched the skin above my right wrist. It would be so good to have burgers again. Too bad I didn't have lettuce and tomatoes or buns and pickles. Mayonnaise and ketchup and mustard!

Maybe I'd crank up the grill and...

No, scratch that. Couldn't go outside because of the spore, but that was ok. I'd pan fry them, slap a slice of cheese on each one, maybe see if Melly wanted one—

The packet of meat slipped out from under my arm, glanced off my knee, and cracked against the linoleum, then slid across the floor leaving a sheen of melting ice behind it. I lifted my arm and stared at my wrist as numb horror spread through me. While I'd been working, the skin had cracked like drying sand. It was red there, in that tiny spot where her thorn-nail had sliced open my contamination suit the day before, red and hot and itchy. Beneath that, a miniscule bump jutted upward, like a boil, so small I wouldn't have been able to differentiate it from the surrounding tissue if not for the color and feel: Brown, like bark or a root, and hard.

I sank to my knees onto the kitchen floor, my gaze automatically seeking the glass-paned door leading outside. She was standing there, her tiny body pressed against the frame, scratching her fingernails against the glass, Melly's favorite rag doll tucked tightly against her chest.

I VERY NEARLY LEFT the meat where it was, would've if my stomach hadn't chosen that moment to cramp from lack of food. But I wasn't a quitter, and I was hungry, and my skin itched like I'd rolled around in poison ivy yesterday.

Without thinking about it, I walked into the bathroom and fumbled through the medicine cabinet until I found some hydro-cortisone cream. Squirted a dob on my skin, covered it with a band-aid.

And then I calmly returned to the kitchen, retrieved the packet of frozen hamburger patties, and proceeded to thaw and cook them, just as I'd planned.

I pulled a chair up to the door and ate one sitting there, off a plate bare of anything else. She was still outside, watching, and finally I couldn't stand it anymore. I just had to know. Right now, not when I finished eating, but in this very moment.

I set my plate down on the counter. My stomach whimpered a bit. I'd only eaten half of one patty, not nearly enough to fill me up.

Screw it. I needed to know. Was anything human left in the spore-bound? Did anything remain of my precious daughter?

My supply of masks was exactly where it was supposed to be, stored in the basement on a rack under the steps. I dug one out, slipped it over the lower half of my face, and didn't bother with a contamination suit. What was the point? That bump was spore. I knew it. She knew it. Tomorrow Mo and the rest of the world would know it, too.

And that urgency was growing in me, pushing me to continue experimenting, to continue learning while I still could.

I pulled down a saucer out of the kitchen cabinet, broke off half a patty still warming in the pan, then took the impromptu offering to the door. My hand trembled like a leaf battered by a gale. I managed to turn the knob and pull the door open.

She watched me, waited for me. When I extended the plate toward her, offering her a bite of supper, she leaned close and sniffed. Touched the tip of her tongue to the cooked hamburger and reared back, her face wrinkled into a frown.

I started to withdraw the plate, oddly disappointed. It was so good, that freshly cooked piece of ground beef. Melly had loved hamburgers. Not as much as hot dogs or ice cream, but they ran a close third. Any hope I'd had that my little girl was still in there withered away and I sniffed in a futile attempt not to cry.

Damn it. Why had I let myself believe, even for a second?

Then her hand shot out and she snagged the beef patty and shoved it into her mouth, and my laughter welled up and over.

"It's good, isn't it?" I said.

She looked at me and grinned around a mouth stuffed full of food. "Mmm mmm," she said, and as much as I wanted to think so, I knew she wasn't really talking. Her vocal cords were still intact, that's all.

But this was progress. Definitely something to share when I filed my report at the end of the day and told Mo his favorite researcher had been infected.

THE NEXT MORNING, I showered and threw on some jeans and a t-shirt, then trudged downstairs and skyped Mo. The bump on my wrist was now the size of a dime. Something moved under the skin, a thin, ropy coil that reminded me, if I didn't think too hard about it, of the vines growing out of her symbiote around her torso.

Strange that the spore was growing so slowly in me, when it had taken the children almost immediately. Maybe that's why they'd turned on the adults. Maybe it just grew more slowly in us, rendering us other, alien. Who knew?

Someone would, someday. I was certain of that. Probably not me, but I was ok with that. Oddly enough, I was at peace.

Mo's face appeared on the central monitor so fast, I was certain he'd been waiting for me to call. "Show it to me," he said, his normally mellow voice now a terse bark.

I lifted my arm, turned my hand around so he could see the back of my wrist. "Two days."

"And that's all it's done?"

I huffed out a laugh. "Isn't that enough?"

"You're sure it's not something else? A spider bite, maybe?"

I was already shaking my head. "It's the spore, Mo."

He leaned back in his chair and his gaze drifted away from the camera. At last, he said, "Let's see if we can remove the growth. If we catch it before it spreads—"

"Mo," I said softly, gently. "We both know it's too late. It's already in my bloodstream."

"You'll run a friggin test before you tell me that."

"Ok."

"Three tests and a biopsy. I want to be sure."

"Sure."

His expression wavered, and for a second, I thought he was going to cry. The moment passed, as moments do, and all he said was, "Report in every day, once in the morning, once at night. I'll assign a research team to help you."

As long as my brain is still my own.

The unspoken words hung in the air between us. I reached toward the keyboard, intending to cut the call, and halted when he spoke.

"Diane."

"What is it, Mo?"

"We're not going to let you die."

We stared at each other for a long moment, then I nodded and closed out the call on the first and last lie Mo had ever told me. The spore was a death sentence. We both knew that, but for all that knowledge, some part of me appreciated that he'd tried to comfort me with that lie.

SHE WAS WAITING for me in the rocking chair, as if she'd sensed me heading toward the porch, her rag doll held to her chest. This wasn't part of our routine, but I let her behavior go. I could note it in the log later, after I'd done what I'd come here to do.

I tore down the decontamination room surrounding the front

door. Didn't need it anymore, did I? And it hadn't been great to begin with. Too many places it could've leaked spore into the house, though it never had.

What did it matter now?

I kicked the plastic sheets aside and walked out, leaving my mask and protective gear inside for someone else's use. "Hello, you."

She cocked her head to the side, and if I hadn't known better, I would've sworn her mouth was trying to smile.

I covered the space between us in a few steps, knelt in front of her, worked up a smile for her, even if she couldn't share or understand it. "You were a bad girl the other day, when you fought me. I wish I could explain exactly why."

"Mmm," she said, startling me. "Mmm mmmmaa."

My heart swelled inside my chest. "That's right, sweetie. I was your mama, and you were my little girl. You were my Melly."

She held the rag doll out to me, her eyes solemn, and I took it and pressed it to my own chest.

"It's time to come home, darling girl. It's time to be my Melly again."

I laughed and sniffed back a tear, shook my head. Of course, she didn't understand me, but maybe when the spore infected me the way it had her, maybe then I could tell her. I held my arms out to her, waited patiently while she scooted forward on the chair and leaned into me, then she was there again, hugging me with her favorite dolly trapped between us. I smoothed down the tendrils that had once been curls and felt her teeth slide along the skin of my throat, but I knew she wasn't going to hurt me. I knew she wouldn't devour me the way she had Matt, when the spore had drifted down her throat, planting a starving symbiote inside her fragile body, forcing her to feed until it grew large enough to fully control her.

We were the same now, me and Melly, on the inside, under

our skin. We were both spore-bound, infected with an alien lifeform humans had yet to understand.

And it was time to go home.

Carefully, I pulled her close to me and stood, ignoring her vines as they wrapped around me and bound us together. I went inside and closed the door, and carried her up to her bathroom for a nice, hot bath.

Good Eats

My husband was one of the first to go.

He'd always joked about the zombie apocalypse, even went so far as to refurbish the basement for post-apocalyptic survival. Enough food for five years, he'd said. Turned out, it wasn't, not the way he thought, but he didn't live to see that. He didn't live to see any of it.

Only it wasn't zombies that got us; it was humans. A bio-engineered virus. Friggin' scientists and their friggin' curiosity. The crops were gone before real panic set in, before hardly anybody realized exactly how bad it was going to get. Everything changed almost overnight. Within a week, by my reckoning.

We were safe for a while, me and the baby. Nobody knew about the basement stash. If we'd lived in Suburbia, everybody and God would've known, but Gabe had gotten a great job in the city, and after, we'd decided to buy a place in the middle of nowhere as a retreat. One by one, our rural neighbors had succumbed, anybody who would've known us, and the roving gangs of cannibals stuck to well-traveled paths, where more people gathered.

Sheer, dumb luck saved us, or maybe there really was a God. Who knew?

My parents fled the city when it got bad. Before they died, they sheltered with me and the baby a while, and we did our best to eke out a living. Crops went first, the game and wild foods not long after, and after that, after people emptied the canned goods out of grocery stores and nothing was left but trees and grass and lifeless brambles, humans turned to the only food source left: Each other.

BABY ELIZABETH was a plump little thing. She'd taken her first step in the week before Gabe died, and since then had learned to toddle along pretty well. But she wasn't cut out for hiking, especially in the depths of forests largely untouched by man. What toddler was?

Traveling by night would've been better, but it was too dark under the canopy's starving branches to make out the trail. I knew how to read a map, could use a compass as well as anybody, but I was afraid to venture far off the trail, afraid we'd get lost. So we walked slowly, kept a careful ear out, and covered our footprints as best we could.

It wouldn't do to have somebody catch our scent and track us. I wasn't afraid of killing another human. In the aftermath, I'd gotten pretty damn familiar with how best to do it. But I also wasn't stupid. A lone woman carrying a child was easy enough to take down. A gang would corner us and cook us for dinner, or worse, eat us while the heart beat and the meat was still fresh and juicy.

The threat of starvation went a long way toward helping a body get over the kneejerk revulsion of eating another human being's flesh.

Determination kept me putting one foot in front of the other, with the added burden of Bethy on my hip and a pack full of dried meat and ammunition slung across my back.

And the seeds, of course. Just in case.

The silence ate at me. The critters that before wouldn't have given human hikers a second thought had either been killed or had learned to silence their songs. Between that and the no talking rule, the late fall air grew oppressive, eerie even, like a thousand eyes were watching us from their hiding places in the sparse under-growth. Sometimes I had to stop and shelter against a tree for a while, one hand wrapped around the hilt of Gabe's rifle, waiting for my skin to stop crawling.

Nobody and nothing was out there that could hurt us. And if there were people out there, pray God they were survivors like us, regular folks trying to find a better way.

Please, God.

THE SUN sank low on the horizon, unaffected by the plight of humanity. Bethy fell asleep draped across my chest. My arms ached under the dead weight. We had to find a place to shelter soon, before full dark fell and I collapsed in mid-stride.

The trail turned and twisted into a steep, rock-slick climb, and I cursed it bitterly under my breath. No more tonight. We'd just have to make do with where we were. Too bad we hadn't found a creek. Fresh drinking water, a quick bath. I sighed and eased Bethy onto a bed of dead, brittle moss fifteen feet away from the trail. A bath would be heavenly, even a soapless dip in icy water.

Hadn't had any soap in ages. Turned out Gabe hadn't planned so well after all.

I slipped the pack off, set it down beside Bethy. Stretched and bit my lower lip, containing a reflexive moan as stiff muscles strained and protested.

And froze, one ear tilted to the soft murmur of masculine voices drifting from the other side of the hill. I held my breath and listened, trying to pinpoint their location, their number, anything that would help me figure out what to do next.

A single word drifted toward me, spoken by a young male, possibly a pre-teen, maybe slightly older. *Dad.*

Hope rose bittersweet, sharply gnawing at my bones. Companionship. I'd been so long without adult conversation, so long without the support of another capable being that tears clogged my sinuses.

I shoved down the need, stuffed it deep inside my gullet, and hardened myself against it. Even if the two males on the other side of the hill were survivors, there was no guarantee of safety, no guarantee at all.

Bethy whimpered in her sleep, drawing my gaze. She had to make it, this chubby little girl topped by wispy brown curls. She was the future, *my* future, and the only guarantee I had.

Something had to survive, someone good and strong. I'd promised Gabe I'd raise her well. It was one promise I'd never break.

I WAITED for full night to fall in a suffocating blanket, then crept up the hill along the trail in the thin moonlight shining through desiccated tree limbs. Careful, slow, steady. My feet slid along the rock, cramming my heart into my throat, and my fingers grappled along the damp leaves, scrabbling for a hold. The smells of mold and decay drifted to me, tickling my nose, and I swiped my forearm across my face, forestalling a tell-tale sneeze.

Another scent. Wood smoke, and with it nostalgia. Evenings in front of the fire, snuggled against Gabe, roasting marshmallows or popping popcorn. Making love while snow drifted down around our home.

I shook the memories off. Those days were long gone, leaving a hollow thirst in their wake.

The ridge crested some ten feet above me. I picked my way there, hesitated at the top. Below, tucked behind a laurel thicket bare of leaves, a campsite had been set up. Light from a small fire glinted off the fabric of a single tent. Two figures crouched by the flames, one almost twice the size of the other.

"Why don't we burn green wood?" a man asked in a smooth baritone.

"Smoke," the younger voice said. "We don't want a huge fire 'cause that'd draw a lot of attention to us."

"You're learning."

There was a smile in that voice, an inviting one. I shifted my hold, aiming for a better look. My hand slipped, losing its grip on the rock anchoring me in place, and down I went, sliding loudly along the trail, scraping skin and muscle away with every inch.

When I'd tumbled to a stop, the voices had ceased. I bit my lip, holding in a moan. Stupid. If I'd stayed still, I could've approached on my own terms. Now they were probably hunting me, creeping through the woods to see who and what I was, maybe laying a trap.

I glanced over, found Bethy's sleeping form still hidden where I'd left her. Dare I call out and let the males know where I was? Dare I trust them before I knew what they were made of?

"Don't move," the baritone said softly from near the top of the ridge some twenty feet behind me.

My eyelids slid shut. I hadn't heard even a hint of his approach. At least I knew where one of them was now. "I'm not going to move. Please don't hurt me or my daughter."

"Where is she?"

"Promise not to hurt her."

He laughed, his voice still so soft I could barely hear him. "Lady, you're crazy if you think I'm going to promise you anything."

A cultured voice, not rough and eager. I could work with that.

"May I stand?" I said, careful to keep my own voice low and unthreatening. Obsequious. "I think I may have sprained my ankle when I slid down the trail."

"Slow and easy," he said.

A teenager stepped onto the trail in front of me holding a long, sturdy stick with a knife tied to it. I could just make the unlikely duo out.

The moon must've risen.

I rolled onto my side, obeying the command to move slowly so as not to arouse their ire. Pushed myself into a stand, tried to put weight on my ankle. It held, though the joint was tender, bruised.

"Where's your daughter?" the man said, so close I nearly gasped.

I hadn't heard him move at all, again. My luck to stumble on someone like him.

But I could work with that, too. And I'd have to trust him, at least a little.

"Over there," I said, pointing. "On the moss. Please don't wake her. It's been a long day."

He slipped behind me, walked over to Bethy, and stood looking down at her for long moments, the barrel of his rifle pointed toward the ground, away from her. "Who else is with you?"

"No one, I swear. My husband..." I swallowed hard, glanced at the boy. "He didn't make it."

"What kind of a fool do you take me for?" the man said.

A retort bottled itself up inside my throat. It seemed like a rhetorical question, said half to himself, half to the boy maybe. I held still, waiting for him to decide what to do with us. Waiting patiently.

I'd learned a lot about patience since Gabe died.

"Alex," he said after a while. "Get the girl."

"Yes, sir."

The kid swung his makeshift bayonet over his shoulder and tucked it into a harness at his back. He moved closer, and I revised my estimate of his age. This kid was maybe ten or eleven, still a couple of years away from puberty. Tall, though, not quite my height, and sturdy, like the stick he carried.

A stick with a knife roped to it, I reminded myself. Another point of danger. At least they hadn't killed us on sight.

The man straightened away from Bethy as Alex approached him. I couldn't see him well in the darkness, shadowed as he was under a thick tangle of limbs, but I could feel his gaze on me.

"It would serve you right if I left you out here, tied to a tree," he said. "Exposed. You'd make good bait."

"Dad," Alex said, and there was a note there, in his voice, that I couldn't quite read.

The man sighed. "Ok. She comes, too, but I'm not letting her in camp with her hands free."

I nearly sighed myself. It was better than I'd hoped for. "My pack is next to my daughter."

"I've got it."

Alex bent and awkwardly picked Bethy up. She gurgled in her sleep, then seemed to accept him as she would me. The man slung my pack and Gabe's rifle over one shoulder and approached me with a rope held in his hands. Dutifully, I held my own out and let him secure them without another peep.

***

THE FIRE had been doused. The man seemed to move more by instinct than sight. I followed him blindly, led by the rope tied around my wrists. Alex was behind us, huffing a little as he toted Bethy up the ridge and down the other side. I could hear them breathing, a little boy carrying a third his weight extra, a little girl catching sleep as she could.

What a world we lived in now.

The man ducked into the laurel thicket, tugging me along behind. Up close, he was huge, easily six three, and broad of shoulder. Sturdy, like the boy. He tied me off around a thin jack pine.

Alex stopped inside the thicket. "Where should I put her, sir?"

"In your tent's fine," the man said.

It was dark in their cubbyhole, too dark for me to make out what was going on, though they seemed to have no trouble moving around.

"Be careful with her," I said.

"Yes'm," Alex said. "I will."

I heard the flap of fabric, then a lamp clicked on inside the tent. Shadows appeared, of a boy kneeling, of a little girl as a lump along the ground. The light was bright enough for me to make out the dome of a second, slightly larger tent and a food bag suspended by a rope from the limb of a nearby tree.

"He seems like a good kid," I said softly. "Where's his mom?"

The man glanced up, half of his face illuminated by the thin light bleeding through the tent. "This isn't social hour, lady."

I nodded affably. "Ok, I'll give you that. Doesn't mean we have to ignore the niceties."

He barked out a laugh, bent to his task reigniting the small fire. It wasn't too chilly out yet, wouldn't be for another couple of weeks, but there was a nip in the air, a hint of the coming winter. I shivered, thinking on it, then relaxed against the tree. Bethy and I were set. No need to worry on things already taken care of.

HE LEFT me there, bound to the tree, as the dew settled on the ground and the night air cooled to uncomfortable. I curled into myself, hunkered against the tree, as the moon passed overhead and the man and boy took turns at watch.

I didn't ask for the thin blanket in my pack, and I didn't speak. What was the point? The man wasn't talking and the kid needed to learn to trust me, if Bethy and I had any hope at all.

She, at least, slept soundly through the night, the first time since we'd hit the trail.

Morning dawned bright and chill, stretching pink and gold fingers into the receding nighttime sky. The man was on last watch. He'd sat quietly at the fire during his turns at watch, feeding it steadily, retreating from it only to prowl the area around the campsite, planting his feet precisely in the cushion of pine needles covering the forest floor.

It dawned on me that they must've been camped there for days, weeks even, for him to know it so well.

Why, though? Why risk the trail when he obviously had the skills to keep himself and his son alive in a less remote area providing better opportunities for food and shelter?

As soon as the question popped into my mind, I remembered my own reasons for being there. My eyes narrowed on him speculatively. Yes, this was something to watch.

When the sun had lumbered fully above the mountaintops, the man picked up a blue ceramic-coated coffee pot and disappeared toward the bubble of an unseen creek. He returned a few minutes later, set the coffee pot on a metal grill over the flames, and flipped the tent flap open. Alex's sleepy face appeared in the opening. Without a word, he crawled into the clearing and quietly slipped out of it again, heading toward the creek.

My arms ached from being held in the same position throughout the night, and grit coated my eyes. I yawned into my arm, ignored the reek of my skin (what I wouldn't do for a bath). I'd dozed off and on, but a deeper sleep had eluded me. Small wonder.

When Alex returned, the man pulled out a vacuum sealed bag of jerky and sliced into it, gave one piece to his son, took another for himself. He stared at me across the small fire.

I smiled. "I have food for me and Bethy in my pack, if you don't mind getting it?"

Why ask about being set free when I knew he wasn't going to? He'd have to unlock the cuffs sooner or later, if only to let me visit a bush.

Grudgingly, the man stuck the jerky in his mouth, holding one end of the thin strip with his teeth, and retrieved my backpack from the tent. Bethy hadn't woken yet, but it was early still. I'd let her rest as long as she needed. God knew we hadn't gotten a lot of sleep since heading out this time.

The man dug through the pack, found a plastic bag full of jerky (venison, honest), and handed me a tough slice.

"Thanks," I said. "I'm Holly, by the way."

The man grunted and started to turn away, then seemed to think better of it. "Tucker."

Ah, a crack in the armor. "Is that a first or last name?"

"Too many questions."

"How else are we supposed to get to know one another in this lovely social setting?"

A smile popped onto Alex's face and was hidden by the jerky being shoved into his mouth.

Tucker shook his head. "Eat while the eating's good."

I winked at Alex, then leaned toward the jerky held in my cuffed hands and stuck it in my mouth. It was salty and tough, but it was better than nothing.

Trust me.

TUCKER LET me loose once our meager breakfast was done. He followed me into the forest, gave me only the most cursory of privacy to do my business, and let me wash up in the creek. The water numbed my skin as soon as the two touched. At least I was cleaner.

After, he rinsed his own cup out, poured me half a cup of coffee, and held it out to me. "This'll warm you up."

I accepted it gratefully and sat with my back to the tree he'd handcuffed me to the night before. The mug was ceramic-coated metal and hot to the touch. Carefully, I pulled my shirt sleeves down over my palms and cupped the mug between them. Its heat seeped into my skin through the cloth, and he was right. It did warm me up.

His gaze was cold, hooded. I didn't blame him. We weren't exactly in a high trust situation.

Alex had sat down on the ground by the fire while his father escorted me to nature's privy. He was watching me the same way. It was a strange look for such a young person to carry.

I blew across the top of the coffee, watched steam waft away from me. "So what next?"

Tucker waited a beat, then two. "Haven't decided what to do with you yet."

"Eat me?" I said, aiming for a light tone.

Tucker snorted.

Alex dropped his eyes and looked away. Poor kid. This must be tough on him. But he was strong. Young. He'd survive.

Tucker squatted beside the fire and poked at it with a long stick. Embers sparked, rising into the morning air with the smoke. Any other time I would've warned him to be careful. Those embers could travel miles, but he didn't strike me as a careless person. Sometimes fire was simply uncontrollable.

But it was incumbent upon us to try. What good was finding other survivors if we burned to death in the desiccated remnants of the forest?

A mewl sounded from within the tent and a sleeping bag rustled. Bethy. I stood up automatically, stepped toward the tent.

Tucker rose more slowly, unfolding until he stood looking down at me across the fire. I clutched the cup, steadily meeting his gaze. He was a big man, fully a head taller than me. Rugged, attracttive even in the dawning day, behind the russet colored beard and mustache covering the lower half of his face.

I expected him to reprimand me, to grab the mug and force me down against the tree, to handcuff me there as he had the night before.

Instead, he said, "I'll get her. Finish your coffee."

It sounded like an order. And Bethy was safe enough. So I sat and brought the cup to my mouth, testing its heat with my lips.

Alex's gaze met mine. His rectangular face still carried the softness of youth, his lips a rosy bloom. They parted as if he were going to speak. Before he could, Tucker backed out of the tent with Bethy stiffening in his arms, and the moment passed without his saying a word.

THE CAMPSITE was their temporary home, I learned over the next few days. They'd fled the suburbs before the cannibal gangs began to form, but after Alex's mother died.

That was a taboo subject. The one time I mentioned it,

Tucker stared stonily at me, refusing to answer. Alex's expression had taken on a stricken look. I wasn't without compassion, so I let it drop. There were more important worries in front of me.

Bethy took to Alex straight off, toddling to him as if she'd known him her whole life. Tucker, on the other hand, had only to look at her and her face scrunched up into a scream. It was odd. She'd always been so friendly to the few people we'd met. Maybe it was his size, or the beard, or one of a dozen other reasons that had nothing to do with anything outside of her toddler-sized whims.

They let us stay with them. Safety in numbers, Tucker said, and we were a relatively low threat. He even gave Gabe's rifle back to me, though he held on to the ammunition. I didn't have to ask why.

We were becoming comfortable around each other. Trusting. Eventually he'd give in.

He left ammunition in the rifle itself, primarily because he'd reapportioned the watch, giving me a good chunk of Alex's time so the young ones could rest.

We drilled daily on what to do if other people found us, going over different scenarios. Alex on watch, Tucker on watch, me on watch. Me and Tucker fighting, Alex and Tucker fighting, and so on, until my mind swam with the possible ways we could escape or evade capture.

It was useful knowledge. I tucked away as much as I could remember, cataloging it for future use, for when me and Bethy were on our own again.

Nearly a week after we stumbled across them, I was on watch, sitting atop the dreaded ridge keeping an eye on the trail leading in both directions. We were remote here, but not so remote we couldn't be found.

The night was balmy, uncharacteristically so, and the stars

cold pinpricks of light against a sooty sky. Tucker had let the fire die down and banked some coals to make it easier to light in the morning, so there was no smoke drifting on the wind, no bats dipping down between the trees, devouring the insect population.

A shudder ran down my spine and I rubbed my arms, not for warmth, but for comfort. The night was eerily empty of sound and movement. Months after the world ended, and I still wasn't used to it.

I hated it, but the silence had its upside. When voices drifted to me, splitting through the night like a knife sliding between skin and muscle, they were far enough away for me to do something about it.

I listened long enough to pinpoint a direction. It wasn't hard. They weren't yelling, but they weren't whispering either. Normal voices. Three men, I thought, maybe a woman. Maybe more. I couldn't tell.

Tucker would be able to, though. The man had an uncanny knack for, well, a lot of things.

I crept down the trail toward camp, clicked my tongue when I was inside the laurel thicket, warning him of my approach. He didn't seem like a man you should sneak up on, so I didn't. By the time I reached the tent, the zipper was already lifting. I stepped back and crouched, waiting for him, and a moment later, Tucker eased out, already holding a gun.

"Men on the trail," I whispered, as low as I could. "Three, I think. Maybe a woman, too, or maybe a fourth man."

"Direction?"

I pointed away from the ridge, felt his hand slide down my arm checking the direction. It was dark out, with only a thumbnail moon to light our path.

"Go back to your post," he said. "Wait for my signal. Keep an eye on the camp. Only shoot if you have to."

I nodded.

"Don't shoot me," he added.

He melted away before I could comment, sliding into the darkness between the two tents as if he were a part of it.

I crept back toward the ridge, my heart hammering against my ribs. We couldn't take that many people, not at night, not without adequate light. Wouldn't it have been better to wait in the campsite and hope they passed us by?

Immediately, I rejected the idea. Bethy and Alex were in the campsite, sound asleep. If even one person slipped past me or Tucker, we'd never be able to protect them. Possibly this was a scouting party for a larger group. If it was, more would come before we could gain enough distance between here and a safer location to not be tracked.

Tracking was so much easier nowadays.

I reached my perch and squatted there, Gabe's rifle held tightly in my hands. The voices came closer, closer. Laughing, joking. Not too loudly. No, they knew what they were about. They knew, and they expected to find nothing.

Boy, were they in for a surprise.

I heard the first gasp when they were almost on top of me, just on the other side of the campsite. Gasp, thud, then a shriek, and a wild mixture of grunts and curses. Feet thudding lightly on the trail, coming right at me.

My heart sank. There were more than the three or four I'd guesstimated.

I raised the rifle, searching for a target, biting my tongue to hold back the curse words bottling themselves up in my throat. No night vision. Wish I'd brought it now, but at the time, keeping the weight down had been more important. A woman could only carry so much, and with Bethy not being able to walk far on her own...

A figure popped into view on a clear spot along the trail some twenty feet away, a thin figure, short, wearing baggy clothing. I couldn't make out features, couldn't even guess a gender or age. What was behind them, though? What if I missed?

I aimed anyway, waiting to see what they'd do, and they kept coming, kept coming.

I squeezed the trigger. The rifle fired, recoiling into my shoulder with a thud hard enough to bruise. Bethy cried out as the figure staggered back and dropped to its knees, her voice not quite drowned out by the scuffle coming from farther down the trail.

Another figure burst into view, stumbled over their comrade. I raised the rifle and aimed, but more people were coming, two or three, not many. Was Tucker among them?

I swore under my breath and lowered the rifle, then slung it across my shoulder and pulled the knife Tucker had given me to wear during guard duty. I couldn't risk hitting him. He had become as much of my future as Bethy. It was time to fight up close and personal, and hope Alex had done what he was supposed to and vacated the campsite with Bethy in tow.

I JOGGED down the trail, praying I wouldn't step on a root and twist my ankle. I wasn't as familiar with it as Tucker and Alex. Hadn't had time to memorize the lay, the irregularities, the hazards.

By the time I reached the mostly hidden entrance to the campsite, my heart was pounding and the air was wheezing in and out of my lungs. I'd carried the knife with the point down and was fully ready to use it, but the jog down the trail had rattled me. I wasn't sure I could keep my hand steady enough to strike well, let alone enough for a killing blow.

Down here it was darker, too, but easier to tell one person from another. Tucker was in the mix, taking on two man-shaped figures, his hands balled into fists twice the size of mine. A third lay on the ground not far from the one I'd downed.

There was a lot of grunting and scuffling coming from Tucker and the other two as the latter tried to take the much bigger man down. I dropped the rifle where I'd be able to find it again and picked my target. Small guy with his back to me, and that's about all I could make out.

Miraculously, they hadn't heard me coming. Not sure how they could've missed me. Running down a trail was noisy.

I rolled my shoulders, throwing off the question of how and why, and crept toward them, aiming for the small guy. If I could get close enough to stab him—

An arm slipped around my neck from behind, cutting off my breath. I stabbed backward, wild in my aim, and caught nothing but air. Damn it. I'd miscounted, or maybe someone had snuck 'round. It wasn't Alex. Whoever held me was taller than me.

And they were dragging me backward, keeping me off balance as their arm tightened around my neck and my head grew dizzy from a lack of air.

They stumbled over something, loosening their grip. I opened my mouth wide and clamped my teeth down on their arm, biting their forearm as hard as I could. Dirty cotton filled my mouth, but beneath that, my teeth found flesh and bone.

They cried out, a high-pitched, nearly inhuman keening. A woman maybe?

Didn't matter. Their body twisted behind mine, slipping to the side, and I stabbed backward again, catching clothing or skin. Another yowl. Their arm twisted, wrenching my head around. I let go and slid to the side, falling into the damp leaf bed, rolling as soon as I hit. Glanced wildly around and spotted a figure cowering so close to the laurel thicket's shelter, their shadow was nearly indistinguishable from it.

The kids!

I scrambled onto my hands and knees and launched myself forward, still gripping the knife, miraculously enough. I raised it high and brought it down. The knife sank into flesh and skidded down their shoulder blade. They twisted around and raised their hands, trying to ward me off, but I was angry now. Bethy had to survive, her and Alex. They were the future, the only hope, and these crazies were threatening them.

I pushed hard against the attacker's shoulder, shoving them down, and leapt on top of them, straddling their waist, pinning them to the ground. The knife came down once, sucking into flesh, and I yanked back and stabbed again, and again, and again, panting my fury into the dark.

They couldn't have her. They couldn't take her away from me.

A hand caught my wrist, holding me tightly. "She's dead, Holly. You can stop now."

I went limp, allowed Tucker to gently pry the knife out of my fist. A shuddery sob escaped, then Tucker's arms came around me and he pulled me away from the person I'd just killed, and I turned into his chest and buried my face there, crying as the night descended into silence.

THERE WERE five of them, so I hadn't miscalculated by much. When my shaking settled down enough for me to think rationally, Tucker sent me to find the kids while he brought the bodies back to camp. We'd strip them down, salvage what we could from the things they carried, then wash the bodies and begin prepping them for preserving. It wasn't cold enough for the meat to keep, and we couldn't afford to let it go to waste.

What a world, right?

Questions buzzed through my head as I picked my way toward the stream and Alex's probable direction of flight. Where had they come from? Why were they on the trail? Was there a larger force behind them, or were they alone and just happened to be out this way?

I'd bet anything Tucker knew answers to some, if not all, of those questions.

I reached the creek's banks, listened to water bubbling over stone and sand, then listened above it for other sounds. Nothing. Finally, I said, "Alex? It's Holly. Are you out there?"

I could barely see beyond the creek. The forest was thick here. Even with the vegetation having died, the tree trunks clustered together with tall laurels and thin brambles. A rustling sounded to my right. I cocked my head, listening. The sound came again, a hair closer. Leaves along the forest floor, I decided. Someone, or something, was out there.

And I'd left my knife back at the campsite, along with Gabe's rifle. Stupid.

Just when I was about to turn around and retrieve a weapon, Alex said, "Holly?"

Relief flooded me. "Yes, it's Holly," I said. "Where are you? Do you have Bethy?"

"Yeah. Don't shoot me."

I shook my head, surrendering to an ill-timed burst of humor. What was it with him and Tucker?

Alex stepped out, brushing aside brambles so brittle they broke on contact. Bethy was draped across his chest, her chubby face buried in his throat. I stepped forward and carefully relieved him of her weight. How he'd managed to get her out of camp without waking her...

"C'mon," I said as soon as she was settled against me. "We have work to do. Five bodies."

He shuddered and glanced away. "Do I have to help?"

If he'd whined or grumped, I would've said yes, absolutely. I knew what kids were like. No one liked chores, least of all the under eighteen set.

But he wasn't whining, he wasn't grumping. He was quiet, resigned even. Poor kid. He'd been through so much already. Why make him do this?

"It's up to Tucker," I said. "But maybe you and Bethy can go back to sleep while he and I do the heavy lifting."

His nod was so subtle, I almost missed it. "Yes'm."

I smiled down at him. "Let's go. Your dad's waiting for us."

"He's not—" He sighed. "Yes'm."

A few minutes later, we were back at camp. Tucker had already carried three of the bodies in and stacked them to the side. A small fire flickered within the stone-edged fire ring.

I stashed Bethy in our tent, which wasn't easy. She was growing like a weed, in spite of the lack of proper nourishment out here on the trail.

When I'd tucked her in, I motioned Alex into the tent behind her. "Stay with her," I whispered. "If we need you, I'll get you."

His nod was easier to see this time. Dutifully, he ducked into the tent and laid down beside Bethy, and I stood back and rolled up my sleeves for the long night of work that lay ahead of us.

TUCKER AND I stripped the bodies down, working quickly by the meager combined light of the fire and moon. The intruders' clothes were filthy, but their skin was surprisingly clean. That made it easier. By unspoken consent, he and I divided our tasks. Tucker stored the goods we'd scavenged in his tent (a pocket watch, some matches, a small treasure trove of stale granola bars), then carried the bodies one by one to the creek.

The water was deep enough and cold enough to store them, if we weighted them down, and there were few predators left to gnaw on the flesh, other than us.

Meanwhile, I examined the bone-saw combo pack Tucker had given me. One handle, four blades, including two bone saws. They were intended for field dressing smaller to medium-sized game. Smaller than human. Deer and the like, I'd bet. I was sure they'd be fine for our purposes.

We'd chosen to work on the woman who'd attacked me first. Tucker helped me get her to the creek so I could scrub her skin down by the precious light of two solar-powered camp lights while he began building the bones of an outdoor oven. Some of the meat would be roasted and eaten now, some filleted and dried on sticks. We'd be creative with the rest. I'm sure he had ideas. I had some of my own.

If we had a grinder and the right seasoning, we could make sausage using the entrails as casings. I had access to both, just not close by, and I wasn't telling Tucker about them, not yet. We'd bury the entrails with his E-Tool and hope for the best.

It was dirty work. When the woman was as clean as I could get her, Tucker sawed her head off at the neck and we strung her up so the blood would drain out of her body. Rigor mortis would set in soon, sooner because we'd moved the body postmortem. Experience is a great teacher.

We had to work quickly, not just because of that, but because these people might be missed. Get the work done and move on. That's what we needed to do. Whether Tucker would agree with me?

I exhaled a burst of air as I scrubbed the woman's blood and excrement off my skin, well downstream from the camp. Maybe he would and maybe he wouldn't. Either way, Bethy and I weren't long for this place.

Though I wasn't quite ready to leave Tucker and Alex behind.

By the time we finished the preliminary work, the eastern sky had lightened over the mountaintops, heralding the dawn. I was tired to the bone, my eyes gritty from the lack of sleep. While I was helping Tucker gather stone from the creek, he caught me swaying on my feet and grabbed my arm.

"Get some sleep," he said. "You're no good to me like this."

I snorted, half irritated at his highhandedness, half grateful for the reprieve. No sleep last night, then the fight and this work. I rubbed the heels of my palms into my eyes, trying to clear the grit away. Yeah, I needed sleep.

"Take my tent," he continued, and finally, I nodded and stumbled off, yawning so hard, I nearly sideswiped the trunk of a massive poplar on my way into camp.

I stripped down outside. So what if he watched? My clothes were filthy from the fight and its aftermath, and I wasn't bringing that into a bedroom, however rough said bedroom was. The rest of me was as clean as I'd been able to make it, which I declared good enough as I entered the tent, picked the sleeping bag on the far side, and stretched out.

I fell asleep as soon as I was horizontal, and woke only when a warm, calloused hand touched my hip.

"Scoot over, Holly," Tucker said, his voice laced with mild humor. "You're sprawled across both sleeping bags."

"Sorry," I mumbled, and scooted over, then I was surrounded by the kind of hard warmth I hadn't experienced in a long, long time.

Something firm pressed against my bottom, and I wiggled. The hand came down in a light smack on my hip.

"Tease," Tucker said.

I shook my head against the sleeping bag, realized he probably couldn't see me even with early morning light creeping across the campsite into the tent, diffused by the domed fabric overhead. How long had I slept? Fifteen minutes? Half an hour? Not long, considering how little daylight there was, and I was still wound tight from the fight.

There was more there, inside me, different needs jangling against each other, each attempting to rise to the surface like blood into a shallow cut.

I turned over and faced him, ran my hands down his chest, his stomach, relishing the fine hair brushing against my palms. "Is this ok?"

"You sure you want to go there?" he said.

In answer, I reached lower and cupped him, then his mouth came down on mine, stoking a fire hotter than I'd ever felt, and he rolled me flat onto my back and slid into me, and for a while, we were closer than any two humans could possibly be.

After, he nuzzled my throat and rolled onto his side, taking me with him, tucking me against him. I smiled and fell asleep again, content with where I was.

WHEN I WOKE a few hours later, Tucker was gone and the kids were up. Their voices drifted to me, Tucker's gruff baritone, Alex's lighter preteen chirp, Bethy's toddler-sized giggles. I rolled onto my back, smiling at the tent's roof, refusing to wince when newly-used muscles ached a gentle protest.

Last night was just the beginning. A lot of work lay before me, and I was eager to get it done.

Patience, I cautioned myself, still grinning. All in good time.

I found one of Tucker's shirts, a long-sleeved black t-shirt, and pulled it over my head. My spare clothes were in the other tent, in my backpack. I needed to wash the others, and soon so they'd have time to dry. But first, I had to get to them.

I poked my head out, a little apprehensive about getting caught half naked. Bethy wouldn't care, but Alex was just old enough to wonder. The campsite was empty, though a fire burned low in the fire ring, beneath a metal spit holding a chunk of cooking meat. I cocked my head, listening, and pinpointed them at approximately where we'd hung the first slab of meat up to drain. Tucker must be working on it.

I couldn't believe he'd let me sleep, but I wasn't going to complain. I'd needed it. Now, I needed to get a move on.

I slipped into the other tent, pulled on a spare pare of cargo pants, clean socks, and my boots, and left his t-shirt on. It was warm and smelled of him, and I wanted him to see me in it, to remind him of the connection we'd forged the night before.

Even now, the woman in me wanted to preen.

I shook my head, then pulled my hair back in a ponytail and headed toward the voices.

"Like this, Bethy," Alex said. "Ay, bee, cee, dee, ee, eff, gee."

I bit my lip against a laugh. He was trying to teach her the alphabet song. Too cute.

They were exactly as I'd imagined, when I found them. Tucker was shirtless in the late morning air, wielding the bone saw on the hanging meat, deftly sawing off limbs. Easier if it were on the ground where he could brace his weight, lean in a little, but we had nothing to cushion the corpse from the ground, where dirt would sully the meat.

Alex and Bethy were sitting on a nearby downed log. He was holding her hands lightly between his fingers and swinging their arms sideways between their bodies.

I reached automatically for my phone to take a picture, and winced. The battery on it had died ages ago. Some habits died hard.

Tucker turned around as soon as I got close enough for him

to hear. His gaze flickered up and down my body, and a small, satisfied smile tilted the corners of his mouth upward.

"You let me sleep late," I said.

He grunted and turned back to the meat.

I shook my head. A man to the core.

Bethy's face lit up when she saw me. "Mamamamama," she jabbered, and toddled to me, her chubby cheeks dimpled in a brilliant smile.

I laughed and held my arms out to her, picked her up, and swung her high. Her giggles pealed across the forest, and for once I didn't shush her. She'd had far too few opportunities to be a child since her birth. Just this once, it would do her good.

Alex stood and tucked his fingers into his pants pockets, his rosy mouth pursed in an anxious frown. "I already gave her breakfast. Hope that was ok."

"Of course," I said. "Thank you."

I shifted Bethy to one hip and held an arm out for him. He shuffled over, sheepish now, and hugged me gingerly, as if he were afraid I'd break. There was an inch wide gap between the hems of his pants legs and the top of his boots. We'd have to go shopping soon. Raid a few houses, maybe find a store that hadn't been thoroughly looted. I knew where to find a sewing machine. It wouldn't be hard to hem pants that were too long, if that's all we could find.

I brushed kisses across Bethy's cheek and his forehead, then set her down and rolled my sleeves up. I'd talk to Tucker about it later, when we discussed whether to stay in camp or hike out. But for now, here we were, one big happy family about to partake in a feast.

***

THE MEAL was as lively as I'd hoped it would be. After last night's scare, we all needed the pick-me-up. Alex and Bethy dug in to the slivers Tucker sliced off without any qualm. Bethy, of course, had no idea what she was eating, and Alex seemed to have disassociated the source from the food.

Whatever he had to do to survive.

Later, Alex followed Bethy into the tent she and I had shared and bedded down beside her. I didn't say anything, just waited for them to fall asleep and the fire to burn low.

Tucker had taken first watch, right at twilight. He tended to move around, patrolling the local area rather than sitting in one vantage point as Alex and I normally did.

Tonight, though, I knew he intended to start at the ridge, so when the kids quieted down, I commandeered one of the solar-powered lamps and walked up, approaching at an angle well within his line of sight. It wasn't a huge hike. I called it a ridge, but in reality, it was merely a sharp-lined hill on this side. The other side was steeper and more treacherous. This side wasn't without problems, but it wasn't a terrible trail, and it was easy to see down from the top of the hill.

Tucker melted out of the shadows when I drew near, rifle in hand. "Everything ok?"

His voice was just loud enough to carry to me. I nodded and found a seat near where he stood, to the side of the trail where the vegetation had died down. "We need to talk about those people."

He grunted. "What about them?"

"I'm worried that they may have been part of a larger group."

"Could be."

"You don't sound concerned."

He shrugged, his gaze on the trail. "We'll deal with it when the time comes."

"Why not move on?"

"Not ready to yet." He lifted a hand, ran it over his beard. "Alex still has a lot to learn about forest survival."

"He can learn it better when he's not being hunted by a pack of rabid cannibals."

If Tucker heard the exasperation in my voice, it didn't show. "We need to preserve the meat first."

"Maybe it's worth the sacrifice if it means protecting the kids."

"Maybe."

I let the silence stretch between us for a few minutes. Why not? I'd made my point. No need to hammer it home.

Finally, I said, "Alex needs new pants. Bethy will need bigger clothes in another few weeks."

Tucker turned his gaze to me. Even in the dim light thrown by the lamp, I could see the heat in his eyes. "Maybe you'll need something bigger, too."

I touched my stomach, sucked in a breath. Yeah, that was a possibility, one I was hoping for. "I'm going to wash up and try to sleep. Wake me when it's my turn at watch."

I stood and started down the trail, and didn't make it far when he spoke.

"I'll be down in a few minutes, if you're of a mind to work on making that baby."

I bit my lower lip, hiding a grin. "Is it really work if you enjoy it?"

His soft, knowing laughter followed me down the trail into the night.

WE DID make love that night, and the next, and the next, as often as we could. I think we were both lonely and in need of companionship, if nothing else.

No one bothered us, though I was constantly aware of the

possibility of others stumbling over us. I didn't mention it to Tucker again. He knew my thoughts, and he knew I'd take Bethy and go if I thought she was in danger.

It's not that Tucker wasn't fully capable of protecting us, with our help. More that I had my own plans.

In between patrols and preserving the bounty of meat we'd procured, I began working with Alex on his reading, writing, and math. We used pointed sticks to etch words and figures into a stretch of bare dirt. Tucker had already been teaching him geography, geology, astronomy, weather, and what history he knew around Alex's lessons on survival, tracking, and whatnot. He'd get a well-rounded education, even if there were few left to share it with.

Two weeks after our first night together, I realized that my period was late. It was hard to tell, true. I'd lost so much weight since the whole ordeal began and didn't always get enough nourishment. Sometimes, I just didn't have one.

But I had that feeling down deep, the same one I'd had when Bethy was conceived. I was pregnant. It was a joy and a sadness, and security, too. Like Bethy and Alex were the future, so was this baby.

If we never got the seeds I'd stashed away in a safe place to take root and sprout, then humans were our only food. The population had to be continued until such a time as someone, somewhere, figured out how to grow other foods.

I whispered my suspicions to Tucker that night, between his watch and mine. We were sitting at the fire, a necessary risk now that fall had firmly set in and the nights were too chilly to go without.

"You're sure?" he said.

I rubbed my palms down my thighs, then clasped my hands together between my knees. "Not one hundred percent. But it feels right."

He stood and pulled me up, then walked me backwards toward a tree. "More practice to make sure."

I laughed and turned around, facing the tree. Let him tug my pants down, baring my skin to the chilly air. "Make it quick. The kids are barely asleep."

He took my hands, pinned them to the tree above my head, and slid into me. "God, you're so tight," he breathed.

I hummed under my breath and arched my back, letting him have his way. The rustle of tent fabric should've caught my attention, but with Tucker behind me, filling me, I barely took note of it.

A hard thud reverberated through me once, twice. Tucker froze, then staggered away from me.

I turned around, tugging my pants up as I twisted, alarmed. How had anyone snuck up on us...?

But it was only Alex. He was holding the E-Tool, staring at Tucker with such virulent hatred twisting his face, it shocked me.

Tucker dropped to one knee, his gaze on Alex. He opened his mouth, then his eyes rolled back and he crashed to the ground like a mighty fallen oak.

I buttoned my cargo pants and rushed over, kneeling beside Tucker with my hands to the pulse in his throat. It was sluggish, but there. I slid a hand behind his neck and gingerly explored the back of his head, and found a gash oozing blood.

"What did you do, Alex?" I said.

Tears glinted off his round cheeks. He sniffed and swiped his nose against his sleeve. "He was hurting you."

"No, we were..." How could I explain sex to a kid who hadn't hit puberty yet? "He wasn't hurting me. Here. Help me get him into the tent so I can bandage that cut."

Alex shook his head. "I ain't gonna help him."

"Alex, please. He'll die."

Might die anyway, depending on how hard Alex had hit him. I'd planned on killing him myself, but not until the baby was born.

"Let him die," Alex said. "He killed my dad, then he killed my mom."

I sucked in a breath. "Alex. I'm so sorry. I thought he was your father."

"Stepdad. I hate him. Hate him so much."

He started crying in earnest then, huge gulping sobs, and his arms dropped to his sides. Good boy that he was, he held on to the E-Tool. Tucker had trained him well.

I stood and walked over to him, put my arms around him and held him until he quieted, soothing him while my mind raced re-formulating plans. This was an unexpected turn of events, but maybe it wasn't such a bad thing. Sure, I could've waiting and killed Tucker on my own, later after the baby was born, to save resources until the kids were grown and old enough to harvest.

On the other hand, we could save those resources now, if I could get Alex and Bethy back to the house and the supplies still stored there. True, some of the food hadn't lasted long, the cured meat, the frozen goods. But I'd been thrifty with what Gabe had stashed away. I had years' worth of canned and dried food left, if I managed it properly, and I did.

Why eat the canned stuff when I could lure in a steady supply of fresh meat with my body and the food I had on hand? Men were so gullible, and I'd learned to manipulate them long ago.

When I was sure Alex would be ok, I stepped back and smiled down at him, my decision made. Strike while the iron is hot, Gabe used to say, right up until I struck him down with a fire iron. It wasn't that I was prescient so much as that I paid attention. I knew when the first alarm sounded that times would be hard, resources scarce, and not a lot of room left in the world for the weak-spined.

So I'd done what I had to do to survive.

I brushed Alex's hair off his forehead. "Go get my rifle, darling. I'll take care of him."

Alex nodded and swiped his nose again, then he let me pry the E-Tool out of his shaky fingers and went to fetch the rifle. Tucker groaned, but I wasn't worried. That blow had been hard enough to rattle him good. If Alex were a few years older, it would've killed him.

But that's what the rifle was for.

I knelt beside Tucker and stroked his forehead as I had Alex's. "Don't worry, honey. I'll make this as quick and painless as I can."

Then I put the E-Tool's sharp blade against his throat and waited for Alex to bring the rifle, happily daydreaming about how good Tucker's flesh would taste when I ground it into sausage.

The Wandering Man

Three smokers into his last trip across the desert, the Wandering Man found Carlita's bones scattered across the top of a smoldering pyre. They were charred black, same as the wood. Looked like wood, too.

He squatted an arm's length away and prodded a femur with the wrong end of his gun, a Benelli Montefeltro Shotgun with a plasma stinger mounted on the barrel. Some of the char scraped off, and the Wandering Man swore under his breath, low and long. There beneath the soot, the symbols binding her soul to the Red Hounds glowed a soft orange-gold.

So she'd sold herself, maybe for food, maybe for safe passage. Didn't matter. The Hounds hadn't claimed her soul yet. He could still fix this, if he went about it right.

He stood and tilted his hat back on his head, glanced at the whitewashed sky, and judged the time by the stifling heat of the blood-red sun suspended above the barren crags of Greenbriar Mountain, some thirty klicks west. A little far out for the Hounds on foot, big as they were. Not so far for the Crowfins. They could've snatched her off the rutted highway, maybe taken her right out of Wayah Pass before she even heard the sizzling flicker of their wings.

He considered the landscape again and the sky, then nodded. Ayuh, Crowfins. That's probably what had happened. Didn't mean the Hounds weren't behind it, only that they'd delegated the hunt.

The wood cracked and the femur slid into the ashes, touching the sharp edge of Carlita's pelvis. Wouldn't be long now before the bones gained momentum and reassembled, fueled by the twined essence of Carlita's soul and the Hounds' blood magic.

Damned if he'd let what was left of her join the Hounds' skeletal army.

He slid the shotgun into the holster at his back, reached into the leather pouch at his hip, and pulled out his journal, a loosely bound collection of anecdotes, spells, contacts, and maps written or tacked onto yellowing parchment. Paper of any kind was scarce anymore, but he always found it when he needed it. Luck of the wanderer, he figured, or maybe he just had good timing. Somebody always needed one of the demon-spawned hunted right about the time he had something to write down.

Three vertebrae rattled together, prodding the Wandering Man into a hurry. He thumbed through his journal, found the magic he needed on a page torn from an ancient copy of *The Sorcerer's Companion*, printed long before the hellholes opened, and held his right hand out over the bones, palm down, fingers spread wide.

"Hear me now, Carlita, you old bag of bones," he murmured, real low so his voice carried to the pyre and no farther. "If you hadn't taken the girl with you, I mighta let the Devil take you straight to Hell. Lucky for you, I'm here now, and I aim to save your eternal soul whether you like it or not."

Her cackling laughter whispered against his ear, carried on the faint breeze lifting sand off the desert floor across his nape and down the collar of his shirt. The Wandering Man bit off a curse, wouldn't have if the spell weren't already started. That's what he got for trekking out this far after a woman who'd spurned him more times than not.

Still, there was the girl, and the vision, and the money he'd get for bringing her in.

A rumble vibrated through the worn heels of his boots, and the bones clicked into place, dragging charcoal and ash behind them.

"Hellfire," the Wandering Man said, then he dropped to the hardpacked earth just as the skeleton, fully re-formed, rose from its ashen grave and stepped toward him, the Hounds' symbols glowing bright and hot enough to burn off the soot. The stench of burning flesh filled his nostrils, and he snorted into the dirt, trying to clear his head.

Another rumble and the earth opened up beneath him, ratcheting his heart into his throat in one leap. *Hellhole*, he thought, and prepared for the long fall into the demon-spawn's dimension.

And cursed again when, instead of falling, his body was scooped up by the unforgiving snout of a Burrower.

Something hard slammed into his shoulder, then the Burrower flicked him off its snout into the air, tossing him upward as if he weighed no more than a piece of spent firewood taken. The journal went flying in one direction, his pouch in the other, and the Wandering Man somewhere in between. He flailed his arms and legs, trying to turn himself over in midair so he'd land without breaking anything vital, for naught. Up the desert floor came and down he went, meeting it stomach first in a thud so hard, the air fled his lungs in a screaming rush.

Flashes of light danced before his eyes, and he sucked air futilely, searching for enough oxygen to feed his starving airways.

Something *wooshed* to his right. Without thinking, he forced his palms flat against the hot desert floor and shoved, rolling to the left onto his side as a burnt out stick as thick as his upper arm, dotted with glowing embers, crashed into the ground right where his head had been half a second before.

He looked up, way up, and there was Carlita's glowing skeleton, the ember-laden stick held high above her bare skull. Smoke whirled around the bones, obscuring the symbols etched into them. Most of the symbols were graffiti, junk added to the mix to confuse the unwary, but if he could find the right one, if he could just figure out which one to break, it'd all be over and he could get on with the job he'd been hired to do.

The Burrower wiggled its stumpy rear out of the hole, looking more like an overgrown, hairless Saint Bernard than the brainless pet of the demon-spawned, except for the brood pouch drooping down from its torso, the scaled snout jutting out of the middle of its face, and a long, crocodile-like tail tapering away from its trunk. It launched itself at the Wandering Man. He scrambled backward, not nearly fast enough. The Burrower opened its mouth, flashing two rows of pointed, black teeth, then it was on him, clamping down on his right ankle so hard, the Wandering Man hollered a curse to High Heaven.

The air behind Carlita's skeleton snapped and hissed, swirling into a murky red portal twice the skeleton's height. A flaming paw stepped through, followed by a long, sinewed forearm and a flat, grizzled face the size of Carlita's torso. The Wandering Man's lungs opened up and he inhaled a rank mixture of dust-dry desert air and the sulfur-tinged stink of a 'tween tunnel.

"Shit," he said, then his brain kicked in, fed by the in-rush of oxygen. He drew his left leg back and kicked the Burrower hard in the snout, dislodging it. Its teeth tore through the tough denim of his pants and the thick hide of his boots into skin, cutting him to the bone.

Blood gushed out, soaking his pants, dripping into terra firma, and sweat broke out along his skin, under the protective layers of his clothing. The Red Hound emerged from the portal and the flames snuffed out, leaving its skin raw and open to the sun's merciless gaze.

"Human," it said, its lipless mouth tilting into a gruesome smile.

The Wandering Man kept his lips firmly sealed together. Talking in the presence of a Hound invited all sorts of trouble he wasn't prepared to deal with, not with his journal and pouch scattered to the four corners. He still had the shotgun and a knife at his waist, but they wouldn't do him any good if he couldn't draw them before the Hound or one of its minions pounced.

Carlita's skeleton hauled the stick back for another swing, and the Wandering Man discarded the plans forming in his rickety brain revolving around his lone weapons. He rolled again, this time toward her and the Hound, and managed to roll right into her shin bones without dislodging the shotgun from its holster at his back, thank Heaven. She tumbled over him, holding her skeletal form, more's the pity, and his head came up just in time to catch a glance of the journal lying open some ten feet beyond the Hound.

Now, if he could get to the journal, he wouldn't need the shotgun and knife. It was a far better weapon anyway. All he had to do was—

The ground beneath him vibrated, and the craziest plan popped into his head. He turned onto his back, ignoring the pain in his leg and the shotgun digging into his back, and pressed himself against the scorching hot sand.

"Human," the Red Hound said again.

Carlita's skeleton snapped upright and shimmied, like a woman settling a dress around her hips.

The Burrower bounded forward, heading straight toward the

Wandering Man.

And he prayed like he'd never prayed before. *Let this crazy plan work, please, let it work so I can get out of this mess and find the girl...*

Carlita's skeleton pivoted around and stepped toward him, right into the path of the Burrower. It skidded away from her, and its hind end slid around. Its tail whipped into the skeleton, knocking it sideways, and the Burrower's front paws splatted into the earth, missing the Wandering Man's injured leg by a hair.

He lifted his hands as it stumbled over him and latched onto the brood pouch, tucked his knees between its stomach and his, trembling from the effort it took not to scream as heated sand scraped into the cuts on his leg. The Red Hound roared as the Burrower skidded past, filling the parched air with waves of sulfur-laden stench, and The Wandering Man held on for dear life, gritting his teeth against the pain throbbing through his leg every time his back hit the hard earth.

Out of the corner of his eye, he caught sight of the journal's cover and let go, rolling away from the Burrower as soon as it cleared him. He stretched out his hands, catching the journal to his chest, and tumbled onto his back.

The Red Hound stepped forward once, then touched one clawed toe to the Wandering Man's stomach, trapping him against the desert floor. "You cannot escape me, Human."

The Wandering Man grinned. In his hand, the journal warmed, and the spell he needed flowed through the pages into his skin. His pouch flew across the earth and into his free hand, then the Wandering Man muttered the words needed to activate the magic freed from the journal. A portal opened beneath him, a 'tween tunnel too narrow for the Red Hound and its slaves. He looked at Carlita's skeleton and made a promise to the piece of her that sill resided on the earthly plane.

Someday, after he tracked down the girl, he'd find Carlita again and smash her bones, breaking the Hounds' blood magic, freeing her soul from its eternal servitude.

He thought he saw her skull dip, as if acknowledging the promise, then the tunnel swallowed him and he disappeared into it, leaving the Red Hound to its fury over being denied another soul.

The Kinder, More Gentle End of the World as We Know It

Mack cared about two things in this world, his guns and his baseball card collection. The woman in front of him was holding neither.

Carol was nearly five ten, raw boned and freckled, with dishwater blonde hair capping her rectangular face. Too awkward and gawky to play basketball. Too girl-next-door to be anything except a kindergarten teacher with a husband in corporate, two point three kids polished to a shine, and a rescue mutt digging up the back yard. Or maybe a cheerleader, the All-American kind who sailed through high school on her smiles and kind words, and went to college where she earned a Mrs. degree.

She claimed to've been an accountant before the end of the world as he'd known it, but anybody could claim anything nowadays. How could anybody verify such things anymore, unless you happened to run into somebody who knew her?

He'd found her a couple of weeks back, wandering around Oconaluftee taking pictures like she was a tourist, while the few Cherokee who'd stayed put eyed her suspiciously. Scouts or rogues should've gotten her long before then, but if there was ever a case of God protecting fools, she was it.

Carol was currently holding a can of SPAM in one hand and a dead, unskinned rabbit in the other. "What's it to be tonight, Mr. McMasters? Fried SPAM or fried rabbit?"

He scowled at her, an expression which did not in any way diminish her Pollyanna smile. "Don't care."

"Oh, now. You have to have an opinion."

He did have an opinion: Steak, seared crisp on the outside, rare in the middle, accompanied by a baked potato loaded with real butter and real sour cream. That's what a man needed to survive the apocalypse, not some goody two shoes with more smiles than brains.

Mack settled for a grunt and turned back to cleaning his guns.

She sighed, but it was one of those happy, June Cleaver sighs. Mother knows best or some such crap. "Ok, Mr. Grumpy Butt. Rabbit it is. I could've skinned it and dried the meat, you know."

He grunted again. What did he care? Food was food, as far as he was concerned, unless it was a thick slab of ribeye.

They were holed up in a rickety Blue Bird school bus parked at the Mountain Farm Museum, conveniently located on the edge of the Great Smoky Mountains National Park just outside Cherokee, North Carolina. Between the resources of the two, natural on one side, man-made on the other, he figured it was as good a place as any to spend the post-EMP apocalypse.

The museum was a collection of buildings gathered from the area, supposedly to represent mountain life back in the day. A log house, a barn, a hog pen, a corn crib, and a few other buildings were scattered around, with an apple orchard and a fenced off garden to boot. The Oconaluftee River ran around one side of the property, another side was a buffer of grassy fields, and the third was the welcome center with its oversized parking lot.

Could've stayed in the farmhouse or barn, but they weren't exactly airtight or comfortable. The bus might not've been in the best shape, courtesy of its decades hauling children around, but it had wheels. Plus, it had space inside for the both of them. The previous owners had pulled out the seats and installed storage space, narrow beds, and curtains. Their temporary home could be moved if bad came to worse.

Worse being the invading army finding them, or worser, the guerillas.

There were other survivors out there, some in town, others hiding in the forest. The area was too far out of the way for the clashing armies to bother them. Sooner or later, he figured, somebody would get around to rounding them up. In the meantime, he intended to clean his guns, admire his favorite baseball cards, and enjoy the view.

And what a view it was. It was dusk, that time of day when mist crept off the river into the valley. The mountains were lush and green, the late afternoon sky on the verge of bursting open with stars. Elk and deer roamed the hills and pastures along with bear, fox, and other wildlife. A barn owl hooted nearby and a lone bat fluttered through the air above him.

Man, this was the life.

Carol had retreated to the rock fireplace near the farmhouse by way of a paved walkway, presumably to skin and cook the rabbit.

Mack had therefore set up shop in the parking lot next to the bus, as far away from her likely whereabouts as he could get without being in the woods.

What had possessed him to save her in the first place?

Her singing drifted to him, an offkey rendition of "The Bare

Necessities," of all things. Loud enough to wake the dead. They weren't inconspicuous (the were in an antique yellow school bus, for cripes' sake), but did she have to advertise their presence to every Tom, Dick, and Dirty Harry out there?

Mack heard the clack of shod hooves on asphalt before he saw the horse. He casually laid down the gun he was cleaning, a Glock 17, touched a hand to the .357 revolver on his hip, and picked up his rifle, a Remington 760 inherited from his dad, bought fresh out of the old man's last tour in Vietnam. The noise was coming from town. Probably Linda come to check on the outskirts. Either that or the damn Chinese army had managed to slip a scout out on horse.

Unlikely. They'd kept their soldiers offshore while they systematically dismantled the U.S.'s electrical grid, beginning with high altitude electromagnetic pulses from the detonation of nuclear warheads, then using portable microwave generators to wipe out anything that was left. They'd effectively dismantled most of the country's information and electrical grids within hours. Commie bastards.

They'd concentrated their post-HEMP attacks on the major cities. D.C., New York, and the west coast had gone down in the first wave, which is what the pansy-ass liberals got for banning guns.

The People's Liberation Army had hit resistance elsewhere. Probably what saved the rural areas, especially in the mountains. Linda's husband had joined a contingent of other armed men and women cutting off the main arteries, paved highways and interstates an invading army could use to penetrate deeper into the otherwise difficult terrain.

Mack hunkered down behind a barrier made of a late model Volkswagen Beetle turned on its side with a dump truck load of fill dirt piled in front of it. It was twenty feet in front of the bus, laid out perpendicular to the road running between Cherokee and the national park. A similar barrier faced the road a dozen feet away from the first, this one backed by a Nissan Juke.

There were other abandoned cars in the museum's parking lot. These had been two of the smallest and therefore two of the easiest to move without power.

And he hated both models, so there was that.

If he'd been stranded with a group of old Army buddies, he would've turned more of the cars over, created a maze of barriers, maybe fortified the bus, which was one of the few working vehicles left locally, thanks to its complete lack of electronics. But he'd been up here alone when the grid went down, one of his semiannual vacation slash retreats, this one coupled with a visit with Linda and Jim. Help had been in short supply, with such a large area to protect.

The horse clopped into view bearing a single rider, a woman of medium build and height with skin the color of river mud and a long, black braid trailing down her back. She was holding a rifle across her lap and the reins in her right hand, expertly guiding the horse with pressure from her knees and light flicks of the reins. Linda, then.

Mack stayed behind the barrier, waiting to see if more people were behind her, but Linda was alone. She stuck to the road, avoiding the elk at the far end of the adjoining pasture, and tied her horse off under the deepening shade of the trees lining the entrance to the parking lot.

Mack stood and waved when she hallooed, and watched her walk toward him holding the rifle in one hand and a small cloth sack in the other.

"'Lo, Mack," she said. "Brought cornmeal for Carol and news for you."

Did Carol even know what to do with cornmeal?

Mack shook the question off. "Bad news?"

"Not good news." Up close, Linda was half a head shorter than him, big boned and tough in a pair of worn jeans and a black

Aerosmith concert t-shirt. "Not bad news either. Reckon it depends on how you take it."

"Just spit it out already."

"Pope's nearby. Got word from Jim down on the line."

Mack's right thigh cramped around an old bullet wound, aching like he'd been hit yesterday. He sucked a breath in through his teeth, let it out slowly, willing the pain to ease.

"What's he want?" he said.

"What's he ever want?"

She shrugged and swung the sack toward the museum proper, Carol's domain. Carol was belting out a bad imitation of Aretha's "Pink Cadillac," apparently oblivious to the fact that there were bad men in the world who'd as soon shoot her as look at her.

Mack nodded Linda on and limped back to his setup, rubbing his thigh as he walked. Pope was back. Wasn't that just a dandy way to top off his week?

MACK FINISHED cleaning the guns he'd set out to work on that afternoon well before the hen party ended. Damned if he'd join them. Carol was sure to find work for him, and his leg still hurt. Last thing he needed was a woman nagging at him to do a chore.

He'd been married once for about five minutes. Tried to stick it out, too. Maybe would've if she hadn't nagged him every waking second.

That and he'd caught her cheating on him.

It wasn't the worst day of his life, but it was down there.

Not a single other woman had tempted him to stay long enough to do more than bed her. Soon as she started hinting, he packed up his guns and his baseball cards and hit the road. Plenty of fish in the sea, present company excepted. He wouldn't touch Miss Suzie Sunshine with a ten-foot pole if she was the last unattached woman on Earth.

"Mr. McMasters!"

Mack winced. Speak of the devil and there she appeared, hollering at him.

"Oh, Mr. McMasters!" Carol called again. "Time for dinner!"

Ten to one Linda was having a good laugh at his expense.

He grabbed the 760 and a flashlight and walked past the visitor center along the paved pathway toward the makeshift outdoor kitchen. The late summer air was mild and dry for once. A gentle breeze blew across the property, accompanied by the gurgle of the Oconaluftee River to his left, just down a bank worn to dirt and protruding tree roots by the feet of thousands of yearly visitors. The women's conversation carried above the sounds of nature, not so much he could ignore it and pretend, just for a moment, that he was alone.

But if he was alone, he'd've had to skin and cook the rabbit, so maybe it wasn't such a bad thing, having Carol around.

He changed his mind as soon as he saw her. She had that Pollyanna, never-known-pain smile pasted on her mug and was setting a picnic table with an old quilt, squat white candles, and paper plates. The picnic table had had to be moved from a nearby roadside picnic area. The quilt had come from the museum. The paper plates and candles were a trade with the grocery store in town and had cost him a pretty penny in venison. Every bit of it had been a pain in his ass. What was wrong with eating by the fire from the pan?

Linda set a plate of sliced apples on the table as he limped past the log house. The apples were from the fledgling orchard of heirloom trees, fenced off to keep the elk out. The fence had been electrified once. Seeing as how a fence alone wasn't much of an impediment to an oversized fox, let alone an elk, Mack figured that was a good idea.

Carol laughed, drawing Mack's attention to the conversation he'd been trying to ignore.

"He did not!" she exclaimed.

"Oh, yeah," Linda said, laughing. "'Ain't no woman good enough to talk me out of my number one baseball card,' he said, then he hit the road in nothing but a pair of pants he hadn't even buttoned yet."

Mack thumped his ass down on one side of the picnic table and stretched his right leg out. Damn thing still ached, just from the mention of that no-account Pope's name. "That's not the way I remember it."

"That's the way Marla said it happened," Linda retorted. "I swear, I've never seen a man who was so gun shy."

"Jim, right before he married you," Mack said. "I had to talk him out of hopping the next flight to Katmandu."

Carol's gaze bounced between them like she was watching a particularly interesting tennis match. "What's this about baseball cards?"

"He hasn't shown you his collection?" Linda sat down across from Mack and plopped a paper plate onto the table in front of him. She shot a reproachful look at him under the sweep of black eyelashes. "Mack has a small but very valuable collection of prize baseball cards. Carries it with him everywhere he goes."

Carol sat down beside Mack, nodding sagely. "Like his guns."

"Be prepared," Linda said. "Mack's motto from birth."

He shrugged, trying to keep his irritation from showing. "A man who can't take care of himself isn't much of a man."

"Yet I was the one who skinned the rabbit." Carol sighed happily, easing the sting of her words. "Grace?"

Linda held her hands out, one to each of them, waiting until Mack took hers and Carol's proffered hands in his own, and bowed her head. "Dear Lord," she said. "Thank you for this bounty we are about to receive. Bless the hands that prepared it, the hands that brought it down, and the hands that ground the cornmeal so we wouldn't have to eat plain rabbit."

Carol cut off a snicker with a polite cough, but Mack had to grin. Trust Linda to put a fine point on things.

"Bless the men and women holding the line," she continued more somberly. "Watch over and keep them. In Jesus' name we pray. Amen."

"Amen," Mack murmured in unison with Carol, then the women finally let go of his hands. There was another reason he'd stayed single. Damn women had to be touchy-feely about every little thing.

They dished out food. Rabbit sliced in thin strips, dipped in the stone-ground cornmeal Linda had brought, and fried in a cast iron pan over the stove. Apples from the orchard. Late summer greens from the museum's piddling garden. Carol had turned them into a salad of sorts using some vegetables she'd traded for mending earlier in the week. It wasn't much. The rabbit was tough and the greens more bitter than Mack liked, but it was good enough, considering what she'd had to work with.

He let the conversation flow around him, ignoring it unless Linda spouted some bald-faced lie about him. Honest to God, he hadn't fled the bed of every woman east of the Mississippi. Look at Linda. Not once had he been tempted, and he'd known her since they were little more than sparks in their daddies' eyes.

Carol's elbow brushed his from time to time, and he ignored that, too. She could've sat with Linda. There was plenty of room farther down the bench, but no, the cussed woman had sat down next to him, like they were a couple or something.

Which they weren't.

"—straggling band of guerillas along the southern line," Linda said, bringing Mack back to earth with a startled thump.

"What about them?" he said.

"Pope is leading his guerillas northeast." Linda's voice was patient, as if she'd already explained. "Crossing the southern line."

"You didn't tell me that."

"You didn't give me a chance to explain."

Carol's gaze was bouncing between them again. "The pope is visiting?"

Mack snorted out a disgusted breath.

Linda just grinned. "Not *the* pope. A guy named Pope. Him and Mack are old Army buddies."

"Pope was never a buddy of mine," Mack said flatly.

"But you had Army buddies?" Carol propped her elbow on the table and her chin on her hand, looking about a decade and a half younger than she was. "I didn't know you were in the Army. I mean I figured, with all the guns—"

"Don't gotta be in the Army to have guns."

"—and the barriers and such, but really, Mr. McMasters. You need to tell me these things."

"Why?"

Linda kicked him with the toe of her boot. "Mack isn't much of a talker. Are you, Mack?"

He scowled at her. "Ain't got nothing to say."

"Sure you do. Have you told her who Pope is?"

"Besides an old Army buddy?" Carol said brightly.

Mack stood slowly, favoring the leg that now had two aches, one in his thigh from the bullet Pope had gifted him, the other in his shin thanks to Linda's sharp-toed boot. "Thanks for supper, ladies. Think I'm gonna turn in now."

Carol whipped her head toward him, her mouth an astonished oh. "But it's not even full dark out yet!"

He waved her off and slung the rifle over his shoulder.

"If you don't tell her," Linda said. "I will."

"Then you just tell her," he called over his shoulder.

"Tell me what?" Carol said, then the women's voices dropped to a low murmur.

He left it to them, walking out by the light of the rising moon and the setting sun so Miss Scatterbrains could use the flashlight. Let Linda explain if she wanted. Saved him the trouble of trying to get Suzie Sunshine to understand.

HE RETRIEVED a bottle of Ron Zacapa from the bus and carried it past Linda's horse onto the road, up to the barricades Jim and company had built before they'd left to defend the bigger threats along Highway 74.

The tension in his muscles eased as he walked. By the time he reached the barricades, the pain was gone and he didn't need the rum. He leaned against a spare sawhorse and allowed himself a tiny sip anyway. The liquor coated his tongue, washing away the gamey taste of rabbit.

He left his mind blank on purpose. A man gets to a certain age and he doesn't want to remember the past, doesn't care to think on the future. Live in the moment. Enjoy life while it's here and all that horse manure.

The shadowed two-lane road leading into the Great Smoky Mountains National Park was empty of everything but leaves in a hurry to vacate the nest. Fall was still two weeks away. The leaves were browning overhead and the air smelled of cool, damp forest and dusty sunshine. There was a decided nip in the air every few nights or so. Not quite time for killing hogs, but plenty of time for canning the last of the vegetables from the garden. If they'd had Mason jars. Or much in the way of a garden.

Maybe next year.

He shook his head, swallowed another sip, hissed as its mellow sting washed away thoughts of tomorrow. They really should put a permanent guard here, more than one gimpy man in a creaky bus and a woman who didn't know the business end of a gun from a hole in the ground. It was safe enough, maybe. They'd gotten word of an outpost south of Gatlinburg, blocking travel on this road, and in between lay miles and miles of uninhabited forest.

A determined man could bypass the roadblock, traverse it, but a whole army? Nope.

Guerillas, on the other hand...

No, he wasn't dwelling on that bottom feeder today, not with a full belly and his best rum for company.

He heard Linda leave, raised a hand in farewell, though he didn't turn around. Heard Carol's footsteps approaching and sighed. Somebody needed to teach her how to walk more quietly.

Somebody. Not him.

She stopped beside him and mirrored his pose. Forearms braced against the sawhorse's top plank, gaze on the road ahead. He waited for her to pepper him with questions, but she just stood there, watching.

Finally he couldn't take it anymore. He held the Zacapa out, passed it to her. She took a shallow sip and, to her credit, didn't so much as inhale sharply when she swallowed. He was surprised she hadn't wiped the mouth of the bottle off first.

"I was thinking maybe I'd pick up some more mending in the next couple of days," she said. Another sip, a contented sigh. "Linda said we should get in some firewood."

He barked out a laugh. "Don't think mending's gonna bring in enough firewood for the winter."

"We have to start somewhere." She took a final, miserly sip, then handed the bottle back to him. "I sent the apple peels and vegetable scraps back with Linda for her hog. She said we could have some sausage this fall. I think maybe I'll learn how to can so we can save it for winter. It can't be that hard, right?"

Ever the optimist. By the time the snow fell, the PLA would be on top of them. That or the guerillas would've wiped them out. Men like Pope didn't give a shit about other men's plans.

Mack sipped from the bottle, sighed as the rum worked its magic. "Probably better to trade for an ax."

"Only if you'll help me chop the wood," she said brightly.

Mack snorted out a laugh. Like he'd let her handle a tool sharper than a boning knife. Which, come to think of it, was pretty sharp. Maybe he should do the rabbit skinning from here out.

Carol turned around and walked away, humming a tune he didn't know well enough to recognize as anything other than Disney.

Mack kept his gaze on the darkening road. Mending for firewood. Fool woman and her fool notions. That's what'd got her in trouble in the first place, that bright belief that the world would turn exactly as she needed it to.

MACK WOKE the next morning to the sound of that infernal woman's offkey singing ringing across the parking lot. He scraped a hand over the rough stubble of his beard, rubbed the sleep out of his eyes. Good thing he'd limited himself to a few sips of rum. Otherwise the combination of a hangover and her caterwauling would be the death of him.

He eyed the sunlight streaming through the sheets duct taped over the bus's windows, makeshift curtains left by the bus's previous owners. It was barely dawn, way too early for anything as upbeat as singing. Too early for breakfast, too, or for her early morning walk, or for...

Mack's gaze landed on the wooden box he kept the most prized cards in his baseball card collection in. The box itself was a one-of-a-kind treasure, ornately carved out of a cherry tree downed by lightning in his parents' front yard when he was a kid. Woodcarving had been a hobby of his dad's, something he'd taken up a decade after being discharged from the Army. It calmed him, kept him from thinking too hard about what he'd done in the service, and what he hadn't done.

Mack was as careful with the box as he was with the collection it housed. When he traveled, he wrapped it in an old quilt and wedged it into the trunk where it wouldn't bang around. And he always kept it padlocked.

Another man would've put those cards in a safe. Mack could not.

He sat up slowly, eyeing the box. Last night when he'd gone to bed, the lock had been secure. Today, it was open, and there was only one person on the face of the planet who could sneak by him and steal the cards.

Pope.

Mack's heart dropped to his knees as he swung his legs over the edge of his cot and planted his feet on the rubber floor. Goose pimples raised on his flesh when the morning's cool air hit his bare skin, but he ignored the chill. His baseball cards. The Wagner and the Ryan and the Robinson.

If the Robinson was gone, he'd hunt Pope down and carve the flesh from his bones with a dull razor blade.

Mack slipped the padlock off and opened the box's lid with trembling hands, and his heart dropped again. The three-ring binder holding some of his memory cards in plastic sheets was gone. Childhood treasures, not worth much to anybody except him. But the Robinson had been in the binder with the other memories, tucked into the inside front flap in a hard, plastic case. Maybe he'd left it out, mixed it in with the others?

He sifted through the ones that were left, stacking them in his left hand as he pulled them out. Wagner, Ryan, a fairly worthless

Mantle, Griffey Sr. and Jr., two cards, but he always kept them together, then the lower grade cards that were still worth something, though not as much as the Wagner. Nothing in his collection could touch the Wagner in value, even the Robinson, and the Robinson was...

Gone.

Mack dropped the plastic-encased cards into the box and closed his eyes, hissing in a breath against the ache in his heart. A memory of his dad came to him, clear as a bell, and of an old man in a suit, smiling down at him, gripping his fingers with a hand that had rocked the world from 1947 on.

The Robinson was everything.

Anger engulfed Mack so swiftly, he rocked back on his bare heels. Pope knew what that card meant to him, knew what it would do to him to lose it, and that sumbitch had still snuck in here and stole it. When Mack got ahold of him, he'd do more than scrape his skin off with a rusty razor. He'd hang the traitorous ass by his thumbs, pour Clorox in his eyes and let them burn out, hold his feet over the low embers of a fire and roast them while Pope watched, unable to do anything.

No, the fire would come first, then the Clorox.

Feet hit the steps leading into the bus, then Carol squawked, "Mr. McMasters! I'm so sorry. I didn't realize you were awake!"

He glanced toward her, barely aware of the flush of red on her cheeks or the way she whipped around and put her back to him.

"Did you hear anything last night?" he said. "Maybe people sneaking onto the bus?"

She shook her head, sending her blandly colored ponytail swinging against her nape. "No, I did not. And I locked up, just like you showed me, I swear. Goodness, I knew you slept in the all-together, but you've been so polite about being dressed, I plumb forgot."

Mack glanced down at his nude body and rubbed a tired hand down his face. In his rush to check the cards, he'd forgotten all about needing to pull on shorts so as not to offend her tender sensibilities.

And that was another reason not to keep a woman around. When a man couldn't walk around in his birthday suit inside his own home, such as it was...

"Get your things together," he said as he grabbed yesterday's jeans and yanked them on. "I have to leave for a few days and I want you safe at Linda's while I'm gone."

"Oh, that's not necessary, Mr. McMasters."

"It's necessary if I say it is," he said flatly. "You've got three minutes."

"But I need to..." She turned around and tapped the white, three-ring binder she held tight against her chest, with both arms crossed over it. "Put this back. Linda was telling me—"

Mack let his hands drop away from the jeans' zipper. "Is that my baseball card collection?"

"—about these, oh." Carol nodded and smiled brightly. "Yes, it is! I can't believe you didn't show—"

"What," Mack said, his voice low and so full of anger he almost choked on the word, "the hell do you think you're doing with that?"

Her smile dimmed and she tucked a loose strand of hair behind her ear. "Well, as I was saying, Linda was telling me about your baseball card collection last night, and when you didn't wake up this morning, I thought, well, I'll just have a quick look-see."

He held up a hand, halting her explanation. "You thought you'd break into my property—"

"Oh, no, I didn't!"

"—and take my cards without my permission."

Her expression wilted and her shoulders drooped. "Well, when you put it like that, but that's not what I intended, Mr. McMasters. Not at all. I just wanted to understand—"

"Shut up." He held his hands out and waited until she walked forward and handed him the binder. "Don't ever touch this again, for any reason. Are we clear?"

Her eyes were round, shimmery pools of azure in her suddenly pale face. "I'm sorry, Mr. McMasters."

She turned around and left, more quietly than she'd come.

Mack didn't bother watching her go and he sure as hell didn't let that wounded look on her face move him. That woman was a menace, a screw loose, wild card, unthinking menace.

He opened the binder, found the Robinson right where it was supposed to be, and closed it again, relieved to his core. Forget Pope. The biggest threat to his peace of mind right now was the woman who'd just walked away from him.

HE DIDN'T feel bad about snapping at her. No sirree, not one bit. That's not why he pulled on clothes and wandered around the outdoor museum until he found her. His belly was eating a hole in his spine, was all. A man had to eat, didn't he? Especially during the apocalypse.

He found her squatting near the cook fire, stirring a pot of bubbling oatmeal sitting on a metal grate over the embers with a wooden spoon he'd carved for her. Steam and smoke wafted toward her pale face. She swiped the back of her hand across a cheek, smearing soot along the cheekbone.

"I'm not mad," she said.

Irritation soured his gut. "What's that got to do with anything?"

"So you don't have to check on me."

"I'm not checking on you."

He heaved a sigh and rubbed a hand down his mouth. This is what he got for leaving the bus. He could've been enjoying the rum he'd barely touched last night instead of being out here getting henpecked by a woman he wasn't even sharing a bed with.

Sharing a bus didn't count. He couldn't have her wondering around on her own, could he? Not after fishing her out of one of Pope's traps.

Mack dropped his hand and glared at the top of her head. "I'm hungry."

"And you expect me to cook for you?" She sniffed and jabbed the spoon into the thickening oatmeal. "That's a fine how-de-do. Take my head off for trying to learn about you, then expect me to feed you?"

"You're the cook."

"And why is that?" She popped up so fast, the smoke rose with her, creating a whirling column in the air around her. "Because I'm a woman? Hmm? Because that's a woman's job?"

"Because I hunt down the—" He hooked his hands on his hips and glared at her. "Why are we even talking about this? Cooking is the only thing you know how to do, woman, that and build a fire. Do you want to build traps and hunt and trade for dry goods with the locals?"

"I want you to stop treating me like a child!"

"You are a child!" he roared. "I found you wandering around the village like the town idiot!"

"I was *curious.*"

"Then the minute I got you back here, you wandered off into the woods and landed face first in a snare. The only thing that saved you is the fact that Pope's greedy ass gets more for live humans when he trades with the damn Chinese!"

She set her fists on her hips, one hand still wrapped around the spoon. "I would've gotten myself out."

"Like hell," he said flatly. "You can barely tie your shoelaces without help."

"I built this fire."

"Because I showed you how."

"And skinned the rabbit."

"Showed you that, too."

"Well, if YouTube was still on, I would've figured out how to hunt and fish and set traps on my own. I don't need you, mister."

"Then why don't you leave?"

She stiffened and what little color she had drained out of her, leaving only her freckles to highlight the curves of her face. "I guess that's what I'll do then."

Her voice was so quiet, it barely crossed the distance between them. She bent and stuck the spoon back in the pot, snagged a daisy shaped potholder one of the Cherokee had traded her for mending, and lifted the pot off the grate onto a flat stone a couple of feet away.

A stone he'd found and carried here, just so she'd have a place to put hot pots while they ate. He'd had to wade into the Oconaluftee to find just the right one, gotten soaked in the process. The water wasn't exactly warm this time of year, either. And he'd strained his back carting it from there to here.

Where was the gratitude?

She turned and walked away, her back ramrod straight, her steps more march than walk.

Something flipped over in his stomach. "Carol," he called. "Come back and eat."

She didn't even pause, just waved a hand at him and kept on trucking, her ponytail bouncing in time to her steps.

He sighed and rubbed the nape of his neck. Infernal woman. Damned if he'd let her ruin his appetite.

Mack grabbed a paper bowl from the stash inside the log cabin, dished some gloppy oatmeal into it, and crouched there by the smoking embers, spooning hot cereal into his mouth. She'd salted it. Found some butter, from where he had no idea. Didn't make much difference. The oatmeal was as tasteless as cardboard in his mouth, but he was too busy trying to figure out how the conversation had deteriorated into an argument to notice.

THE BOWL was barely half empty when Mack noticed Carol walking down the road toward Cherokee pulling her suitcase behind her, the big one with the squeaky wheel. He dropped his spoon into the bowl and let out a disgusted snort. It's not like he didn't have a clear view of the road coming and going from where he sat. Did she really think she could run away without him knowing about it?

He shook his head, picked up his spoon, poked at the congealing oatmeal. She'd be fine. The only trouble she could get into between here and there was tripping over a crack in the asphalt, or maybe running across a wild animal. A fox or skunk, maybe, or an elk...

Mack stood up so fast, his head spun. He turned and scanned the narrow valley for the herd of elk roaming it. Nowhere in sight. Didn't mean they weren't around, just that they'd moved into an area he couldn't observe from where he was standing. She knew to stay away from them. They'd had that conversation after he caught her trying to sneak close enough to take a picture with her camera.

He'd confiscated the camera, but that hadn't dented her determination. God in His infinite wisdom had given her a double helping of that trait.

The clatter of hooves on asphalt reached him, drowning out the squeaky suitcase, then Linda trotted into view, riding a roan. She was moving faster than normal. Must be something important.

Mack dusted his jeans off and set the oatmeal on the table to take care of later. He happened to glance at Carol again. She stopped dead in the road, then turned abruptly around and marched back toward the museum's parking lot.

He let out a long sigh. It wasn't relief. Not a chance. Or if it was relief, then it was only there because her being here meant he didn't have to chase after her to make sure she didn't get hurt.

Linda reached Carol long before Carol reached the parking lot and paused. The two women had a brief conversation, then Linda spurred the roan on and trotted ahead.

Mack was nearly at the bus by the time she tied off her horse and jogged to him. He lifted a hand and hailed her as she drew near. "What's up?"

"Pope." Linda stopped well out of arm's reach, her expression grim above the collar of a threadbare work shirt. "He wants to meet."

Mack bit off a hard curse. "He's not getting the Robinson."

"He didn't mention word one about it. Leastwise, that's not what got back to me."

"Then what?"

She shrugged. "Dunno. Jim wants you to come to the line. Says you're the only one that's ever been able to talk sense into Pope."

"I'm the only one crazy enough to take him on, you mean."

He shook his head, scuffed a boot heel against the asphalt. Carol had made it to the entrance. The suitcase's squeaky wheel whined sharply like it had come out of the factory ungreased. He wasn't going to fix it either. Carol's suitcase, Carol's responsibility.

Linda turned and followed his gaze. "What's that about?"

"What's what about?"

"Carol. The suitcase. You piss her off or what?"

He shot her a hard glance. "I caught her with her hands on my baseball cards."

"Oh." Linda drew the word out as she turned toward him. "You didn't tell her what they meant to you?"

"I thought you did."

"I told her about Pope."

Anger shot through him and he let loose a ripe curse. "You had no right to air my personal business."

Linda's expression hardened. "Cool your jets, Mack. I said I told her about Pope. Didn't say I told her what passed between you and him."

He sucked in a breath, hissed it out slowly, and with it, let go of some of the anger. "Sorry."

"Yeah, yeah. You going to apologize to her?"

"The hell for? I didn't do anything."

Linda shook her head. "The older I get, the more clueless men seem. Say you're sorry, Mack. Smooth things over."

"Nothing to smooth over," he muttered.

Carol walked up to them then, dragging that squeaky suitcase behind her. She looked right at Mack and said, "I just remembered something."

He spat on the ground, crossed his arms over his chest, and glowered. "Yeah? What's that?"

"I'm not a quitter." She turned the suitcase upright, pushed the handle down, then walked over to him and hugged him hard, resting her cheek against his crossed forearms. "I'm not a quitter, Mr. McMasters. I shouldn't have walked out just because you were mad at me, but I promise not to touch your baseball cards again unless you say it's ok."

Linda put a hand over her mouth, stifling a snicker, but Mack just glanced down at Carol, appalled, his heart a floppy mess inside his chest. The hell was she doing hugging him?

"My dad gave me the Robinson," he blurted out, and winced. Hadn't meant to say anything at all, wouldn't have if she hadn't gone and messed things up with a hug.

"Jackie Robinson?"

Her breath was a warm, gentle breeze across his flesh, raising goosebumps. He resisted the urge to push her away and settled for scowling at the crown of her head. "Who else would it be?"

"I don't know a thing about baseball except what I saw on your baseball cards."

"Well, it's time you learned."

"Ok." She stepped back and beamed up at him. "I'm going to work in the garden while you and Linda have a nice chat."

She patted his arm and bounced away, humming "Bippity, Boppity, Boo" under her breath.

Linda reached out and cuffed Mack's shoulder. "Good thing she came back, huh?"

He turned his scowl on her. "Is it pick on Mack day?"

"That's every day of the week. Tell her why the Robinson's important, Mack."

He grunted and rubbed his chest over the flutter of his heart. Fool woman was going to give him a heart attack if he didn't watch it. "Send word back to Jim. I'll meet with Pope, but only if he needs me to."

"Will do."

"And Carol has to stay with you, if I go. I'm not leaving her here to fend for herself. Next thing you know, she'll drown in the river trying to save the fish."

"She's not nearly as stupid as you think, Mack."

"I didn't say she was stupid," he retorted. "Just flaky."

"I hope to God you didn't tell her so." Linda shook her head as she backed away. "Go talk to her. I'll send somebody out to spell you tomorrow so you can hightail it down to the line."

Mack nodded and watched her go, then his gaze fell on the suitcase. He was going to have to talk to Carol about leaving her stuff laying around. Putting the suitcase up was her responsibility, not his, just like it was her responsibility to oil that damn squeaky wheel.

He rubbed his chest again, then let his hand drop and hopped into the bus. Rummaged around the tools he'd managed to scrape together for some oil, and went outside and squirted it on each of the rollers, wondering all the while what song Carol was singing as she worked.

MACK DIDN'T go talk to Carol, not on purpose. He'd had every intention of avoiding her until she bebopped into the parking lot with a plate of fried oatmeal.

"Waste not, want not!" she said in a voice so chipper, he expected cartoon birds to start flying around her head.

He sneered at the plate. "What's that brown stuff on it?"

"Cinnamon sugar, Mr. Grumpy Butt."

"Where did you get—?"

She huffed out a breath. "Just try a piece already."

He picked up a slice, sniffed, and caught a whiff of cinnamon. It was still warm and a little soft.

Carol tapped the bottom of his hand gently. "Eat it before it gets cold."

"Fine," he snapped, and stuffed it into his mouth. The cinnamon sugar melted on his tongue, paving the way for the thick oatmeal. He'd half expected it to be as gloopy as breakfast, but it wasn't half bad. Sure as hell beat eating it out of a bowl.

She stepped back, grinning. "See what happens when you try new foods?"

He swallowed and wished for some water to wash it down. "Yeah. You get shot in the back by your friends."

"Is that what happened with Pope?"

That was one memory he wasn't dwelling on, and he sure as hell wasn't going to explain it. "Close enough."

"What does Pope have to do with your baseball cards?"

"Who says one has anything to do with the other?"

Her mouth turned into a pitying frown. "If you don't want to talk about it—"

"I don't."

"I mean, it's your business and all."

"Yup, it certainly is."

She sighed and patted his elbow just below the sleeve of his t-shirt, but she didn't say anything, just stood there looking at him. Waiting.

A stiff breeze blew down the valley, ruffling her hair, bending the tops of the grass growing in the field. Leaves drifted by, bouncing across the pavement like tumbleweeds, and an owl hooted in the forest, a low, mournful plaint.

"Fine," he said. "I'll tell you."

"Ok."

"My dad was in Vietnam. It messed him up some." He eyed her, waiting for her to interrupt, but she just kept on looking at him with those big, innocent eyes. "When he came back, he fell into drink, then fell in with the wrong crowd."

"I'm sorry," she murmured.

He shrugged it off and let his gaze wander to the road. Three does stood there, picking their way across the asphalt from the woods to the field. Good hunting soon, if he was still here.

Did Carol like venison?

"He tried to commit suicide a coupla times," Mack said. "Not the way you think. Not with a gun to his head or a handful of pills, just a slow, downward spiral. Then we were in the airport one day. Going to see my grandma, I think, and there was this man there, this black guy wearing a suit. And my dad just stopped and stared. 'Who's that?' I said, and he said, 'My God, that's Jackie Robinson.'"

Her mouth parted into a delighted oh. "Then what?"

"Then my dad marched right up to him and said, 'Mr. Robinson, can I get your autograph?' But for the life of us, we couldn't find a pen and paper, so Dad shook Robinson's hand and they talked for a minute before our flight was called. Things got better after that. A lot better. Dad quit the drugs, he got a steady job. Him and Mom split, but it was still good. Still better.

"Later, and I'm talking years here, but later, Dad told me that meeting Jackie Robinson was a turning point. Seeing him reminded Dad that you can still make a difference even when life hands you a pile of shit. Dad died not long after, and I found that baseball card stuck in his Bible, and I..."

The words petered out as suddenly as they'd started.

Carol sighed happily. "That's a great story. No wonder that baseball card means so much to you."

"Yeah. They all mean something. My grandpa gave me the Wagner."

"The what?"

A grin threatened to burst out, but he just shook his head. "Honus Wagner. Maybe I'll show you someday."

"I'm looking forward to it." She pressed the plate of fried oatmeal into his hands. "I'll leave you to your guns and such so I can get some mending done. Get some exercise while you're at it. You're getting a little bit of a belly."

He scraped a palm across his midsection, appalled all over again. "I am not."

She grinned and bounced away. "Don't worry, Mr. McMasters. The ladies are going to love it. I certainly do."

Heat crept up his throat into his cheeks. "I've worn the same size jeans since I was nineteen," he muttered, but if she heard him over her singing, she didn't turn around.

Mack picked up another piece of fried oatmeal and took a bite. Crazy woman. Next thing, she'd have him running laps around the parking lot, working off his nonexistent belly.

***

WHEN THE fried oatmeal was demolished, Mack set about doing chores around the museum. Checking the rabbit traps he'd set out along the river, past the museum. Cleaning the men's bathroom so Carol wouldn't have to. Scavenging downed limbs to use as fuel for the cook fire and chopping them into smaller pieces with a handheld ax.

As surprising as it was, Carol was right on one thing. They needed firewood. The oncoming winter had been a tickle in the back of his mind, one he'd happily ignored during a normal season as he'd rather move to a warmer locale than fiddle with firewood.

Moving wasn't much of an option now. Sure, the bus was mobile, but what were the odds they could sneak it past the PLA moving north and east from Columbia and Atlanta respectively?

No, better to stay here where they had people they could rely on.

With that in mind, he changed into shorts, a light t-shirt, and running shoes, strapped the holster holding the .357 onto his hip, and set out for a slow jog down the road toward the national park while the sun was still strong overhead. It would've been nice to run without having to think, just let his mind wander while he worked up a sweat, but he was running for a purpose.

And it wasn't because Carol said he had a belly. Because he didn't.

Instead, he kept an eye out for downed trees of a size that could easily be pulled out, cut into rounds, and split for firewood. Should've done that weeks ago, after the barriers were up, but he really hadn't thought that far ahead. Too much time alone, too many years being a tumbleweed.

He watched for deer sign, too, and bear. Either would be good for food, though bear was fatty as hell. The fur would come in handy. He could trade it to one of Linda's cousins for something Carol needed, lard and whatnot, and they could tan the hide and use it for—

The sun reflected off something in the tree line along the side of the road. Mack slowed, his gaze fixed on that spot. It was up in a tree, about eight feet off the ground. Not far from the road.

The back of his neck crawled and his gut twisted as instinct kicked in. He scanned the forest, searching for people or game or whatever was out of place. Nothing.

But there was that glint again, and this time he recognized it for what it was: A game camera, set with the lens pointing toward the barriers placed across the road near the museum's entrance.

Mack climbed the bank and found the tree, then shimmied up it and detached the camera. Damn thing was recording, though how he couldn't tell. For one, the EMPs should've wiped out most of the working electronics, even the small stuff, unless somebody had had the forethought to stash it away in a Faraday cage, or maybe traded it with an importer.

Like, say, the Chinese army.

Mack didn't know a thing about these types of cameras, though, other than what they were used for, to monitor the activity of wild food animals. His gaze drifted thoughtfully to the barriers. Animals, or maybe people.

The skin on the nape of his neck prickled again and he stifled a curse. Damn it, they were being watched, probably by more than this camera. Bad thing was, he walked this road every couple of days. Maybe he'd missed the camera the last time he'd been out. More likely, it had just been installed. If so, it signaled trouble for them and the town, and he had a good idea where that trouble was coming from.

They'd made do until now with just him on guard, because the folks in Gatlinburg had cut off access on that end of the road. But if Pope or another band of scumbags had taken the trouble to figure out a way around Cherokee and Gatlinburg both and had an eye on this strip of road, well. Maybe it was time to get serious about guarding this side of town.

Mack picked his way down the bank and jogged back to the museum, carrying the camera. He'd send up a flare, get some help out here, and tomorrow, he'd head to the line and have a little come to Jesus talk with ol' Pope.

LINDA SENT one of her nieces out to check on the solitary flare Mack sent up at dusk, and the niece came back an hour after Mack told her the problem with her brother in tow. The two of them set up watch on the road behind the barriers. The relief watch would come in the next morning to spell them right around the time Mack took Carol to Linda's so he could go play diplomat.

Hell if he'd leave her at the museum alone, even with two guards standing watch. No telling what type of trouble she'd get into on her own.

Carol was delighted with the game camera, which shouldn't have surprised him. She turned it over in her hands, examining it from every angle, her eyes wide with wonder.

"I thought all the electronics were goners," she said that night when they'd retreated to the bus for sleep.

Mack shrugged as he settled onto his bed near the middle of the bus. "Think this might have been imported."

Her head shot up and her mouth formed a soundless *oh*. "The Chinese brought it in?"

"Or gave it to somebody who traded it for something until it landed in the wrong hands."

"The wrong hands," she murmured. "You think your Pope has something to do with this."

"He's not my anything."

She hummed a tuneless note soft and low. "Mind if I

disassemble it?"

"Be my guest," he said, then lifted it from her hands. "Tomorrow, at Linda's. Bedtime now."

"I'm not a child."

Mack shook his head. She'd uttered the words without a hint of rancor. "All the more reason to get some sleep. Us old geezers need more than the whippersnappers holding down the fort outside."

Carol laughed and patted his forearm. "You're a funny man when you put your mind to it."

"I am not," he said gruffly, though he couldn't quite hide his own smile.

EARLY THE next morning, Mack and Carol walked the short distance from the museum to town, waving at the guards on their way past. Two young women this time, each with a small armory worth of weapons at her disposal. Their horses had been unsaddled and turned out into the field with the elk.

Naturally, Carol wanted to take pictures.

Mack hardly had to bite back a sigh. Maybe he was getting used to her. The idea should've panicked him, would've if he'd thought too hard on it. But his mind was clear and focused on the task ahead. It would have to be if he wanted to outmaneuver that rat bastard Pope.

He left Carol at the new Dairy Queen where Linda had set up camp so the locals could drop by and get help if they needed it. As the chairman of the tribal council, she felt that it was her duty to remain accessible during her people's time of need.

That was the official line. Not long after the shit hit the fan, she'd told Mack that with the federal and state governments out of the way, the Eastern Band would have a much easier time taking care of themselves.

Carol was happy to stay behind and sat down at an out of the way table with the game camera and a small tool kit she'd packed in her travel bag.

Mack shook his head and set out for Jim and the line on foot, following the roads. Linda had sent along an escort, four young men and women intended to rotate into positions on the line so four others could come home for a short leave.

The day was warm, warmer still because he was walking and carrying a backpack. The Robinson was in there. He never went anywhere without it. But it was tucked away in a hidden pouch, where it would be difficult to discover among the guns, ammunition, and other supplies he'd brought.

Collectibles weren't worth anything anymore. Food was more valuable, ammunition more valuable still.

Toilet paper was as precious as gold, for cripes' sake.

They reached the main section of the line a few hours later, mazes of barriers set up blocking the exit off Highway 74 toward Cherokee. Mirror lines of barriers were set up along every point of entry. They couldn't protect the town from people coming in through the forests. The area was too big for that. But they could sure as hell block the roads off.

Jim came up the road to meet him, as if he'd been waiting for Mack to get there. His broad face carried more wrinkles and his hair, normally shorn close to his scalp, was brushing the collar of his denim jacket. He hailed Mack as the escort slipped past them toward one of the motels where headquarters for the hastily scrambled militia was located.

"About time you got here," Jim said when Mack drew near. "Hard to get your lazy ass out of that cozy bed, huh?"

"Cozy my ass," Mack retorted, grinning. "You've got easy digs here, sleeping in a cushy motel room, no wife to nag you about picking up your socks."

"My wife sends word every day nagging me to pick up my socks."

Mack laughed. "Yeah, she would. She nags me often enough and I'm not married to her."

"She's an equal opportunity nagger." Jim's laughter faded and he jerked his chin toward the motel's office. "Let's talk inside. There's a lot to go over and not a lot of time to discuss it. Pope's on his way here."

"Already?"

"He sent word as soon as you neared the McDonald's. Supposedly he'll be here by supper, or if not, then by lunch tomorrow. The liaison he sent was a little vague on the whens."

Mack cussed under his breath. "Linda tell you about the game camera?"

"That and some other stuff. Come on."

They walked side by side down the road into the motel's parking lot. The motel had been built in the '70s. Two stories, metal doors for each room. A coke machine stood outside the office next to a snack machine, neither working, not far from a wooden rack holding brochures for local and regional attractions. Santa's Land, Oconaluftee Village, Unto these Hills. The EMP had wiped out more than the electronics. It had decimated the local tourist trade.

Not such a bad thing. Look at all the traffic jams they'd avoided.

The office had been converted into a strategy room. Kerosene lamps had been set around the room for light. One burned on the check-in counter, which had been cleared of computers, telephones, and other items needed to run the motel. Maps were pinned to the walls and covered with flags showing the last known locations of the various armies in play.

Mack had lost count, but evidently Jim had not, considering the number of colored flags pinned to a map of the US.

A local map had lines drawn on it denoting where roads had been barricaded. That was of more interest, but there was plenty of time to study it later.

Jim ducked into the back and came back carrying two folding chairs. "Best we could do on short notice."

"This is fine." Mack set his chair up next to Jim's, in front of the plate glass window fronting the office, with a good view of the parking lot and the road beyond. "Give it to me straight, Jim. What am I really doing here?"

"You're really here to deal with Pope."

Jim settled onto his chair and laid his palms flat on his muscled thighs. He'd taken to weight training in the Army and never quit. Worked out every day and twice on Sundays, if Linda was to be believed, and on that Mack believed every word. Jim was disciplined in a quiet, holistic way. Mind and body working together to support the spirit or some such.

Mack preferred finding his harmony at the grip end of a gun, but to each his own.

"What does he want?" he said.

"No idea. He sent a letter by his liaison, called for a parlay. Said he needed to restock his troops. Wanted to trade for supplies, if you can believe it."

Mack didn't believe it. There was something else going on. He could feel it in his gut. But what?

Jim shifted his feet against the worn linoleum floor, his gaze trained on the view. "I should probably be suspicious, since he mentioned you by name, but I can't figure out what his angle is."

"If it's me he wants, he could've skirted Cherokee and come in the other side, got the drop on me while I was sleeping. He has to know that end of town has almost no defenses."

"Linda fixed that."

Mack grunted. "Needs more than a couple of guns up there."

"We'll get there. Maybe. A scout came up today on horseback, riding in fast."

"One of yours?"

"One of the white locals from down Sylva way. Said they got word that Atlanta was still standing. The National Guard's got it covered with the help of a lot of citizens with guns."

"That's the thing about the South," Mack said mildly. "Everybody's got a gun."

"Or two or three."

"Or four or five."

Jim grinned at him. "Why stop with five?"

"My sentiments exactly."

"Is that how you got your woman? She impressed by your gun?"

Mack's mood soured. "Carol isn't allowed anywhere near my guns."

"I meant your—"

"I know what you meant. Does Linda know what a perv you are?"

"She's thankful for it every damn night and sometimes during the day, too." Jim stretched his arms back and laced his fingers together behind his head. "Pope's up to something."

"Then we'll deal with it."

"Yeah."

They fell into silence, watching the road and the shifts changing outside, and the wind blowing autumn into the mountains along with trouble.

POPE ARRIVED at the line just after lunchtime driving a cherry mid-'60s Ford pickup truck. He got out with his hands held over his head, turned when asked, didn't make a fuss when he was patted down and his weapons were confiscated.

That alone made Mack uneasy. Pope never did anything without good reason. Giving up his weapons? He must want something pretty damn badly, and Mack had a funny feeling it wasn't supplies.

Three other vehicles had followed Pope, but parked on Highway 74 at the bottom of the exit ramp, a respectful distance from the line. All three were older model vehicles. One was a Volkswagon Bus with a mural of Jimi Hendrix painted on the side.

Jim had designated one of the motel rooms as a conference room and had the furniture cleaned out and a card table and chairs brought in. That left plenty of space for the three of them to sit without one of them having his back to the room's lone road-facing window.

Mack sat between Jim and Pope, not bothering to hide his scrutiny of his former frenemy. Pope had aged a great deal more than Mack or Jim had since their Airborne days, though he was still a lean, wiry sumbitch under the black shirt and cargo pants he wore. His once-blonde hair was brown now and streaked with gray, and his green eyes were emotionless under a deeply lined forehead, despite the slight smile twisting Pope's thin lips.

Mack's stomach clenched. What his ex-wife had seen in Pope, he had no clue. Anybody with a brain could see the man was trouble just by looking at him. Even Carol, and she walked into trouble whistling Disney so often, he'd lost count.

They sat nearly simultaneously, Jim to Mack's right, Pope to his left. Mack leaned back in his chair, skewering Pope with a glower that would make any sane person turn and run.

"What do you want?" he said.

Pope's smile widened a hair. "It's in the letter I sent Jim here. I'm sure he's let you read it."

Mack's eye twitched at the smug arrogance in Pope's gravelly voice. Sumbitch just couldn't help himself, could he?

"I read it," Mack said flatly. "Food and water and, what, fresh clothes? You could've gone anywhere for that. Why trade with us?"

"I like spreading the love around, especially to old friends."

Jim barked out a disbelieving laugh. "Old friends my ass. You tried to kill Mack."

Pope leaned forward, still smiling. "If I'd wanted him dead, he'd be rotting in a coffin six feet underground right now."

"While you made off with his woman." Jim shook his head. "I think our price just doubled. What do you think, Mack?"

Mack forced his hands to remain exactly where they were, resting on the edge of the table, relaxed as if he weren't at all bothered by what was going on. "Triple it and maybe he'll go away."

Pope sat back in his chair, his hands on his thighs. "I think you're going to want to hear what I have to offer."

"The day you have something I want," Jim began.

A horse galloped into the parking lot and slowed to a stop outside the motel in clear view of the makeshift conference room. Linda slid off and dropped the reins onto the ground, then hollered for someone to take care of her effin horse loud enough to be heard all the way back in town.

Jim stood. "Duty calls. You two try not to start World War III while I see what the ruckus is."

"The Chinese beat me to it," Pope said.

"Asshole," Mack said mildly.

Pope just smiled.

Jim walked out shaking his head, leaving the room's door wide open.

Linda's voice carried clearly through the air. "Where's Mack? I need to talk to him right now."

Jim spoke too low to hear, then the two of them came into the room, Linda first. Her cheeks were flushed dark red and her eyes were lit with an unholy fire. When she spotted Pope, she marched straight toward him, reared back a balled-up fist, and, quicker than Mack could react, knocked Pope in the jaw so hard, he teetered backward in his chair.

And swung his head toward her smiling. "Nice love tap you've got there, sweetheart."

"Where is she?" Linda said, the words so low and angry, Mack could barely understand her.

Jim caught her arm and hauled her back. "I told you to let me handle this."

"I'm the goddamn chairman," Linda spat out. "She's my responsibility."

That funny feeling in Mack's gut morphed into a sick queasiness. "She?" he said, but some part of him already knew.

"Carol," Linda said, a hair more calmly. "She went up to the museum to harvest some apples and never came back. We can't find her, Mack."

He forced his expression to remain neutral, forced his hands not to twitch, but his mind seethed. He'd told her to stay put, told her again and again exactly what she needed to do while he was here. Stay with Linda. Don't leave town. If something happens, find shelter and hide until he could reach her. How hard was it to do what he told her to do?

Pope's smile had grown into a self-satisfied grin during Linda's outburst. "Problems in paradise?"

"Oh, you muck rooting, sheep loving tallywacker," Linda said. "There's going to be a serious problem here if you don't hand her over."

Any other time, Mack would've admired the insult, but he had bigger fish to fry. Said fish being the woman he'd *told to stay put* under threat of house arrest.

"Her who?" Pope said, arching bushy eyebrows. "Lost

someone?"

Linda lurched forward, dragging Jim with her. Jim managed to haul her back before she reached Pope, but it was a close thing.

Mack speared Pope with the calmest gaze he could muster. "What do you want?"

"You know what I want. Same thing I've always wanted."

"You're not getting the Robinson." Not after Pope had put a bullet in his leg and stolen his wife. "She doesn't mean anything to me, and even if she did, no woman is worth that much."

Pope's smile had grown wolfy. "We'll see how you feel when I start sending her back to you in pieces. After my men have her, of course. Strangely enough, nubile young women like your little friend tend to avoid us."

Linda screamed a bloodcurdling war cry. "I'll rip your throat out if you so much as harm one hair on her head."

Jim yanked her back with a hiss. "You're not helping."

"Oh, she's helping," Pope said as he stood. "Meet me at the bottom of the exit ramp. Bring the card."

Mack leaned back in his chair, kicked his legs out, and crossed his arms over the rapid patter of his heart. "You're not getting it."

"Yes, I am."

Pope slipped past Linda and Jim with the lithe grace of a mountain lion. He'd used that grace to his advantage in the Army, sliding into enemy territory for purposes both official and personal, and he'd slithered back out again like the snake he was.

Linda watched him go, panting her anger into the late summer air. As soon as he was out of earshot, she whipped her head around and glared at Mack. "You can't let them keep Carol. You know what they'll do to her."

Mack's throat chose that moment to close up on him.

Which was just fine, as Jim answered for him. "He knows, Linda."

"Then he needs to haul ass back to town and get that baseball card."

"And let Pope win?"

Linda jabbed her elbow back, catching her husband in the ribs. Jim's breath whooshed out of him and his grip eased enough for her to wiggle away from him. She strode forward and slammed her fist into the table in front of Mack so hard it bounced.

"No baseball card is worth a woman's life," she said, nearly growling. "Even if you don't care about her, I do, and you owe me, Mack. You owe me."

He stood slowly and met her hot gaze with ice. "I don't owe you shit."

"Who took you in when that ass shot you, huh? Who took a broken man and pieced him back together again when his wife ran out on him, when the Army turned its back on him?"

Mack looked at her for a long moment, knowing she was right, and just not caring. The Robinson was everything. It wasn't just a symbol of the bond he'd had with his dad, and of the man who had unwittingly saved his dad's life, just by being in the right place at the right time. It was a reminder that even when life hands you a shit hand, you can hold your head high and make the world a better place.

The world needed people like Jackie Robinson in it.

The world needed people like that.

Mack shook his head mutely and walked out, his heart a leaden ache above the greasy spin of his stomach.

MACK RETRIEVED his backpack from the office and was halfway to town when Jim caught up with him riding one of Linda's roans.

"Helluva thing," Jim said.

Mack grunted. Yeah, it was a helluva thing.

"We can take him, maybe," Jim continued. "If he doesn't have men waiting at the ready, just beyond our sight. Carol might get hurt in the crossfire though."

"Not my responsibility."

Jim laughed. "Man, she became your responsibility the day you took her home."

Mack stopped dead in the middle of the road. "I didn't take her home. I took her to the museum so she wouldn't be such a damn nuisance in town. Clicking away with her camera like she was there on vacation. Who does that?"

"A tourist?"

"Exactly!" Mack said. "We're in the middle of a crisis situation and that airhead is running around playing tourist. She hasn't got the brains God gave a goat."

"You know she has a Master's in business, right?"

Mack glared up at Jim, whirling around so fast, the horse sidestepped away from him. "How the hell do you know that?"

"Well." Jim shifted his grip on the reins, easing the horse's restlessness. "I sat down with her, person to person, and had a conversation with her. Interesting woman. I can see why you like her."

"Like her!" Mack sputtered. "I can barely stand eating at the same table as her!"

"That why you gave her the run of the museum, because you hate her so much?"

"Hate is a strong word."

"So you do like her."

"I didn't say that."

Jim stuck his tongue in his cheek. "Uh-huh. Well, you might want to decide right quick whether you like her or hate her, as Pope's planning on throwing her to his men any minute now."

The knot in Mack's gut jumped into his throat. He closed his eyes and pinched the bridge of his nose between his fingers. For cripes' sake. When had he gotten so damn wishy washy? And over a scatterbrained, tone deaf woman, no less.

"I just need a minute to think," he said.

"Think quick, my friend. Time's a-ticking."

Jim guided the horse in a wide circle and headed back toward the line, leaving Mack standing there with his brain and his heart warring with each other.

THE LINE was just like it had been when he'd headed in the other direction. Barricaded, manned, a little menacing if you happened to be on the wrong side of it.

Linda met him there and threw her arms around him. "I knew you wouldn't walk out on her," she whispered. "I knew you couldn't do that to her."

Mack stiffened in her embrace. "I didn't say I was here to get her back."

"You showed up, didn't you?" She kissed his cheek and let him go, drawing back enough to smile at him. Relief shone from her eyes through the tears glistening there. "Want me to go down with you?"

He shook his head as he eased back. Beyond her, he spotted Jim standing in the middle of the road grinning like a loon. That was fine with Mack. At least he wasn't the only crazy one on this side of the barricade.

He slipped past the line, carrying his backpack on one shoulder, and walked down the exit ramp, examining the cars still sitting on the highway below. Pope's cars, four in total, but Mack was of a mind to agree with Jim on that. Reinforcements were probably nearby and they probably numbered in the plenty. Pope had a way about him that drew people in. If you weren't careful, he'd chew you up and spit you back out again, and doing so wouldn't make a dent in his heart.

Pope had always been a cold bastard. Being in the Army had only magnified that trait.

He slid out of the truck he'd driven earlier and walked up the exit ramp, stopping just shy of the halfway mark. "Thought you'd change your mind."

Mack pulled the .357 out of his hip holster and aimed it at Pope's heart, nice and steady. "Is that why you think I'm here?"

Pope just grinned. "You're not crazy enough to shoot me with my men down there. I let my lieutenants have a go at her. They said she was tasty."

Mack's hand tightened on the revolver's grip and anger burned through his hesitation, strengthening his resolve. "Linda will kill you for that."

"Linda won't get anywhere near me."

"You don't know her very well." Mack smiled coldly. "Let me see the woman."

Pope raised a hand without turning around. Behind him, two rough-looking men opened the VW bus up and yanked Carol out. Her hands were zip tied in front of her and her shirt was ripped at one shoulder seam. Her hair was a disheveled mess, too, and was that a bruise under her eye?

Mack let the backpack slide off his shoulder and dropped it to the road out of his way. "Get her up here so I can make sure it's the right woman."

Pope threw his head back and laughed long and hard. When he finally stopped, he wiped fake tears from his eyes and huffed out a sigh. "That's the flimsiest excuse I've ever heard for getting a hostage close enough to steal her away. No dice, Mack. Show me the card."

"The woman first."

"Not a chance."

His men were walking her closer anyway, close enough for sunlight to glint off the tears streaking through the dirt on her face. Close enough for him to see the blood on her knees where she'd fallen. Close enough for him to see that by God that was a bruise on her cheek, and on her arms where her t-shirt didn't cover.

Slowly, Mack reached toward his backpack, keeping the .357 pointed at Pope's heart.

"Don't do it, Mr. McMasters!" Carol yelled. "Don't you dare give him that baseball card. I can handle anything these yahoos dish out!"

"Aw," Pope said. "She still calls you mister. Isn't that so Victorian of you."

Mack arched an eyebrow, his hand still two feet from the backpack. "I should've shot you a long time ago."

"And yet, here we are." Pope held out a narrow hand. "The card."

"She can come get it."

"Not until I see it."

Carol shoulder butted the guy next to her, a thin kid who didn't look old enough to shave. "I swear, if you give him that card, I'll put castor oil in your oatmeal!"

Mack snorted. She'd do it, too, but tough luck. He was on a mission here and he aimed to see it through. He reached down and pulled the Robinson out of an unzipped pocket, then held it up for Pope.

Here was his daddy's life, right there between his fingers. All these years, Mack had held onto the card thinking he could draw courage and inspiration from it, but that's not where the courage and inspiration lay at all. Those were there, in his memory, in his heart. The card was just a reminder. What mattered most was that he'd never forget, not that he held onto a piece of cardboard at the expense of a woman's life.

"Set her loose," Mack said, "and let her bring it to you."

"How do I know that's the real deal?" Pope said.

"You'll just have to take my word for it."

Pope nodded and raised his hand, waving the men behind him forward. And they all came forward, like they were too curious not to, dragging Carol along with them when she resisted. They were a ragtag group of various sizes, shapes, and colors. Most carried guns or knives at their hips. None had been stupid enough to draw their weapons, a wise move given the small army Jim had assembled behind the barricade.

Finally, they pulled her even with Pope and he shoved her forward. "Get the card so I can see it."

She spat at his feet. "Eat elk poo."

Someone snickered, setting off a rash of titters. Pope just shoved her again, nearly knocking her off balance.

She glared at him, then turned her nose into the air and marched toward Mack, who sidestepped her path and kept the .357 pointed at Pope. When she reached him, she whispered, "I told you not to give him that baseball card."

"Shut up," Mack said gently. "Where did they hurt you?"

"They didn't lay a hand on me except for the kidnapping, but what does it matter?" she hissed. "Now's your chance. Shoot the rat bastard so we can go home."

"I heard that," Pope said, "and it wounds me to my core."

Mack ignored him and stared down at her. Slowly, the knot in his gut eased and he found his laughter again. "Rat bastard?"

"That's what Linda calls him. That and a few things I can't repeat."

"Ladies," Pope called. "My man Bob here's got an itchy trigger finger just waiting to squeeze away."

"Yeah, yeah," Mack hollered back. He pressed the card, still in its case, into one of her hands. "Take this and set it down halfway between us, then walk back here. We'll have your hands free in no time."

She shook her head, sending her hair in a wild shimmy around her rectangular face, her eyes as wide as saucers. "No way. I know what that card means to you and I'm not letting you give it up for me."

His humor died abruptly. "I'm suddenly remembering what a pain in my ass you are."

"See?" she said brightly. "Better to let me go back and take my chances with them. Good riddance, right?"

He would've agreed with her a week ago. Now, he knew better. The world needed people like Carol, just like it needed people like Jackie Robinson. People who knew better times were ahead, if they were willing to work for them. People who kept a smile on their face even when the shit hit the fan.

"Take this to him," Mack said, "and I'll put new chinking in the log house so you can have a decent roof over your head this winter."

Her mouth opened and closed. "You'd do that for me?"

"I'll do it for me. You're just tagging along."

She smiled at him then, that bright, sunny smile that melted all the anger right out of him. "I've got a secret."

"Yeah?"

"Yeah. Those guys weren't so great at watching me. My pockets are full of all sorts of things, and I know where they're camped. Dang fools didn't even blindfold me, even though Pope told 'em to. 'Course, that might've been because I bit the first couple that got too close to me."

Mack grinned as he holstered the gun. If she really knew where Pope was camped, it'd be no trouble at all to sneak in under the cover of dark and get some payback. Sooner rather than later. Pope never stayed in one place for long. That was the one thing they had in common, or did before the PLA invaded.

He turned her gently around and helped her along with a small push. "Get going, woman. We've got firewood to split."

"Yes, sir, Mr. McMasters, sir."

"Call me Teddy."

She looked at him over her shoulder, one dirty eyebrow arched. "Teddy?"

"Yeah, well." He rubbed a hand over his nape, fighting to keep the blush down. "There's a reason everybody calls me Mack."

"I like Teddy," she said simply. "You might want to pull that gun back out, though. You may need it when I shove this card down Pope's throat."

Mack laughed and watched her walk toward the other man. Yeah, the world needed women like Carol in it, especially when times were tough.

And so, as it turned out, did he.

The Infinite Bright

ndiri saw the flash through the narrow view afforded by the airplane's window. She reached across her sleeping son and jostled her husband's arm. "Did you see that?"

Harij held up his book. His eyes were flat and annoyed behind the rims of his glasses. "I see words running in lines across the page."

She let her hand fall away and turned back to the window. They'd climbed above the clouds after takeoff. She'd been enjoying the view, imagining herself floating through the air like a cloud herself. Golden hued and perfectly formed from wishes and dreams, perpetually suspended in an ocean of blue.

Now those clouds were a boiling orange and red mass beneath the plane. Her gut clenched tight under the rapid beat of her heart. The airplane shuddered once, as if someone had shaken it hard, and a woman across the aisle gasped.

The seat belt sign flickered on. The intercom crackled and a male voice said, "Ladies and gentlemen, the captain has turned on the fasten seatbelt sign..."

Indiri ignored the announcement and leaned forward, peering around her family. The woman was short, plump, and pale beneath a wildly curling cap of brassy yellow hair, and wore a thin, flowing shirt decorated with brilliantly colored hibiscus.

"Are you all right?" Indiri said.

The woman attempted a smile, jiggling her sagging jowls. "Just nervous is all. It's my first time on a plane in years. All this turbulence!"

Indiri smiled reassuringly. "It will be fine, I'm sure, or the captain would say something."

The woman pointed upward. "Isn't that him talking about the turbulence now?"

"He would say more if it was truly bad."

Harij held up his book. "A little quiet please."

The woman smiled sheepishly. "Sorry."

Indiri waved off her concern. Flying always made her husband grumpy. He'd been staring at the same set of pages since takeoff. It was his way, she thought, of alleviating the stress of flying. This trip to see his parents...

She glanced down at their son sleeping peacefully between them. Devid was the very image of his father, small and slender, round smiling face, inquisitive gaze. Well, she thought, turning toward the window. Normally smiling, laughing, playing. Normally happy, for a child who was anything but normal.

Normal in his own way, she amended. Every child had a base norm, regardless of where he fell among the norms of other children.

The clouds hung below the airplane like a bubbling pit of fresh lava.

"What do you think caused that?" she murmured to herself.

"I don't know," Harij said.

She reached blindly toward him, holding her hand out to him, and felt him enclose it in his own.

"I'm sure it's nothing," he said.

"It doesn't look like nothing."

"But what else could it be?"

She turned away from the hellish view and faced him. "If it were important, the captain—"

"Probably doesn't know what it is either." He squeezed her hand and smiled, the barest curve of his lips. "Even if they did, would they tell us?"

"Yes," she said firmly. "Of course. That's their job. The crew, the attendants."

He dropped their joined hands onto their son's legs and rested the back of his head against the seat. "I wish I'd brought another book. This one is tedious."

Surely he'd known that before he'd brought it aboard, as he'd been reading it while they were packing. Still, she played along, hoping to ease his anxiety. "What is this one?"

"*The Curious Incident of the Dog in the Night-Time*. It's about a boy..." His eyelids fluttered open and he looked down at their son. "I thought it would help me understand."

Her heart twisted in her chest, just a little. "Has it?" she asked gently.

"Perhaps I should've read Sherlock Holmes first."

The reference confounded her, as she'd never read either, but she let it go. That he was trying was enough.

Devid stirred in his seat, yawning sleepily. The plane lurched forward and down, shaking violently, rattling the contents of the overhead storage. Indiri's teeth clacked together as the plane veered sharply to the right, tilting so that her long hair, pulled into a sleek ponytail at the base of her neck, swung sideways and brushed the top of her son's head.

Just as abruptly, the plane leveled out, though her heart

continued to hammer wildly in her chest. She thought perhaps it might be building a new home for itself behind her sternum.

The woman across the aisle leaned forward and caught Indiri's eye. "Things have settled down now, thank goodness."

Indiri's smile had abandoned her. "Are you all right?"

"I don't know." The woman laughed and patted her voluminous chest with beringed fingers. "How's that for honesty? I'm Patty, by the way. Patty Long from Missouri."

"Indiri Patel from Georgia. My husband Harij and our son Devid."

"Oh! I have a grandson named David. What a coincidence!"

Harij tucked his paperback against the armrest, unbuckled his seatbelt, and stood. "I think I should stretch my legs."

Indiri pressed her lips together, restraining a protest. They'd only just come out of that turbulence. What if there was more and he was caught in the aisle?

She clasped her hands into a knot in her lap, hiding them in the folds of her sari. Traditional dress, to please her in-laws. Why had she worn it? She'd have been more comfortable in a suit. One of the ones she wore to work, perhaps, or something more casual. A tunic length sweater and leggings.

Harij had worn casual clothes. Jeans and a long-sleeved polo! Why did she cling to this notion that she could please his parents by dressing as a proper woman should?

Outside, the clouds had frozen into a violent, bubbled mass. Curiously, the noise from the plane's engines had dissipated.

"Your son's a handsome fellow," Patty said above a sudden burst of conversation from the other passengers. "You must be very proud of him."

"I am," Indiri murmured, and it was true. For all his differences, Devid was a good son, helpful and devoted, quite bright in his own way. At the age of three, just two years earlier, he'd found a screwdriver and taken the vacuum cleaner apart when it had broken.

Then fixed it as if nothing had ever been wrong.

Yet he couldn't speak, couldn't articulate his thoughts beyond basic gestures. He seemed to live in a world of his own making, one which few others could enter, let alone understand. How could she explain these things to a stranger, that her beautiful, beloved son was so differently abled?

The words failed her. Instead, she said, "Are you travelling alone?"

Patty's laughter was a tinkling sound, like chimes blown together by a light breeze. She touched the man sitting to her right, on the other side from the aisle, nearly hidden by her voluptuous form. "My husband came with me. Darn thing fell asleep as soon as he strapped in. Can you imagine?"

"Devid, too."

"There's something about transportation. Puts him right to sleep. I have to drive wherever we go."

A flight attendant paused in the aisle and smiled at each of them in turn. He was tall and slender, clean cut. The starched white collar of his shirt, just visible above his dove gray suit, was a sharp contrast to the darkness of his smoothly shaved skin.

"Ladies, how are we?" he said. "A bit shaken?"

"Fine, hon, just fine," Patty said, though she was still pale.

Indiri nodded. "Thank you, we're fine. My husband is stretching his legs. If you see him..."

"I'll point him this way," the attendant said, then stepped forward and repeated the conversation with the people in the rows behind them.

Had the engines stopped?

Indiri leaned forward and glanced back through the window, but all she could see was a sea of clouds infused with the colors of a dying sun, stretching toward the horizon. It filled the view, as if eternity were compiled entirely of a bright, infinite expanse.

The intercom keyed on, filling the cabin with a babble of panicked voices. Out of the corner of her eyes, she saw Patty's hands clenching the armrests. The intercom cut out abruptly, and was replaced by the worried conversations eddying through the passengers.

Harij appeared in the aisle, blocking her view of Patty, and sat down. "You didn't have to send someone to fetch me. I was coming back."

"I didn't..." Indiri bit the inside of her cheek. If she continued along those lines, it would lead to a fuss, fraying her nerves. One of them needed to remain calm, in case Devid awoke. "I thought perhaps you were looking for a parachute."

Humor lit his eyes, chasing away the irritation. She'd fallen in love with those eyes, their expressiveness, their warmth. The kindness of his heart was reflected there.

"Should we be worried?" Patty asked. "I mean, this doesn't seem normal, does it? I can't even hear the engines anymore."

Indiri had been on the verge of reassuring the other woman again, until that last statement.

Harij shook his head and opened his book. "I wish I'd brought another book. This one is tedious."

Devid inhaled a stuttering breath, and the plane tumbled and jerked. Someone screamed, high and thin. Patty, Indiri thought as she gripped the armrest with one hand and pressed the other against her son's stomach, above his tightly buckled seatbelt. The oxygen masks dropped down, swinging with the plane's motion.

Indiri gasped and squeezed her eyes tight. The engines roared to life, the airplane settled into stability.

A perky male voice said, "Ladies, how are we? A bit shaken?"

She glanced up, swallowed past the choking dryness in her throat. The oxygen masks were gone. The same flight attendant stood in the aisle, smiling beatifically between her and Patty.

Harij was no longer in his seat.

"My husband is stretching his legs," she said numbly.

"I'll point him this way."

Outside, the clouds frothed and boiled in a dance unto themselves.

SHERLOCK HOLMES," Harij said, shaking his head.

"What?" She'd been watching the clouds again, measuring their plane's progress against the sky below. Had they shifted any? Had they changed colors? Weren't they a little darker now, tinged black around the edges?

He held up his book. "A little quiet, please."

The woman across the aisle squeaked. "Fine, hon, just fine."

"Ladies and gentlemen, the captain has turned on..."

But the sign had been on the entire trip, save for a brief moment after leveling out, not long after takeoff.

Indiri's tongue clung to the roof of her mouth. Such a bizarre flight. She pulled her bag from under the seat ahead of her, dug through it for her cellphone.

"I thought it would help me understand."

"Should we be worried?"

"Ladies, how are we?"

Ah, there it was. She held it up, triumphant, ready to check the time. It had been a long journey. Surely they were close to their destination.

"Kali Yuga," Harij said.

She frowned at the phone's black face. Hadn't she charged it last night? She hit the on switch, fiddled with it for a moment, and, finally, his words registered in her brain.

"Kali Yuga doesn't end for—" She dropped the phone into her

bag and stuffed the whole into place under the forward seat. "You've never believed in such things before."

"I've never seen such things before. Look."

She followed his pointing finger toward the window, expecting to see a bull with one leg tethered among the clouds. Dharma reduced to the bare minimum. The view hadn't changed since that first shudder ran through them and the clouds became molten. "What is it?"

His hand dropped. "Nothing."

"Why this sudden interest in the end stage?" The final of four stages of the universe before it ended, or as some preferred to put it, when it renewed and began again. The age of the demon Kali, ruling over an immoral, degenerate world.

"I said it was nothing."

He seemed petulant now, which puzzled her. Aside from his grumpy irritation while flying, he was a calm, even-tempered man, not given to fits of emotion. His rational side nearly always won out.

"Are you feeling well, my husband?"

The Curious Incident of the Dog in the Night-Time was back in his hands. His gaze was intense behind the rims of his glasses. "I wish I'd brought another book," he said slowly. "This one is..."

"Tedious," she murmured. "So you've said."

"Many times," he agreed. "Why is that?"

"I don't know."

Across the way, Patty patted her nearly invisible husband's leg. "Can you imagine? Can you just imagine that?"

RUMOR DRIFTED through the passengers like waves along a shoreline. The ocean of murmurs touched the sand here and deposited a word, touched it there and deposited another.

"Engines cut out...glide down...pilot had a heart attack."

Unsubstantiated, Indiri thought. The captain or co-pilot would have made an announcement if something tragic had happened. It was their job to inform the passengers, to calm them.

Surely the flight attendants would've said something.

Indiri waited for someone to come along and explain, waited through half-finished conversations interrupted by violent turbulence.

How could Devid sleep through such?

Yet sleep he did, stirring only when the aircraft's shaking became extreme.

Or did he stir and then the aircraft jittered?

She tried to remember which it was, but the events were jumbled together in her mind, overlapping one another like the folds in an ancient sari. All of one cloth, pleated out of order.

"I just had the biggest sense of déjà vu," Patty said. "Don't you hate it when that happens?"

Harij lifted his head from the book and turned his head toward their row mate.

Indiri leaned across Devid and placed her hand on his arm. "Harij, be gentle."

"Déjà vu," he said precisely, "happens when there's a glitch in the matrix."

Patty threw back her head and laughed, a full belly laugh. "*The Matrix*! I thought for sure you were gonna light into me with some scientific mumbo jumbo."

"She knows you well," Indiri said sweetly, "and has only just met you."

His flashed a boyish grin at her. "Predictability is the first sign of old age."

"Stiff joints are the first sign of old age."

"One leads to the other." He tucked the paperback against the armrest and shifted forward in his seat. "I think I should stretch my legs."

Alarm washed over her, raising goose bumps along her skin. Her hand tightened reflexively on his arm. "No, don't. Please."

The flight attendant appeared in the aisle, absent his usual smile. "We've heard the rumors being passed among the passengers. Please rest assured that everything is fine."

If everything was so fine, why hadn't he simply made an announcement over the intercom?

The attendant moved on (Why hadn't she caught his name that time?) and Harij's hand pressed against hers. "Your nails are cutting into my skin, Indiri."

Horrified, she released her grip on him. "I don't know what I was thinking."

"You're upset. We all are. Why don't you switch seats with Devid, sit next to me for a while?"

She glanced at their son, sleeping so peacefully, and slowly shook her head. "We shouldn't wake him."

Harij's eyebrows shot up in his sweet, round face. "He's been asleep for hours! If we don't wake him soon, he won't sleep tonight."

"I have such a bad feeling." She placed her palm there, over the apprehension gathering under her heart. "We shouldn't wake him."

"Then at least walk around. Sitting for such a long time is unhealthy."

"Of course. I will."

Dutifully, because he'd suggested it and some part of her wanted to please him enough to comply, Indiri rose and passed gently by her son and husband, careful not to jostle either one. She'd walk for a while, up and down this aisle once, perhaps twice. That should please her husband. Four laps should appease his concern.

***

INDIRI MADE her circuit of the aisle, noting random passengers as she passed. A woman and two small children. A businessman wearing a sharply tailored suit. An older gentleman reading a thick paperback with a tattered cover. Curious, she gazed out the windows beyond them, surreptitiously attempting to compare her side of the sky with the far one.

It was as she had seen, like a bed of molten lava arrested before it cooled and hardened into rock.

She would've returned to her seat then, but when she approached him, the gentleman who had been reading closed his book, leaving his hand between the pages as a temporary bookmark. The cover caught her eye, and the title.

The Mahabharata: An abridged translation.

Once upon a time, in the days of her greatest curiosity, before university and motherhood, Indiri had read Mahabharata. She glanced down the plane, toward where her family sat, her brow furrowed. What a coincidence, for Harij to mention Kali Yuga, and for this gentleman to be reading the very text in which the mahayuga, the four stages of the world, were described.

Or was it a coincidence?

The gentleman looked up, his bushy white eyebrows arched high on a wrinkled forehead. She smiled and moved on, and returned to her seat, thoughtful now. The plane had been remarkably calm during her procession. She paused in the aisle, staring down at Harij and Devid, wondering.

"Did he wake?" she said.

Her husband shook his head. "Not once. Do you want me to—"

Her hand shot out, touching his shoulder. "No. Don't wake him. I think..."

Harij looked up at her, smiling. "You think what?"

What did she think?

The intercom keyed on with a squeal to rival Patty's. "Ladies and gentlemen, the captain has turned on the fasten seatbelt sign. Please return to your seats and fasten your seatbelts. Thank you."

It was the flight attendant's voice. She would know it anywhere now, having heard it so many times.

Harij grasped her hand and tugged, capturing her attention. "Time to sit."

She nodded mutely, slipped by his knees, being careful not to wake Devid. Once seated, she tugged her seatbelt around her waist, fastened it, and waited, her gaze drawn again to the unchanging view.

The unnatural view. Clouds were not supposed to look like that. Even the sun's light could not achieve that effect.

"Ladies and gentlemen," the captain said.

Or perhaps the co-pilot. Indiri hadn't bothered learning their voices. This was supposed to have been a routine flight, another in a series of flights they'd taken across the continent from their home in Atlanta to the home of Harij's parents in Washington state.

"Our communications with air traffic control in Seattle have been interrupted."

A buzz of voices filled the cabin, passengers tittering to one another over the unusual circumstance.

"We expect that this is a result of the shockwave that hit us at thirteen forty-five."

Indiri's eyelids slid shut. That coincided roughly with the first round of turbulence. She'd have to check the time on her cellphone to be sure, but...

No. Her phone's battery was dead.

"Please remain calm. Thank you."

Patty moaned and rocked in her seat. "Oh dear, oh dear."

Indiri's gaze met her husband's. "I don't think it was a shockwave."

"No," he said after a moment. "Well, yes, it could've been, but a shockwave alone doesn't explain the clouds."

"What does?"

The question seemed to surprise him. "A catastrophic event?"

"Such as?"

He paused. "A nuclear strike? A meteor?"

She frowned, thinking of the site in Russia that had been devastated more than a century past. What was it again? Some unpronounceable place name. "Wouldn't those have similar effects?"

"If the meteor was big enough."

"And those could cause..." She held a hand toward the window and the unnaturally tinted clouds. "That?"

He shrugged. "Possibly. Or the cause could be something entirely different. There aren't enough data to speculate."

"Data," she said, huffing.

"That's what scientists work with," he said, unperturbed. "You knew that when we married."

"I knew you were a geek when we married," she retorted, though there was more teasing than irritation in her voice.

"And you were right. Which is why I should've brought the latest Star Trek novelization along."

"You were trying."

His eyes fell to Devid, and his expression was tender, kind. "I always shall."

The flight attendant appeared in the aisle, and Indiri finally caught a glimpse of his nametag. John! A lovely name. Strong, implacable. Perfect for a man about to deliver solemn news.

And by his expression, she was sure whatever John intended to say would be quite solemn. He opened his mouth to speak.

Harij shifted in his seat. His elbow slid off the armrest into Devid.

Devid's eyelids fluttered and he raised a chubby hand to his mouth.

The plane bounced in the sky as if someone had bumped it

from behind. The flight attendant gasped and braced himself between the seats as they swayed and tilted. Indiri's gaze bounced around the cabin, taking in more than her brain could process at once.

The terror in her husband's eyes as he reached toward John. Patty screaming into a fist, her husband waking at last with a startled yelp. A book flying through the air, its pages fluttering between a tattered cover.

The moon drifting in pieces along the far horizon, just visible through the window across the cabin.

She shushed Devid, calming him, and the plane righted itself.

"Harij," she said, her voice trembling. "I think I know what happened."

"You want to talk about that *now*?" he squawked.

"Look out the window."

He turned automatically to hers, and she reached out and pressed her fingertips into his jaw, gently pointing him in the right direction. John's gaze followed as well, and Patty's, and soon, everyone was staring at the broken moon as a thick silence descended around them.

"My God," John said faintly.

"God didn't do this." Harij rose slowly. "Man didn't either. Couldn't have either. We lack the technology."

"An asteroid?" Indiri said.

"I don't know."

"ATC is gone," John blurted out, then clapped a hand over his mouth and closed his eyes. "I wasn't supposed to say that."

"Too late," Harij said. "What is an ATC?"

"Air Traffic Control." John's hand fell to his side and he stared bleakly at them. "We got word, just before the shockwave overtook us. About the moon, then communications ceased in mid-word and when we tried to reconnect—"

"Someone deduced that they were gone." Harij was facing the other side of the cabin now. His shoulders were rounded into a near slump and his hands were limp at his sides. "That's only about half the moon's mass out there."

Indiri wanted to ask where the other half was, but she already knew. If an asteroid had hit the moon and only half of the orbiting body was hanging in the sky now, the other half must have collided with Earth.

Her mind stuttered over the damage that much material could do when it hit a planet at a high velocity. How fast did the moon orbit around the Earth? How fast had the asteroid been travelling? What trajectory had it been on when the two collided?

She discarded the math immediately. Physics had never been her strong suit. That's why she'd drifted into other interests at university. Languages and drama, and then Devid had come along.

She looked at him now as the pieces assembled in her mind. The jumbled folds of time repeating itself. The turbulence coinciding with Devid's restlessness. The clouds, oh, the clouds!

The airplane should've burned up in the atmosphere, yet here they were, flying above the remnants of a ruined Earth, alive.

Or were they?

"I'm going to talk to the captain," Harij said, jarring her from her reverie.

John nodded and scraped a narrow hand down his mouth. "I'll get you in. Tell him you're a physicist, you know about these things."

Yes, Harij should go, for now. He should figure things out from a scientific perspective. She already had her answer.

Indiri rested her hand on her son's as her husband walked to the front of the airplane, and sang a lullaby to help her darling sleep.

Love in a Winter Garden

When Edith was three, her mother taught her to read from scraps of faded newspaper glued to the walls of their cardboard home. The written word had fascinated her ever since, drawing her through the field school served by itinerant teachers like a pirogue along the ripa, and then into a rare scholarship at the makeshift college on the outskirts of Uptown.

These things were true, but they were not what Edith was thinking when her foot knocked a molded book loose from the muck along dingus path. She was thinking

what a shame, no children

and wondering

who read this one last

What a shame because she loved books and they were precious rare nowadays.

No children not because she had no children, but because there were no children left to be had.

She left the book as it was, to decay into dingus with the other remnants of Uptown.

Long burnt out, if not literally then certainly in every other wise.

Her hip ached by the time she made Shanty, dragging her sledge behind her. Duchamp was waiting for her on his throne, the withered stump of an ancient baobab rumored to've come from the Mother herself as a seedling

careful now, careful, carry it gentle

then transplanted in the arid, far from the fertile loam of the flooding ripa.

Shanty was like that, perched between desert and garden. Like the baobab, it had once been fertile and ripe. Like the baobab, it had never reached its full growth. Like the baobab, it was now beyond death and useful only for rest.

That was before Edith's time, when the baobab came. Before Duchamp's time, too, though if time had a rival, it was him.

The baobab had no rival, only an unfulfilled yearning to reach the potential of its species, long faded now.

Duchamp grinned a toothless smile at her as she approached. His skin was leathery brown and shriveled around his bones, but his eyes were bright and his memory sharp as a freshly chipped stone. He was the sage of Shanty, the center of its knowledge, and, as far as she could tell, the only thing keeping the land from devouring the ragged clump of haphazardly built shacks under the sun's shimmering heat.

Edith let the sledge's handles fall onto the ground with a clank, slipped her satchel off, and set it atop the pile of gear it carried. "Fabler," she said, respectful.

"Wanderer," he replied. "Uptown whence?"

"Ya-ya, that's where I been. Was the same as ever it was, empty and gone."

She squatted beside him, dropped her knees to the hardpacked earth by the sledge, nearly regretted the yellow dirt stains she'd wear on her skin when she left. She thought about telling him of the book, of the cover so ruined the title was indecipherable, of pages molded beyond recognition, and thought better of it. The days of books and fairy tales were gone.

When she was settled, she said, "News come whence?"

"Monkey carried a tale."

"Monkey, eh?"

"Little hairy creature, long tail?"

Edith bit back a laugh. "Know what a monkey is, Fabler."

"You met her, ya-ya?"

"Never in my day."

"Then how you know what she is?" He shook his head, an old man chastising the young, then dropped his palms onto knobby knees and smacked his lips together. "You want to hear monkey's tale or no?"

"If thee and time allow," she said, the traditional plea of a wanderer to a fabler.

"Oh, it do, it do. We get on with it, then." Duchamp's back straightened and his gaze wandered past hers toward the ripa's winding journey some half-day behind her. "Was in the day long back when monkey crossed the ripa."

He paused expectantly, and Edith, knowing well her part, said, "Ripa whence?"

"Flat and wide, whence she crossed. No bridge then, ya-ya? But monkey, she clever. She wait on the bank, wait for a pirogue, and lo, one come along. Was cheetah and her kin, a litter of three cubs all thick with fur and little sharp teeth and blind yet, 'cause they still too young to see. Monkey say, you got room for me? And cheetah, thinking monkey make good meat but too stealthy to run meat off, she say, ya-ya, but you pay."

Edith dug out a spare bladder full of nut milk and handed it to him. "How monkey pay?"

"That the thing, ain't it?" He unscrewed the cap, lifted the bladder, sipped once. A dribble of liquid escaped his mouth and slid down his chin, and he rubbed it off with the back of one hand. "Monkey got no chit. She got naught but clever and nimble, so she think a bit and finally say, cheetah, you a good mama, ya-ya?

"Well cheetah, she bristle over that. I the best mama, she say, and monkey soothe her. Course, course, monkey say. I just mean, you want what good for the cubs, ya-ya? Mollified, Cheetah agree, so monkey say, if I help the cubs see, is that chit enough?"

Behind Duchamp, a woman drifted into the open, out of one of Shanty's ramshackle huts, carrying a clay pot in her spindly arms, her feet shooing stringy chickens out of her path. Amaris, kin of a sort, in the way of Shanty. Edith sighed. She'd have to speak now whether she wanted to or not, but not yet. Not until Duchamp finished his story.

"Was it chit enough?" she said.

"Cheetah be like any mama. She know the blind-time is a grave danger and her heart tell her if her young see now, it may save them. But she also know monkey is clever. She look for the trick, but the longer she look, the less trick she find. Finally she say, you make the cubs see now, then I carry you across the ripa.

"Monkey is clever, but clever without wisdom is naught. If she help the cubs now, cheetah eat her quick, nom-nom, and monkey likes her hide where it is, not in cheetah's stomach. She say, one now, one in the middle, one on the other side.

"They bargained for a bit, but monkey held firm and finally cheetah give in, thinking no doubt that her teeth would find monkey either way. Cheetah pat the nearest cub on the head with a sharp-clawed paw and say, you start here. Monkey say, not that one, this other one, then monkey scamper into the far side of the pirogue and lay her hands on the smallest cub's eyes. A tock later, monkey's hands fall away and the cub blinks and looks at his mama and mewls, and cheetah so pleased, she forget all about pouncing on monkey."

not for long

Duchamp sipped another drizzle of nut milk, then handed the bladder back to Edith. "Good stuff, Wanderer. You make your own self?"

"Got it in trade," she said. "Milk for baubles taken out of Uptown."

"Good trade. Where was monkey?"

"On the pirogue..."

outwitting cheetah

"...curing the cubs."

"Ya-ya." Duchamp smacked his lips and grinned. "Along across the ripa them went, cheetah and her cubs and monkey, and monkey, she be good for her word. Halfway through the journey, she lay her tiny paws on the blind eyes of the second cub, and lo! She see well as the first.

"Now, cheetah think she get some good bargain out of this deal. Three cubs over the blind-time well before it ends and some monkey meat throwed in for good measure? Yessiree, some good bargain. She watch monkey careful while the ripa's far bank comes close, and monkey, she watch careful, too. Soon as the pirogue touch the dirt, monkey leap straight over that third cub, nimble quick, and onto cheetah's back. She place her hands over cheetah's eyes and puts all the blind she stole from the cubs into cheetah."

"Clever monkey," Edith murmured.

Duchamp held up a crooked finger and wagged it at Edith. "Cheetah clever, too. She reach behind her with a sharp-clawed paw, searching for that tricksy monkey, but monkey already scamper away. True to her word, she cure that third cub, too. Just as cheetah's ears figure out where monkey is and her paw reaches out, monkey whispers a secret to the cubs."

"What secret?"

"The secret of the cheetahs." Duchamp's grin fell away and his gaze took on a far away look. "One meat tastes just like the other."

The area around the baobab fell silent. In Shanty, the women gathered and began preparing the midday meal. Sweat trickled down Edith's back, and she felt more than saw the morning's cool humidity give way to the afternoon heat.

At long last, she said, "Did monkey get away?"

"Why you ask after things you already know?" Duchamp's gaze sharpened on hers. "Amaris been looking for you."

He closed his eyes and began to hum softly under his breath.

Edith, justly dismissed, pushed herself awkwardly off the hard-packed dirt and started toward Shanty.

"Edith," Duchamp said softly.

She half turned toward him. "Yes, Grandfather?"

"Cheetah nearly got monkey that time, you ken? Her claws missed monkey by scarce a hair."

Edith paused for a moment, but when his humming resumed, she hobbled toward Shanty, stretching her tale-cramped legs as she went, her satchel slung across one shoulder. The sledge she left where it lay.

EDITH WAS born into the winter, same as Shanty. After the bombs fell on Big City and the creeping sickness stole out of the ruins, the hale and whole, those not touched by the poison, fled into the wilderness.

Thus were the shanty towns birthed. They were all alike, though not at first, for they were made of what people brought with them. Wide glass screens that once held moving pictures, plastic bags full of wondrous foods, whole piles of paper money. The detritus of their former lives.

A very few brought books, and those were treasured more highly than food, eventually.

Later, though, when their before lives began to lose the luster, when paper money was good for naught but kindling, that's when every shanty became the same.

Edith came along much later, when them that were still trying began to understand exactly what the creeping sickness had done. Women's menses dried up and men's seed withered in their loins. She was the only babe for so long, they thought her the last.

Then, along about the time when Edith should've begun her own menses, Amaris
  given by God
came screaming and shrieking into Shanty, bringing sharp and spite
  green glass shards
into Shanty's quiet despair.

Nothing was the same after that.

EDITH'S MOTHER was waiting for her on the edge of Shanty. Hamisi's shoulders were crooked one higher than the other from carrying water from the ripa to Shanty day after day, year after year. The men were all gone, the meat rare as books, and the only way to get vegetables and grain to grow was to plant seed in the backwash of the ripa's floodwaters.

Edith had done her time in the fields, and in the grassy plains hunting deer, and in the ripa itself, drawing hand-knotted nets through the murky waters in search of untainted fish.

"Uptown whence?" Hamisi said as Edith drew near.

Edith shrugged her satchel off her own shoulders and set it down at her mother's feet. "No food, no men."

"The creeping sickness?"

"None for years there now."

"Never hurts to ask." Hamisi brushed a bare toe against the satchel. "What you bring back?"

"Baubles. Some for you, some for the rest." Edith tried for a smile. It wobbled on her face and fell away. She should be happy to be here, happy to bring small treasures to the women of her line. "Dried meat. Caught a deer on my way in. Skinned it and left the meat to dry. Picked it up on my way out."

Hamisi harrumphed. "Coulda been stole."

"Nobody and nothing out to steal anything anymore."

Even cheetahs were gone now, though truth was, they'd never lived nearby anyhow. Cheetahs came from the Mother, like monkey and the baobab. The only large predators near Shanty were too shy and canny to let humans see them. Not even drying meat drew them out into the open anymore.

But their sign, scat and pawprints and the remnants of meals, those were easy enough to find.

Amaris stole up on them, her expression sly. "Hear you say baubles?"

Hamisi exchanged a wry glance with Edith, an apology where none should've been needed. "Later," she said and shooed Amaris back to her chores.

Edith took the dried meat from her satchel and left it to Hamisi to divvy it up. She'd portioned off her share already and tucked it into the food box lashed to one end of her sledge. Hamisi would take care of the rest, doling out the tough protein as it was needed best. Duchamp would get a share, and Hamisi and the other women, and even Amaris with her grasping little paws.

Edith frowned and picked up her satchel, and followed Hamisi into Shanty. "Any corn to grind?"

Hamisi smiled over her shoulder, and though it was a tired

smile and small, it was still a smile. "You brought the meat."

"Corn still needs grinding." And she was one of the few possessing muscle enough to rub stone against stone anymore.

When had the women lost their strength?

She shook the question off and emptied her mind of anything but familiar routine as the evening meal was prepared. The rhythm was old and soothing, the labor rough, and soon a song gathered in her throat and murmured out of her. Around her, the squawk of chickens gave way to Shanty's chorus, nearly a dozen voices joining together as one, spiraling into the blue above them.

After the meal was cooked and eaten and the sun had faded into a wash of pink and gold clouds against the darkening sky, Edith gathered with the women around the central cooking pit. A fire flickered and popped there, casting long shadows around the circle. Duchamp joined them, leaving his baobab stump to participate in the hen session.

Gossip, Edith thought. Naught but words spread from shanty to shanty by wanderers such as herself. The women fingered their baubles, admiring necklaces of glass beads created when the bombs fell and fires burned the cities. Edith segued into a tale she'd heard, long ago, of how it was then, of tall buildings faced on all sides with huge sheets of glass, of stores carrying enough meat to feed a village ten times over, of hulking balls of metal zooming along streets paved with gold and silver, carrying people along.

She'd never seen the gold and silver herself in her journeys through the ruined cities, but it was part of the tale and she was a faithful fabler, when needs must.

When the tale wound down and the women began to drift up and away from the fire toward their huts, Hamisi said, "Books whence? I been dying for a new tale."

Edith thought of the book she'd stumbled over on dingus path. Books aplenty in the ruins. Not many left what could be read. "I'll pick some up in trade, if any can be found."

"Books," Amaris said from the other side of the fire. "What you need books for?"

Hamisi exchanged a telling glance with Edith, but her voice was calm, even. "To be carried away on the fable, same as Duchamp's tales."

Amaris's expression twisted. She turned her head and spat into the yellow dirt. "The devil brung us books."

Edith was so shocked, her mouth gaped. "What?"

"He brung us books, and books was what chased us from the cities to Shanty. Everybody knows that."

A woman passing nearby clucked her tongue, though whether in agreement or admonishment, Edith couldn't tell.

"Books did no such thing." Hamisi rose slowly, her joints popping as her limbs and back straightened. "Was the bombs what rained fire down and burned out the cities."

"And bombs was built from books." Amaris rocked back on her heels, her expression triumphant and challenging. "Best to plaster over them words now, lest they escape and cause more mischief. I'm doing it my own self. You'd best, too."

Edith bit back the anger rising inside her, struggling for the patience of a good wanderer. "Them words will lead us out of the wilderness," Edith said. "You mark my words."

"Daughter," Hamisi said, her hand gentle on Edith's arm, a quiet warning to keep the peace. Go along to get along. That was Shanty's way. "Help me store the dried meat. These old bones don't hardly reach much no more."

Edith turned dutifully from Amaris's smug spite and followed her mother away from the fire's heat and light, from the protection it offered once, long ago, against night predators. Those beasts were no more and would be never again, though their lack had not kept danger from the world of woman.

* * *

EDITH CREPT out of Shanty the next morning, when the sun's leading edge touched the horizon, her sledge piled high with the makings of her kin. Duchamp was already sitting cross-legged on his stump

old man to the bones

meditating or maybe sleeping. She left him be, picked up the sledge's shoulder pull-ropes, and walked slowly out of town, letting the air's biting chill chase the sleep from her head.

She'd dreamed of the burning time, of glass melting in fire, of children turned to ash, of wind tunneling through the empty remnants of civilization, scattering survivors before it. The dreams had unsettled her all the more for the surreal knowledge of never having witnessed such with her own eyes. Nor had Hamisi, or Duchamp, or any of the men before they'd left. No one alive could carry such tales firsthand, though plenty enough was handed down.

Her feet led her along dingus path, winding near and away from the ripa's coiling journey. It lay like a sinuous snake under the warming sun, dank and dark and mysterious. Tempting.

Duchamp's tale from the yester popped into her head. When a fork appeared in the path, she took the one leading away from the ripa, away from cheetah and monkey and the lessons of that tale. She needed to go to Big City anyhow. Hamisi wanted books and books she would get, Amaris be damned. Books caused the fires. Edith snorted and leaned into the ropes, jostling the sledge in her hurry to put that woman behind her.

Jal caught up to her at the next fork, the one coming from Uptown, long about the sun's midtime. He was a big man, tall and rawboned, his muscles firm from years of hauling sledges up and down the countryside, searching for trade among the sparse settlements, hoping for signs of rebirth in the abandoned towns. They were friends, in the way of the wanderer, sharing food and gossip

185

and, occasionally, a spot by the watch fire.

Edith's heart warmed at the sight of his broad smile, easing the last of her crankiness over Amaris's nonsense. "Ho, Jal!"

"Ho, Edith!" he called. "Whence come you?"

"Shanty of my mother," she said, and slipped the ropes off her shoulders. Her skin tingled to life where the harness had numbed it. She paid it no mind. Hazards of a wanderer. "Uptown whence?"

He slipped his own harness off and stretched his long body sunwise. "Uptown, ya-ya. Big City before that."

"Was headed that way myself, maybe."

"Good digs there. The clicker's slowed down enough to enter the city's heart."

"Welcome news!" She clapped his shoulder, would've kissed him if the stink of travel weren't clinging to them both. "Sit down. Rest a spell. Share some dried venison with me. I've got a fresh haul."

"Trade it for a surprise."

"We're trading for news."

"The news is free," Jal said easily. "Sides which, you're gonna want what I'm willing to trade for some venison."

They sat under a tree so dried out it was unrecognizable as anything but a roost for woodpeckers. Their joints groaned and popped, and Jal moaned as his bottom hit the hard earth. "I'd give anything for a patch of grass right now, something cool and soft."

Edith grinned as she dug in her satchel for the venison jerky. "Ain't been cool and soft here for generations. Where you see the grass?"

"Big City." He dug in his own satchel, pulled out a pouch of nut milk, and offered it in exchange for the jerky. "Down in the heart, like I said. Was more there, too. Machines and books and—"

"Books?"

"Ya-ya, more'n one man can read in a lifetime, stacked row

upon row, higher than my head."

"A library," Edith murmured, the very idea a reverent hum in her heart.

"That'd be it."

"How'd it escape the bombs?"

Jal shrugged. "Who knows? Lots left there, outside the blast radius, still in the heart. Maybe it was a small bomb. Maybe Big City was bigger than our ken."

"And the clicker said it was safe?"

"Safe as baby's breath."

She laughed and sipped the nut milk, handed the pouch back to him along with some of the corn pone Hamisi had wrapped in threadbare linen the night before and tucked into the satchel. "I'd like to see that. Mother was asking for books."

"She'll find plenty there."

"Is that the surprise we're trading for?"

"Naught doing!" Jal's eyes twinkled, mischievous as a magpie, and he jerked a thumb at his sledge. "Found a stack of cardboard wrapped in plastic. Good as the day it was minted, you ask me. I figured that'd make good trade, if you're of a mind."

"I'm of a mind. Thank ye kindly, wanderer."

"Welcome as always, friend."

They sat in silence for a moment, chewing on the tough jerky, watched the sun top its arc in the sky and head back toward the horizon. A spare breeze skipped across the earth, stirring dust against their skin. Edith grew drowsy in the heat and let her eyelids droop. No need to rush. Big City wasn't going anywhere, and as long as the company was friendly...

"Something else, Edith."

She roused from her dozing, stretched and yawned. "More'n cardboard and books?"

"More'n all that plus some." His gaze slipped away from her

toward the horizon, toward the road leading to Uptown and Big City beyond. "The machines I was telling you about?"

"Ya-ya. What of them?"

"One's a printer."

Her breath froze in her lungs, cleaving her tongue to the roof of her mouth.

"Works good, I reckon, though I didn't test it."

"But we could, ya-ya? We could test it and print books again, maybe reclaim the ones lost to us or gather up the fablers' tales, or—"

"Edith," he said quietly. "It's not that simple. There's another, on the outskirts, other side from Uptown."

She drew back, puzzled. How could it be bad, those two printers? How could that not be the thing they needed to jostle the shanties out of their misery, to learn again as men and women once had, to regrow into something more than hardscrabble and hunger?

"It's been seized by a group of burners. They're printing up leaflets as to how books was the cause of it all. I've seen them posted along dingus path here and there, and I've heard the whispers among the shanty folk."

"Amaris," Edith said, her voice a bare whisper. "She said as much, that books were the devil and ruination, but I paid her no mind. She's always nattering nonsense into the wind."

Jal nodded. "Best pay more attention, friend. It's not bad now, just low rumblings every now and again, but be careful all the same. Tuck your books away deep. Don't let strangers see them."

She hadn't needed the words of caution, but took them to heart anyway. "Thank ye for the news."

"Welcome, friend."

They traded books and cardboard for jerky and the reed mats and baskets Hamisi and the others made from the ripa's bounty. Not long after, they broke camp and parted ways. Another time, Edith might've tarried and shared Jal's company a while longer.

Now, a deep urgency gathered like a stone in her gut, replacing her earlier languid mood. She wanted to see the machines for herself, wanted to watch them in motion, and she wanted to find one of those leaflets. Those'd be near Uptown, she reckoned, at the cross-roads where news was shared and passed along.

As soon as that was done there, she'd return to Shanty with a book or two for Hamisi, courtesy of trading with Jal, and measure the damage those leaflets were doing among her kin.

RAIN SWEPT in that afternoon, muddying dingus path with its quick patter. The sledge's runners caught in the mud, forcing Edith off the path before her precious cargo was ruined.

She found shelter under the rusting roof of an abandoned shanty house and checked the books and slabs of cardboard she'd gotten in trade. Jal had had the good sense to keep them wrapped in tattered plastic, and that was protection enough. She settled against the sledge with her head cushioned by her satchel, and drifted into sleep to the steady drum of raindrops against the tin overhead.

It took her another day to reach Uptown and the news posted on the boards, and it was as Jal had told her. A flyer tacked to the board proclaimed books to be the true evil behind the bombs, books and the knowledge they wrought. Them what could read nattered off the message to them what could not, and all walked away muttering under their breaths as they bypassed the ghosts of Uptown for points beyond.

In a moment when no one else was around, Edith stepped up to the board, a freestanding slab of wood nailed to a leaning post under a makeshift roof, and fingered the flyer's paper, stuck her nose close to it and sniffed. Fresh printed, was her guess, and she'd handled enough paper in her time to know the difference. Knew the sharp pinch of fresh ink in her nostrils anyhow.

What puzzled her was the machine that had printed it. Years back, in the days of her youth, a passing wanderer had let her borrow a textbook for the season, then answered what questions she could of the contents when she passed that way again. Between the two, Edith had learned the magic of such wonders as electricity and currents, of machinery and fuel. Remnants of a by-gone day, long faded from this world.

One thing was certain. To run the printing machine took more than want to. Someone had figured out the old ways, and she wanted to meet that someone more than she'd wanted anything in her life.

THREE DAYS LATER, Edith approached Shanty laden with fresh trade from Uptown. She'd tucked the books into her satchel, hiding them from prying eyes. Two books, one a bulky leather-bound volume, the other a book of poetry. Hamisi would like the poetry. Her feelings on the other were anyone's guess.

Laughter drifted out of Shanty, the titters of women, the deep chuckle of men. Her heart leapt. Had the men returned? Could that really have happened at this late date? Or was it a pack of wanderers brought by coincidence and naught else?

Duchamp was sitting as he ever was, atop the baobab with a thin cloth wrapped around his legs. His torso and arms were bare to the sun and more gaunt than Edith remembered. She dropped the sledge's harness and squatted beside him in the yellow dirt.

"Fabler?" she said, soft and gentle.

His eyes opened sluggish as the ripa in the drought season. "Wanderer. Uptown whence?"

"Ya-ya. Same as it ever was." She glanced beyond him to the women gathered around the central cooking fire, to the two men sitting easily among her kin. "Strangers come now."

"Been here a day or so." Duchamp swallowed and smacked his lips, then grinned slyly at her. "You be wanting another tale, eh? Maybe one about elephant?"

Dutifully, she scrounged out a fresh pouch of nut milk and handed it to him. "I know the elephant."

"You seen her, then?"

"Never in my day."

"Then how you know her?" He cackled and sipped the nut milk, drank more deeply the second and third times he brought the pouch to his mouth. "That good stuff, wanderer. Good stuff indeed."

"Should be, for the cost of barter."

"You got an ear for the barter," he said, then he handed the pouch back and dropped his gnarled hands to his knees. "One day, elephant woke to the sun high overhead. It burned down on her, drying out her hairy old skin. She lifted her trunk to it and said, sun, why you gotta burn so hot?

"Well, that sun, he so far up in the sky, he hear naught of elephant down on the ground. So elephant turn her back on sun and lumber to the ripa for a cool drink to cut the parch in her throat."

Edith had a sip of nut milk for elephant

wash the dust down

capped the pouch and set it aside. "Elephant whence?"

"In the Mother, a-course. All comes from the Mother. You wanna hear this tale or no?"

"Beg pardon, fabler."

Duchamp narrowed his eyes on her, but he was grinning still so she took no umbrage. "Elephant lumber to the ripa, but when she get there, the water be dried up. She sniff around the banks, finds enough for a sip or two, then she turn to the sky and lift her trunk to sun. Why you gotta burn so hot, sun? say she, but sun too far up to hear and don't care nohow.

"Elephant, being no fool, points herself upstream and wanders for a bit, hoping for water. Soon as sun dip down below the land, she find a good pool and drink her fill. Thinking she onto something, elephant bed down there, next to the pool, and sleep a good long while.

"Next morning when she wake, though, sun done dried up that deep pool, too, leaving only a handful of water for elephant. Elephant raise her trunk to sun and curse the blue heavens. Sun, that old rascal, he hear a peep or two and squint down, but elephant, she just a tiny creature to him and he pay her no never mind. Him got a job to do, same as all creatures, and he gonna do it long as it's his to do, ya ken?"

"I ken, fabler," Edith said.

"You ken enough to know what's ahead?"

"Never heard this tale before."

"And you ain't got naught for a guess?"

She thought about it for a minute, ruminating on the possibilities. Sure, she could venture a guess or two, but that might take the fun out of it. "No, fabler, I haven't a guess."

Duchamp tapped a bony finger to the side of his nose. "Thought you was better with the tales, wanderer. How you gonna take your rightful place on the baobab if you can't guess the tale?"

"It's not my place to guess."

"It's all creatures' place to guess." He shook his head

weary soul

and rubbed his knees with palms like parchment. "Elephant, she decide she gonna do something about that rascal sun, so she set her feet toward the mountains far, far away. Travel by day, she does, while her hairy skin withers and wrinkles in sun's heat. Travel by night, she does, when the water's aplenty and the air cool and crisp.

"The mountains rose up, higher than she ever seen, almost high as sun, but the first mountain ain't high enough. No, she's looking for something better, something to take her right up where she could teach that sun a lesson or two. Next day, she come to a second mountain higher than the first, but still not high enough.

"The days pass such like. Elephant wander along, growing thin under sun's curious gaze. The mountains ain't never good enough, though they rise higher and higher and higher still.

"Finally, elephant come to the tallest mountain of the lot and she make a deal with it. Mountain, say she, if you let me climb to your peaks, I'll stop the sun from drinking up your water. Think of the trees you could have then! Think of the birds and beasts you could have!

"Now, mountain think this a pretty good deal, for she just as tired of the sun beating down on her as elephant. So she open a trail and show elephant the way, and pretty soon, elephant nears the top in the deepest, darkest of the night.

"If moon was awake, maybe she woulda warned sun what was to come, but moon slept on, as she does every now and again, and sun rose as he ever does, shining as bright as he could, lighting the day for the earth below.

"Elephant greet him, trunk raised high. Sun, she say, you gotta stop shining so hard the water dries up.

"Sun just laugh and burn all the hotter. I got my place, he say, and you got yours.

"My place is to drink from the ripa, elephant shout, angry now. My place is to wander the savannah and tamp down the earth and nip the grass before it grows too high. How can I do that when the ripa's low?

"But sun don't see the problem. Far as he's concerned, they each doing what they was meant to do, him tending the sky, her the land.

"Well elephant, she don't take that so well. She leap in the air and wrap her trunk around the sun, and though he scorch her skin to the bone, she won't let go. I'm gonna teach you, she say. I'm gonna teach you to burn so hot.

"Mountain, seeing what elephant is about, open wide and try to swallow the sun, and elephant try to help, stuffing what she can of that great heavenly ball into the earth.

"Sun was determined, too, and scared, for he knew only the sky and could never dwell beneath the earth where his fires might die. He panic and rip himself in half, scything off a good third of his body in sacrifice to the land. Mountain swallow that part whole, down, down, down she swallow, and shiver as the cut off part of sun consume her flesh and turn it hot with the fire of the heavens.

"Elephant's trunk slip off the smaller sun, and he escape into the heavens, settling into a higher plane where creatures of the land can never again reach him. Winter come then, dowsing the land in ice and snow, freezing the ripas and lochs, for only sun's fire can fill the land with heat.

"Mountain, being as mortal as all creatures, can't hold what little bit of the sun she swallow. It belch out of her, flowing in great ripas of orange and black fire. Elephant see this and race down the path mountain opened for her, though she lost her hair and now wears skin so gray and withered, even clever monkey mistake her for an old woman."

Edith glanced up at the sky, squinted into the light. "Sun ever come back down again?"

"Only when the bombs fell." Duchamp smacked his lips together and his eyelids drifted closed. "Go on now, daughter. Like the sun at night, I need rest."

She stood quietly, stretched out the kinks in her muscles and bones, and dropped a kiss to his weathered cheek. "Sleep well, grandfather."

His hands twitched on his knees, jerking his robes away from the baobab's base. She knelt again, winced as her own knees popped and cracked, and shifted the cloth aside. There, partially hidden in a hole at the base of the stump, was a worn copy of *Pride & Prejudice*

> *her mother's soft voice reading to her, a finger tracing the words*

but that wasn't what caught Edith's eye. Behind that, to the side, also covered by Duchamp's clothes, a sprig of green jutted into the air.

The baobab had sprouted, and that could mean only one thing.

Tears gathered in her eyes and she sat for a moment more, head bowed, listening to the old man's breath whistle in and out of his chest as he drifted into sleep.

EDITH PICKED OUT voices long before she reached the central cooking fire. Amaris cried

> *sharp like a knife*

"Tell us of the ever-burning fire, Elias!"

The man beside her leaned back, rubbing his palms down muscled thighs. "The fire that brought the cleansing."

"Aye, that one," the women said, their voices overlapping like water rippling over the ripa's rocky bottom.

Hamisi sat stiffly at her place by the fire, her expression hard as stone amid the laughter of the others. Edith slipped her satchel off her shoulder and dropped it to the ground, then squatted beside her mother. Hamisi acknowledged her with a curt nod, and Edith would've greeted her, but Elias raised his hands and laughed and began the tale.

"Long ago," he said, his mouth stretched in a practiced smile, "there was Big City, and it was an evil place. The people were sinful in their greed and lust and wanton disregard for the Mother. Knowledge was hoarded among them that had and shared through a magic called internet and in books printed on the skin of dead trees."

Edith opened her mouth to correct him, but Hamisi's hands twitched a warning in her lap.

"There was a man called Adam and a woman called Eve, and together they lived in Shanty, shunning the sinful knowledge of city, for God gave them the everything they needed. Harvest from the land, fish from the ripa, the barter trails, friendship and kinwise, and all that was good and holy.

"One day, the great serpent Devil slithered into Shanty. Adam, he said, why do you toil under the hot sun? Eve, why do you wither in the river? The city has better ways, vast machines to do your work, more knowledge than your mind can hold, and an infinite supply of food. You would never have to live by the rhythm of the land again!

"Adam was a wise man and chased Devil away with a long cane, but Eve, being merely a woman and gullible

arrogant fabler

grew curious. That night, under the cover of the moon, she crept out of Shanty and journeyed into Big City. And lo! It was exactly as Devil said, and more. The streets were paved with gold so fine, it shone under the magic lights decorating the buildings, as bright as the moon and all the stars put together. The people were dressed in clothes so beautifully woven, they seemed more like moonlight than cotton and wool. Eve followed a crowd into a building, and marveled at how cool and even the air was inside. As she watched and wandered, people stuffed more food into their mouths than their bellies could hold, growing fat on the riches of invisible hands. They fornicated openly, there on floors made of smooth stone, and begged Eve to join them.

"Eve refused, for she had only ever known Adam, as was good and right. She fled Big City and arrived at Shanty just as dawn was breaking over the land.

"Adam, now. He'd slept right through Eve's sinful wanderlust, and so he rose not knowing what his woman had done. Eve held her tongue that day, pondering the many wonders she'd witnessed, but on the seventh day, she could hold her tongue no more. She sat Adam down and told him of Big City, of the fineness of the food and cloth, of the abundance and joy, and after hearing this from his woman, Adam, too, was tempted to go.

"The next day, they set off, and by sunset, they had arrived. And so entranced were they by Big City and its forbidden knowledge, they forgot their home in Shanty, forgot the righteousness of God and the path he had chosen for them.

"God, on seeing this, grew angry. If his people could not live on the bounty he provided, he would make sure no bounty was left to be had. But God, like Devil, was canny. He would not destroy the people; they would destroy themselves. He opened his mind to the meanest of humans, sharing a knowledge beyond what they could ken, and bade them to spread these evils far and wide. War broke out upon the land, and pestilence, and humans grew so angry, they threw bombs at each other, cleansing the land with a fire so great, it burned for forty days and forty nights. From sea to shining sea, the fires raged, destroying everything in their paths, and the people of Big City perished in the flames."

"The ever-burning fire," Amaris murmured softly, her eyes wide and wild.

"Ya-ya, that," Elias said. "But God was not without mercy. He had spared two of each animal, ferrying them into the Mother on a boat made of timber and light. These innocent creatures were not to blame, he reasoned. They would repopulate the land and renew it with their shat and spit.

"A few people managed to escape their fires and fled to Shanty, Adam and Eve among them, but because of their sins, God decreed that people could never spread so widely across the earth as they had before. For their disobedience, God cursed Adam and Eve, shriveling their organs so they would never again bear fruit.

Eventually, their sins spread to the other people, until today when there is no one left alive to bear children."

The women had grown silent during Elias's tale. Now they stared mournfully into the flickering flames, their hands cupped over their own shriveled wombs. The other man threw something into the fire, sending sparks flying into the darkness gathered around them, then Elias sighed and spoke again.

"We live with the sin of knowledge, my friends," he said. "Until we renounce it and return to the path God intended for us, we will remain like the desert, barren and dry, and Shanty will die without the children needed to renew her."

Edith stood abruptly and laughed, sharp and bright. "You speak the nonsense of an addled fool, stranger."

Hamisi's hand shot out and grasped Edith's, and her ragged nails dug into Edith's trail-hardened flesh. "We owe our guests the courtesy of a listen, daughter."

"Not when the speaking is untruths." She turned her head and spat into the dirt, ignoring the disjointed murmurs of her female kin. "Books caused the fires. Bah! Books are tools, a way to pass stories from one to another, nothing more. If they are evil, then so is this man and the words he speaks."

The men rose slowly, their eyes glinting darkly, and faced Edith squarely.

"Our words are true," Elias said quietly. "We have no need for lies."

"Yet you spread them all the same."

"We spread the Gospel."

"I've read the Gospel," Edith retorted. "And that isn't it."

Amaris rose and marched on Edith, her face contorted with rage. In her hands, she held a book, and before Edith could stop her, she threw it into the fire. "That's the lie, sister, there in the fire. There in your mind. Lies, every word! You're the sinner here, not these gentle men."

Edith stepped forward to meet her, and Hamisi rose abruptly, placing herself between them. "There will be no more such talk, Amaris. Go home. Rest your anger."

Amaris laughed

a cold, bitter wind

and said, "I have as much right to speak as she does."

"Aye," Hamisi agreed mildly, "but I tend the stores and decide who gets what. Mind your tongue if you wish to fill your belly on the morrow."

Amaris glared at Edith, then whirled and strode to her shack. The men exchanged glances, then Elias nodded, respectful. "The Gospel was ne'er meant to bring discord. Best we leave now."

Hamisi shook her head once, sharp. "On the morrow, when the sun rises. That's soon enough. Thank you for your tales."

"And for your hospitality."

The men turned as one and walked to the far edge of Shanty, stepping carefully among the legs of the women silently watching their own tale unfold. When they were out of ear's reach, Hamisi dropped Edith's hand, her face suddenly weary.

"Edith, tend to Duchamp," she said. "You can share news of the outers on the morrow."

Edith bit her tongue, holding her peace. She had plenty to say, none of it on the news she carried in her heart. Her gaze caught on the fire and the embers from which it sprang. The fuel was not wood or dried dung, but the pages and spines of Shanty's precious few books, now no more than fodder for the flame.

DUCHAMP HAD vacated his throne during the recitation of the twisted Gospel. Edith peeked into his shack on the outskirts of Shanty, watched his chest rise and fall in shallow, wheezing breaths, then dragged her sledge to his home under a starless sky. She secured it under the lean-to attached to the side of the flimsy tin and cardboard building and harrumphed.

In all the fuss, she'd forgotten the cardboard she'd traded for.

It took only a moment to unload it and store the tattered plastic away for later use

good covering for a window, maybe

then she laid down crosswise in front of Duchamp's open door, using the satchel as a pillow.

The books were hard and lumpy under her head, but she paid that no mind. Small burden to bear. Her mind fixed on the book she'd found moldering in dingus path some days back, and regret stung her sharp. If she'd been able to save that one, if it had been in better shape...

No, she thought. Some things were beyond saving and that was one of them.

Sleep claimed her swiftly, gobbling her up like cheetah with an antelope. Her dreams were orange flame and glowing embers, and in them she saw the faces of her kin. Hamisi and Duchamp, and even Amaris, their expressions stoic as stone.

Whispers reached her ears, disturbing her slumber, and the thumps of feet on the earth. She blinked her eyes open, squinted against the soft glow of the predawn morning, her skin sticky in the mist clinging to the land. Elias and the other man were shadowed blocks against the horizon. They spoke quietly with the woman standing between them, a slim figure composed of sharp angles and jangling beads.

Amaris.

Edith watched them for a while, watched their embraces, their intimacy, and felt nothing, not anger or spite or antagonism. Maybe having the men to herself would calm Amaris's bitter hatred. Maybe it would distract her from the malevolent belief that sin had driven

God to destroy the world.

Man had done that, and woman. They'd needed no help from God.

Hamisi stepped through the cloth fluttering in her doorway and spoke sharply enough for the tone to drift across the courtyard to Edith. Amaris's head bowed, then she touched each of the men in turn and scurried off. Edith kept watch until the men paid their respects to Hamisi and dragged their sledges out of Shanty and the sun was full in the sky.

A waiflike figure caught her eye, coming from the river, and she huffed out a laugh. Duchamp on his way back from the ripa. He'd stepped around her in the night and likely had a new tale for her.

Footsteps shuffled across the courtyard, and Edith swung her head toward them. Hamisi with Duchamp's breakfast, porridge cakes steamed in banana leaves, by the looks of it, carried from wanderer to wanderer along dingus path.

Edith sat up and watched them both approach, and managed a smile for her mother. "Do I get a portion?"

"Ya-ya," Hamisi said as she squatted beside her daughter. "Never know when you're coming and going, but I knew you wouldn't leave that old coot."

Edith laughed as she stretched her arms skyward. "Naught doing. Someone had to watch him with strangers in Shanty, ya-ya?"

"If they be strangers." Hamisi handed off one of the breakfast portions and lowered her voice. "They'll be back. We've heard the tales of them passing shanties up and down river. The Gospel they carry—"

"Pure nonsense," Edith scoffed, though she kept her voice soft and easy.

Hamisi nodded. "Maybe so, but the women believe."

"Amaris believes, and she's tupping the men, both of them at once by the looks of it."

"She's young and lusty."

Edith threw her head back and laughed until her throat hurt. "Not so young lust should addle her brains."

"She had naught to addle," Hamisi said mildly, setting Edith off again. Hamisi shook her head, her mouth turned down. "Jest if you like. The men carry trouble. Mark my words. Naught good will come of their travels."

A foreboding snaked down Edith's spine, chilling her, but Duchamp was upon them and she was loathe to heap such upon his ears.

HAMISI REFUSED the books, as Edith had feared her mother would after the previous night's tales. The books would journey with her, then, to Big City and perhaps beyond.

"You just returned," Hamisi said, her hands flapping this way and that over Edith's tunic, dusting it clean. "Dingus path is patient. It can wait another day or two."

Amaris's laughter jangled through the air, like cheetah's screech, and Edith shook her head, her belly filled with a sudden urgency. "There are things there, things I can't share as of yet. Things I need to see with my own two."

"Your own two," Hamisi scoffed, but she stepped back and perched bony hands on her hips, and her mouth pursed once more. "Journey safe, daughter. Watch for the Gospel men. They grow in number, even as our own men tarry from our hearths."

Edith searched for reassurances, for the words to numb her mother's worry, and when they failed her, simply nodded. "I'll be back, quick as I can. Put the cardboard to good use. The cold is nearly upon us."

Hamisi let her hands fall and turned away, and Edith dragged her sledge to the baobab. Duchamp sat there crosslegged, his hands folded in his lap. A light shone down upon him, glittering against the dirt surrounding the stump. She considered breaking his meditation, and thought better of it. Duchamp would have another tale for her when she returned. There was time enough for that, before the baobab's sprout sapped his bones of their strength.

She was twenty paces away when his voice drifted to her.

"Granddaughter."

She turned and lifted a hand to her forehead, shading her eyes from the sun's glare. "Yes, grandfather?"

"Remember cheetah and monkey on the ripa?"

"Yes, grandfather."

"The cubs were blind. The mother was not."

She waited for him to say more, waited through a hundred slow heartbeats for him to explain. Finally, she called, "Yes, grandfather," and hefted the sledge down dingus path toward the answers waiting for her there.

BIG CITY was nearly a month's journey along dingus path, shorter by pirogue, toward the mountain range that from Shanty was a mere smudge along the horizon. Edith traded for passage on the ripa when she could, floating past mud daub huts and voices carrying across the floodplain fields. The harvest time had come. Wheat grew short and stubby and golden under the sun, side by side with corn and beans and whatever else woman could find to grow. Here and there, men mingled among the women, and Edith wondered if they were of the shanties or, like Elias and his companion, wanderers with poisonous tongues.

She put out upripa of Uptown, took down a deer three days beyond it. A fine buck with a spread of antlers wider than her shoulders

good trading, that

and enough meat to feed a small shanty for a week.

She stripped the hide and sliced meat off, and traded the lot later that day for another day's journey on the water, save a small portion she'd cooked for herself.

The urgency to move that had gripped her in Shanty intensified with every step, every paddle stroke. Not just the urgency to discover for herself what lay in Big City, but the urgency to return to her mother and Duchamp, to show her kin that evil lay not in knowledge, but in the hearts of humankind.

If they would listen. If they would believe.

The worry of it all gnawed at her, and though she ate sparingly of her stores

had to save them, savor them, for the long journey

her belly refused to rumble under the power of hunger. It was simply beyond her then.

Days after leaving Uptown, she reached the outskirts of Big City. The mountains were bigger here, though still a day or two's journey away. Long avenues of broken pavement cut across the land, overgrown with weeds and trees. She avoided those, especially avoided the animal trails forged over them by herds of animals passing around the hot zone. Other wanderers would travel those paths, and she had no urge to mingle with other humans, whether friend or foe.

Her shanty's clicker had died long before Edith had taken on the mantle of wanderer. It was a shame, really. Such had kept her from fully exploring ruins from the bygone, and thus reduced Shanty's clout on the trade routes. There were other ways to tell, though, if not because of human intervention, then through the earth itself.

Still, her belly fluttered and cramped, and her skin tingled as if a chill wind had blown across it, though the day was warm and dry. Wanderers had misjudged before, and the results had been terrifying.

The ragged edges of Big City shifted from clusters of houses

like Shanty, only finer

lying low along the plain, to abandoned shopping centers and business parks, their wide paved areas dotted with rusting chunks of metal. In the distance, the tall buildings circling the rubble of downtown

never seen it, only heard the tales

beckoned her forward, a siren song tugging at her heart. Jal had described the printing places to her, told her the street names and landmarks, what was left of them, and she'd memorized them, faithful to the duty she'd eagerly assumed on her thirteenth born day.

Still, she chose her path carefully, once she left dingus path behind her. Three times the sun set on her journey, and three times it rose before she heard the voices of men drifting down the decrepit streets

it would not do to be seen

and though it shamed her to do so, she hid and watched them in secret, fearing discovery after the lies Elias had passed on to her kin.

What would they do to her, these men? What fate would befall her?

She'd never been afraid of wandering before, but now, if they found her books...

Her thoughts lingered on the memory of pages feeding the fires of home, and her heart mourned the loss.

She visited the city's heart first and stood on the edge of the blast zone, beyond the dust-filled crater left behind by the bombs. Only one had fallen here. Only one was needed. The explosion had destroyed the heart, then radiated outward, consuming life on the outskirts like fire through a forest.

Quicker, maybe. She'd seen a forest fire once, when she was young and had strayed too far from the trading paths. From a distance, she'd stood on the plain, far removed from the ravenous heat. The fire had raged like a monster, devouring trees and animals fleeing from its wrath, an orange and red beast belching black smoke and ash.

She'd told Duchamp of her journey, when she'd returned to Shanty. He'd nodded sagely, smacked his lips together over toothless gums. Said, "Spring follows the winter, granddaughter," and laid a comforting hand on her narrow shoulder.

"Yes, grandfather," she'd replied, head bowed, but she'd never understood.

Still didn't. Maybe she never would.

FROM THE CITY'S dead heart, Edith backtracked and followed Jal's directions to the library, skirting the print shop he'd told her of, the one where men already toiled. No need to see it, she thought, but her heart leapt with fear, not unconcern.

The library would be enough, then the other printing machine, just to see if such wonders truly existed.

Vegetation grew in twisted spurts along the city's abandoned streets, breaking through concrete and asphalt, through glass into buildings and the rusted hulks of abandoned vehicles, up signposts and streetlamps. Here and there, her keen eye detected abnormal growth. Five- and seven-leaved clovers, an oak fully three feet around that she could look over while standing on flat feet.

A fox with a second head jutting out of its shoulder darted past her through a clump of wildflowers. She paused there, in the middle of the street, her mind fighting with her heart. Jal had said it was safe, so safe it must be.

Still, she hesitated for a good, long while, considering the danger to herself and her kin, her heart a haphazard beat in her chest.

The sun had sunk behind the broken skyscrapers by the time she found the bronze lion. It loomed over the surrounding courtyard, towering over pavers arranged in circles around its pedestal, its back to the pillars of the building it guarded. The library had been insulated from the blast by the buildings behind it, saved from destruction by mere chance, or maybe by its length from the city center.

She stood in the growing shadows, between the sentinel and its host, gazing up at the building's façade, savoring the words inscribed over the doorway into the building itself.

That humans had once had the power to build such things and fill them with the wonders of all the world's knowledge...

Her shoulders eased down, relaxing, and she smiled. A quiet contentment sank through her, erasing her fears. It felt like home, standing there with one foot on the bottom step. It felt like welcome.

She stored the sledge in an out of the way spot, where passersby couldn't see, if any made it this far into the city. Dug metal and bone picks out of her satchel, shrugged it onto one shoulder. The steps were smooth and wide, carved mechanically, she imagined, and set together by the finest stone masons. Jal had said the front doors were intact and locked, and so she found the glass doors now.

No trouble to unlock them. She'd learned that decades before, in Uptown, under the tutelage of Duchamp himself, before age had confined him to Shanty and the baobab throne. These doors were different than the wooden and metal doors she'd unlocked with her tools before. They were thick glass framed in black metal. The lock was much the same

a simple deadbolt, easy pickings

but when it was taken care of, she had to pry the doors open, and that took some doing. She was sweating by the time she'd grunted and heaved and pushed one side open far enough to slide inside. Rusted, stuck. She slipped into the cool, dry interior and dropped her hands to her knees, her head hanging as her breath panted in and out of her lungs. Whew. Time sure had a way of jamming things up.

The thought tickled a faint memory of a story Duchamp had once told her, in long ago days tinged with heat and sunshine and the lapping of water against the ripa's banks. She let it pass from her mind, unexamined, and pushed the library's door shut behind herself.

Then took out her tools and locked it back by feel, on an impulse that came and went so quickly, it barely touched her heart.

The soft whisper of readers past reached out and wrapped itself around her. She rose slowly and felt her way deeper into the library, her arms outstretched in the growing gloom, sliding her feet in front of her along the smooth, polished floor, one foot then the other.

She bumped into tables, apologized under her breath, felt her way around them. Wished for a torch, but flame would be too dangerous here, in the dry remnants

spines burning down to ember

and she couldn't bring herself to risk the library, now that she'd found it.

Some time after she'd entered and her knees and shins were bruised with all the bumping she'd done, soft lights flickered on overhead, illuminating the room. Her gaze snapped upward, and in spite of the fright it had given her, she laughed at her own silliness. Jal should've warned her that the building was automated and still had power of some sort.

Maybe he'd wanted her to discover the wonder of it herself.

After a moment, she nodded. Yes, it was better this way.

She turned in a slow circle, studying her surroundings. It was surprisingly orderly, as if someone had come through only the week before and cleaned it. In front of her, opposite the entrance, a long, wooden desk curved in a half circle, bracketed at the edge of the light's glow by wide staircases ascending to an upper level. Signs hung over the desk. One read "circulation" in big, bold letters. Another had broken and twisted around, obscuring the text.

She approached the desk and stood on tiptoe, wondering if she dared go around and explore behind it, to learn of the men and women who'd worked there, overseeing the great stores of knowledge held within the library's confines. A buzzing sound filled the air, coming from behind the desk. She dropped back on her heels just as a hologram popped on, rising through the dusty air in the form of a smiling woman dressed in sharply white clothing.

"How may I help you?" the woman said.

Edith's tongue clung to the roof of her mouth for longer than she'd ever admit.

"How may I help you?" the woman said again, and this time Edith found her voice.

"I'm looking for..." She paused. What was she looking for exactly? Books, certainly, but of what sort? Farming? History? Something to detail the wonders of automatic lights and people appearing out of thin air?

The woman smiled. "Let me access the catalogue for you. If you need further assistance, just say so and I'll come right back."

Edith nodded, then cursed her own stupidity. The woman wasn't real. She couldn't see Edith or react to her, could she?

The woman faded away and was replaced by a giant question mark, then it, too, faded and an image of a book appeared. The book flipped open, its pages rippling in an unseen breeze, turned by unseen hands. Finally, it stilled and settled on a page, which slowly enlarged until it filled the hologram's width with a box hovering above rows of letters.

"Ah," Edith said, stumped. "Can't you just point me to the

history of the war?"

The woman appeared above the box, her image smaller, but still smiling. "Which war would you like information on?"

"The war that..." Edith paused, considered the time frame. The old calendar had been forgotten. How much time had passed since the bombs fell? Did the library even hold information from that period, or had the people here had time to gather it before they fled the city?

"The last war?" she said at last.

The woman smiled again. "The last war for which we have books are the skirmishes of the early twenty-first century. Are you interested in these skirmishes?"

"Not those. A later war."

The woman's image froze for a moment, as if she were thinking, then the image flickered once and she said, "Perhaps I could direct you to the newspaper archives?"

"If it pleases you, then I'd like to go there, yes."

Five minutes later, Edith was upstairs, having followed a trail of lights embedded in the floor to her destination. The room the holographic woman had led her to was filled with ancient machines bearing the faintest hint of dust along the tops of their screens. Rows of cabinets sat to one side, each drawer marked with tiny, typed letters. She pulled a drawer open, stared at the neatly packed white boxes, and closed it again. If the answers were there, she would never find them, as she had no hopes of learning the secrets of both boxes and machines in her first go.

She turned instead to the newspapers scattered across the tables of the two sitting areas, and to the rows of newspapers hanging from bamboo rods against the wall. Beyond that, opposite the machines, were large, bound volumes labeled in gold lettering on various colored covers, but those could wait. She needed the most recent news first.

A copy of *The New York Times* dated August 21, 2036 caught her eye, not least because of the headline splashed across the front page.

WASHINGTON FALLS!

Edith's brow puckered into a frown. Was that a person? A place?

She slipped the satchel off her shoulder and set it on the floor, then knelt at the round table and gingerly picked up the newspaper. The pages were brittle in her fingers, dry. She held her breath as she carefully unfolded the pages and spread them in front of her across the table. The words were a tiny, black scrawl decorating the yellowing pages, sorted into columns, interspersed with black and yellowish pictures.

She squinted at the text, leaned closer for a better view. The overhead light brightened, startling her. How had it known she needed more light?

No, she thought. That wasn't important, not just yet. Plenty of time to puzzle such marvels out.

She leaned closer to the newspaper again and began to read, slowly at first as she adjusted to the size of the text and scope of the story unfolding, skipping unfamiliar words

come back to them later with a book of words, had to be one here somewhere

absorbing the history of the last days of civilization.

Into the night she read, until her eyes grew dry and dusty as the pages in her hands, until she could scarce prop them open. Then she curled up on the floor with her satchel as a pillow and slept, dreaming of a nothing so great, it filled her mind with its blackness.

THE LIBRARY held her attention for another day. She poured through old newspapers, piecing together the war's culmination, then skimmed backwards through the days and weeks and months leading up to the end of it all.

In between, she skimmed the stacks, weaving through tall shelves filled with more books than she'd ever seen. Small, circular mechanical beings wove along the floor, sucking up what dust there was. She followed them for a time, grew restless with their meandering paths, and instead focused on the titles printed across the spines of rows of books.

Once, she pulled a book from its shelf and flipped it open, running her fingers along the smooth, white pages, searching for the feel of the words themselves. It smelled of must and ink, of summer days and the mineral scent of a fresh rain.

The holographic woman appeared at the end of the aisle, beamed down from the ceiling perhaps. "Would you like to check that book out? We can hold it at the front desk until you're ready to leave."

A cart rattled slowly up the aisle toward Edith, and she stared at it, bemused. The wonders of this time, the sheer majesty of the gadgets. How much easier had life been for these people? How much smoother had their lives run?

Elias's voice echoed to her from memory

long ago, there was Big City, and it was an evil place

and she shivered. He was wrong. She felt no evil here, and if there was evil, it was not within the heart of this building.

Objects could not hate, only people.

Carefully, she replaced the book, aligning its spine with the edge of the shelf. Plenty of time for it later, when she'd studied what was needed. Plenty of time for learning after she brought news of this place to Shanty.

* * *

THE NEXT MORNING, bright and early, Edith pried the front doors open, locked them behind herself. Her head was full to bursting, bouncing between news of the before days so rapidly, she was dizzy from it. What would she tell Hamisi? How much should she share, how much to hold back? What would Duchamp think of it all?

Her steps were slow as she retrieved her sledge and picked her way along the empty streets toward the place where Jal said the printing machine was housed. The day was gloomy and dank. Dark clouds blocked the sun, threatening a storm later. Edith paid them no mind. She'd have shelter soon enough, and besides. The land needed rain, here as much as anywhere.

The sledge's runners ground along the broken sidewalks, scraping weeds and detritus away. She became aware of an echo of footsteps behind her, following at a discreet distance, only when she stopped to rest her shoulders. The noise halted, and she twisted around, water pouch held at her side. The streets were empty behind her, save for a stiff breeze heralding the arrival of a steady rain. She heard that, too, bearing down upon her like an army of pellets hurled through the air.

If she called out, would the person following her answer?

The rain hit her before she could decide. She ducked into the recessed doorway of an abandoned store

half price, everything must go!

dragging the heavy sledge in behind her, and waited out the storm, half curious whether the one following her would catch up or remain lagging behind.

Perhaps they wondered where she went. She had no reason to hide herself, except from the Gospel men.

She hunkered down in the doorway watching the wind drive the rain sideways onto the street beyond the doorway. She'd emptied her satchel of books, and wished for one now to pass the time. Instead, she waited and watched, and studied the contents of the abandoned buildings across the street.

When the storm paused, she heard the footsteps again and waited for them, unafraid of what the sound would bring. Still, she brought her skinning knife out, held it loose at her side. Unafraid didn't mean unprepared.

Through the glass fronted shop, she caught the hazy figure of a man. When he stepped into the doorway, hands up and open in the gesture of peace, she nodded at the Gospel man who was not Elias, but Elias's companion. He was a big man, like Elias, bulky and muscled in the way of them toiling under hard labor. Plowing fields, maybe, or pulling sledges laden with raw materials. His dark hair was shaggy but clean, and his eyes were a piercing gold under thick eyebrows.

"Wanderer," he said, respectful.

She nodded. "Fabler. Shanty whence?"

"Ya-ya. Hamisi sends word, asked me to watch for you on dingus path."

"We're far from the path."

"There is always a new path."

She nodded again. That was true enough. "You've watched for me. Duty done."

His mouth clamped into a firm line within his beard. Not an unfriendly expression, merely a thoughtful one. "You're looking for the other printer. We couldn't get it to work."

So the Gospel men were the ones using the first printer. She kept her counsel, waiting for him to continue, or to leave, which she thought she might prefer.

It occurred to her then that she'd been alone on the trail too long to well tolerate the company of other humans. Perhaps that's why she never tarried long in Shanty. Even her kin, her mother, were too many to bear.

The man's hands eased down to his sides. "I can show you."

"I know the way, fabler."

He grinned at her then, and the expression morphed his face from gently stern to handsome. "I know it better. Come on, now. I can haul the sledge for you. Least I can do, after Hamisi's hospitality."

"You bring her some good meat," Edith said, sharp as cut flint. "That's trade enough."

"Ya-ya," he replied, easy now, still smiling. "But then I'd miss the company of a beautiful woman."

"Pshaw. Naught but flattery."

"Naught but truth."

And because his words felt honest, she let him take the sledge's harness, adjust it to his broader shoulders, and guide her to the printing machine so she could judge for herself whether it worked or not.

THE GOSPEL MAN lead her through the city, down broken streets into overgrown alleys. Kenzo was his name, and it fit, much as Edith fit her. He came from a place where men gathered, some seeking refuge from the harshness the world had become, others simply because they had nowhere else to go.

"The men of our village," Edith began.

Kenzo's voice softened. "Hamisi told us. It's the same up and down the ripa. Men leaving their women, fleeing the withering sickness. The wasting away."

"Why didn't they return?"

"Even now, men have their pride."

That made no sense to her, but Kenzo seemed reluctant to say more, and she was likewise reluctant to push for answers.

Maybe she wouldn't like what she heard. What if the men had abandoned their wives and daughters...

She let the thought trail away. *If* was a terrible game to play.

"You've seen our men then?"

He shrugged against the harness, his gaze on the deserted street stretching out before them. "Hamisi didn't say their names. There are other places like ours."

"We miss them."

Kenzo grunted.

"The women have grown weak without their men," Edith said. "Corn needs grinding, fields need plowing."

"You think it's shameful, them leaving."

That gave her pause. "I guess that depends on the reason they left."

"I can't answer to another man's heart."

"Can you answer to yours?"

He stopped abruptly and stood there in the street, his head tilted back on his neck. "You're asking why I went along with Elias."

"I'm asking why the Gospel men are spreading rumors and untruths, aya."

"We're trying to stop the bombs from falling again."

She laughed, hard. "You see any sign of them bombs being built? You see any way we can throw them at each other?"

"If we study the books—"

"We might maybe learn better," she said flatly. "We're dying, Kenzo, dying out as a species. Dying out as communities. Amaris was the last child born in Shanty, and me near on a decade and a half before her. How long you think we can go on without children being born? How long do you think we can survive?"

Slowly, his piercing gaze met hers. "I'm fertile."

His words stirred heat in a place she'd thought dead. She pushed down the need, meeting him with a challenge instead. "You going to repopulate the entire earth?"

"Only my part of it." He turned to her full on, beseeching.

"Come to the Gospel, Edith. Lay with me and bear a child, be a part of the rebirth."

She laughed again, softer. "The rebirth we need lies in books. We can build on that, protect ourselves. Learn the old ways, aya, but follow a different path. A better one."

"You really think people won't walk down the same dingus path?"

"There's more than one path. You said so yourself."

"Clever woman." He grinned, shook his head. "You could still lay with me."

"I don't take Amaris's leavings."

"Who said I was her leavings? Maybe she's mine."

"Now who's being clever?"

"Seems the only way to deal with a woman like you." He shook his head again and leaned into the harness. "We'd best get moving, we want to find that other printer before sunset."

She let him start forward, leading the way a few steps. The heat he'd aroused in her lingered uncomfortably on her skin, and though she tried not to, her thoughts returned again and again to the idea of carrying a child within her womb, at long last.

THE STORM waxed and waned throughout the afternoon, delaying their progress. They wound up sheltering for the night in the lobby of an abandoned building. Kenzo told her a tale she hadn't heard before, of monkey and gator on the ripa. Edith vowed to carry it back to Duchamp for his ever-growing collection of stories.

"You make an able fabler," she told Kenzo.

They'd huddled together without a fire in the dank recesses of the lobby, against a stout wall. Wasn't quite cold enough for a fire, wasn't quite warm enough without one. Kenzo had encouraged her to sit close, arm to arm, where his larger body could shelter her. She would've been a fool to decline.

"I like stories," he said. "The wilder, the better. Elias says stories should have a kernel of truth in them, but I like the ones that stray far afield the best."

Edith kept her counsel about Elias and his kernel of truth. If ever a man needed to be acquainted with the full truth, it was Kenzo's brother. "That's why I like books. They hold so many stories, so many journeys."

"Ya-ya."

She searched for a hint of disapproval in his tone and found none. "If I had the paper, I'd write down Duchamp's tales."

"You should, someday."

"Reckon there's paper at the print shop?"

"In plenty. If I'd known you wanted it, I would've..." He laughed, a slow, soft rumble. "Would've made a good trade."

"Paper for a baby?" she said, arch and a little sly.

"Paper for stories." She felt him shake his head, resettle against her. "There's more to the world than making babies."

She grunted, yawned, rubbed her face against his arm, searching for a softer perch for her head. "More than stories, more than babies. There's more in the world, Kenzo, more than we ever dreamed."

"Dream now, wanderer," he said, and she drifted away on sleep's winding ripa.

I'M TOO OLD to bear a child," she murmured later, still half asleep.

"What, thirty winters, aya?"

"Thirty-three."

He laughed softly, bussed the top of her head. "Old woman."

"Feel old sometimes." She yawned and shifted against him. "Old as the mountains. Old as the ripa winding through the desert."

"The world is young yet. Look. There's the dawn."

Her eyelids refused to open, for she was warm and comfortable and drowsy still. "Not yet," she said, and he laughed again, and the sun rose without them.

THEY MADE the print shop when the sun reached its zenith, high overhead. It beat down upon them through a thin layer of hazy clouds. Kenzo stashed the sledge, stretched his arms overhead, and sighed gustily. "How do you stand it, woman?"

Edith had already climbed the dingy, broken concrete steps leading into the building, around a stout poplar that had taken root in a crack and now towered above her. "Stand what?"

"Hauling this thing around." He kicked the sledge gently and frowned down at it. "No wonder you've got no fat on you. A man likes a woman with a little padding."

She laughed and turned away from him. "What woman can rest long enough for her body to grow soft?"

"My woman," he muttered under his breath, but she ignored his grumbling and tried the door. Kenzo could find another woman to cushion his rutting. What did she care?

The print shop was molded and overgrown, much as the outside had been. She stood in the doorway overlooking a machine that was as mysterious to her as the dark of the moon. Beneath the rust lay a power she could feel down to the marrow, but it was long dead now, crumbled away beneath the ceaseless march of time, barely sheltered by the building falling into ruin around it.

Kenzo moved behind her, brushing his body against hers. "I'm sorry."

"Why?"

"You wanted it to work."

"I wanted to see it," she corrected gently, though she couldn't quite suppress the disappointment in her voice. Yes, she'd hoped for better, but at least now she knew such things truly existed. "Was the other one like this?"

"No, it's different." He hesitated for a moment, and when he spoke again, his words dropped between them, carefully spoken. "It's smaller, less complex in some ways, more in others. We found a book that helped us fix it. One of the Gospel men knew how to power it."

Edith nodded. "As easy as harvesting wheat, then."

He laughed, and his laughter echoed around the ruins. "As easy as that."

She waited for his mirth to end. "Can it be salvaged?"

"Everything can be salvaged, if you work hard enough at it."

He sounded like Duchamp, and so, she bit back a scalding response. Strange how the old man's teachings could reach her even here.

"We've heard tales," Kenzo said. "Of other cities, other machines. Could be a way to fix this one."

Other cities! The thought stole her breath. She'd known it was a possibility, somewhere deep in her mind, but she'd discounted it, or forgotten, or ignored it in favor of the path before her.

When had her world narrowed to the stretch of dingus path marking Shanty and Uptown and the other settlements in between?

"Or another one somewhere," Kenzo continued, "in better condition."

"I want to print books again." The words burst out of her, like a seed sprouting into sunlight. "I want people to read again, not just me, not just the few here and there. Everyone."

His hand skimmed up her back and came to rest on her nape. "Elias will stand against you."

Let him, she thought. She glanced up at Kenzo's profile, wanting, of a sudden, for him to be different. "And you?"

He jerked his chin at the machine. "Why is this important?"

She let her gaze drift to the silent machine, laying dormant under the decay and ruin. If she listened hard enough, she could almost hear the clack of paper running through the rollers, of ink being pressed onto the surface, of people standing nearby overseeing the process. She could almost smell the sharp pinch of it all in her nostrils, and the beat of anticipation in her gut as the first page landed at the end and was read.

And in the reading, enriched the world with its goodness.

Kenzo's hand twitched against her nape, bringing her back from the past. She shook her head, unable to articulate the feelings and thoughts rumbling around inside her. "It just is."

"I think I could study you for a thousand years and never understand you."

She glanced around and up and found his gaze on hers. His eyes glinted in the light streaming through cracks in the roof, and were unfathomable.

"I have something else to show you," he said, his voice rough and gentle. "Near the base of the mountains outside the city."

"Away from the road back to Shanty."

"Ya-ya. Some sights are worth the journey."

"Some things are," she agreed, but she was thinking of this machine and others like it, and not of his hand against her skin.

KENZO LED her out of the city toward the mountains, hauling the sledge behind him as if it weighed no more than an infant in a sling. Her own shoulders were straighter for the lack, and she was grateful to him.

Though they were on a journey of his making, not hers.

She calculated the time since she'd last left Shanty, tamped down the kernel of urgency prodding her to return as quick as she could. There was more here to see, more to learn, and a good chance of trade along the way.

Trade was always good.

They talked little, rested less. The path was wide and packed hard, as if many feet had trod it, and wound away from Big City through long fields of knee-high grass. Bison grazed there, roaming in herds so large, Edith's eyes grew round.

"Good eats?" she asked Kenzo.

"Good eats, good fur, good bones." He shot a sly smile at her. "For the right woman."

She pshawed him

persistent man, clever, clever

and trained her gaze on the forest blanketing the foot of the mountains. Smoke rose in thin curls, reminding her of the growing cold. She would've asked Kenzo about the smoke, but he'd sidestepped every question she'd peppered him with.

The last question had been met with a gruff, "You never had a surprise before, woman?"

She'd pulled a face at him, one a child would make. He'd laughed good-naturedly and made a face back.

The playfulness, now. That had surprised her.

Now, though, with the mountains growing tall against the sky

elephant must've climbed these

and smoke rising from the forest's canopy, she had an inkling of his big surprise.

Or thought she had until they reached the forest's edge and she saw what lay beyond.

"Kenzo," she breathed, for there in a clearing stood houses made of hewn logs and mud chinking with rock columns climbing one side. She'd never seen the like, only heard of them from stories in books or from fablers and wanderers.

Six in all, she counted, of varying sizes spaced far enough apart for privacy. Not like Shanty, where the hovels huddled close together like children whispering secrets. There were small plots for gardens, she thought, surrounded by stacked rock walls and split wood fences. Tufts of plants grew within, none she recognized. Not enough for a proper food plot.

She vowed to wiggle the details of it out of Kenzo before nightfall.

A horse roamed the clearing, tearing up dying grass and vegetation with strong teeth. This amazed her so much, she nearly dropped her satchel and ran to the creature for a good pet. She hadn't seen a horse since a wanderer brought one through when she was, oh, five or six winters old.

"I thought they died out," she murmured.

"Sturdy creatures," was all Kenzo said.

He finally stopped near a small, round structure situated roughly in the center of the clearing. The base was a round wall of stacked rock capped by a shingled roof. A handle was affixed to one of the posts holding the roof up and a sturdy rope dangled down into the walled circle.

She peered into it, discovered a bucket. The scent of cool water and dank drifted to her. Kenzo's hand gripped the back of her tunic and tugged her away from the wall when she leaned too far over, trying to catch a glimpse of the depths.

"A well," he explained, "for water. Easier than settling near a ripa, if you've the proper tools to dig one and know where to source the water."

She glanced up at him, as amazed by this as by the horse. "Everyone gets water from the ripa."

"Everyone who lives near a ripa gets there water there," he corrected gently. "We want to live here, we have to find another way to get water."

He let go of her tunic, shrugged out of the harness, and left the sledge there, near the well. She, in turn, dropped her satchel on the sledge and hoped the horse wouldn't eat it.

"Three men live here," Kenzo said as he walked toward one of the log houses. "Me here, in this house. The other buildings are for storage, and over there is a barn for the horse. We're hoping to trade for a cow or two, some lambs or goats."

"You're making it a proper settlement."

"Naught doing. There's a proper settlement up the path a ways. This is our home. Two or three men to a grouping, for safety and shared labor."

"Men only?"

"Ya-ya, to the date." He stopped in front of one of the houses, gazed up at the dark, shingled roof. "This is a long tale. Rest with me inside. Eat, have a shower."

"A shower?"

He grinned at her over his shoulder. "A bath standing up, in clean water from the well. Hot water piped through metal tubes to a cistern attached to a wood stove."

"That's where the smoke comes from," she said, and couldn't help the wonder in her voice.

"That and from cooking, and for warmth. It gets colder here than in Shanty. The mountains..." His voice trailed off and he shook his head. "Time for that later. Come. Welcome, friend."

She followed him up sturdy chinked rock steps, through a door made of planed wood, into the house Kenzo had built, her mind full to bursting with the questions tickling her tongue.

THE ROOM she stepped into had a rough wooden floor and a ceiling a good two feet over the top of Kenzo's head. The walls had been smoothed over with plaster, seemed like. At the far end, on a layer of rock, a rusted hunk of metal squatted with a newer metal box attached to the side. Heat radiated off it.

The water heating contraption Kenzo had told her of.

There was a small wooden table, four spindly chairs with reed-woven seats

like Hamisi's baskets

and a braided rug underneath. To the right, beyond the stove, was a doorway covered with worn cloth rather than a door. This, at least, was familiar. None of the shacks in Shanty had a proper door.

Shelves lined that wall, filled with books and simple pottery and crocks. She wanted to pry, to open the lid of each one and test the contents for herself, but it seemed rude. Humans had forgotten so much, but not the courtesy of a visitor in someone else's home.

He'd been polite enough when he'd visited Shanty with his brother, whatever the words he'd spoken.

"Talk first," he said gruffly, "or a good cleaning?"

Her first instinct was curiosity

a bath standing up, in clean water, not the muddy ripa

but curiosity was two-pronged. There was the wonder, the marvels, the surprise on the one side.

And on the other were the questions.

"How long have you known of such ways?" she asked.

"My father's father," he replied, and pulled a chair away from a table. "Sit. This will go easier then."

"Is it a hard talk we're having?"

"Mayhap." He waited for her to sit gingerly in a chair, then pulled another one up in front of her. "My father's father's father, really. Too many fathers, a few generations back. He foresaw the bombs falling, gathered supplies, carved out a home for himself at the base of the mountains, and waited. When the first bomb fell far away, he took his family there. His wife, a daughter, and a son."

"Your grandfather."

His eyes gleamed pleasure. "Ya-ya. The father of my grandfather had stocked his new home with books and tools, medicines, food, seeds. Animals. The horse is descended from stock he and his family nurtured through the coming winter until today."

A breathless knot was gathering in her chest. "You've had these things all along."

"Some. We were waiting."

"For what?"

"For the right time. For the men to grow restless with their lot, for the women to grow restless with their men. For signs of spring and renewal."

"How long since you built the house?"

"A few winters."

"And the men you were raised with?" she asked, her voice sharp and high. "Did you teach them these things? Did they learn of wells and clean water and horses and tools?"

The pleasure had died from his gaze. He watched her carefully now, cautious. "We did, all that we knew."

"And yet they left their women to squalor in shanties where we dug in the land hoping the ripa wouldn't flood too high this year and wash away our homes." Her fingers clenched into fists in her lap, and her nails dug into her palms, drawing blood. "They left their women to starve, to eke out a living, to trade for meat with their bodies if nothing else was at hand. They left them childless, riddled with guilt and suffering, to live in luxury here, in the mountains, among plenty."

He stood slowly and gazed down at her. "The women could've come, too."

"How?" The word burst out of her, sharp as a chiseled stick. "How were we to know?"

"When we deemed it right. When we had built these homes and laid back enough food and knowledge for the women to want to come."

"What woman wouldn't want this?" she shrieked, and he knelt in front of her and covered her fists with warm, calloused palms.

"What woman?" he said. "We're going out, now that we've made homes for the women of our choosing, for their kin and neighbors. We're clearing land around the settlement, up the forest path, for more houses and fields to plant."

"But we must accept the Gospel," she said, her voice strangled and bitter. "Accept the Gospel as Elias says, or battle starvation on the ripa."

"No," he said, firm. "You're welcome here with or without acceptance."

She looked at him, at last, looked right into those golden eyes. "To be your whore."

"No," he said again, still gentle. "Be my woman and live here, or don't and live in one of the other houses. I'll build you one, if none are to your liking."

The angry bitterness drained out of her, leaving her tired and weak. "Why would you do that?"

"Because we need the women as much as they need us." He shifted in front of her, squeezed her hands. "We weren't meant to live apart. We weren't meant for men to gather in one place and women in another."

"Stronger together," she murmured.

"Together, aya." He squeezed her hands again, emphasizing the word. "Not apart. Be my woman."

Her mouth curved into a tremulous smile. "Told you, fabler. I don't take Amaris's leavings."

"Then don't. I never lay with her, not fully. One time, yes, just to hold her, just to see." He barked out a laugh, shook his head. "Too sharp for my liking."

Humor filled her, and she laughed, too. "You like your women with a little padding."

"And a gentler tongue." His hands fell away from hers and he stood. "My brother is welcome to your kin. I'm for a different path."

She nodded mutely, let him pull her to her feet. He showed her how they'd built the stove, where they filled it with water, and how they carried it to the bathhouse through pipes. Her thoughts buzzed in her head, like a swarm of bees over clover. Before he gave her a roughly woven towel and a cake of soap

trade with women up the way, such fine soap

and showed her how to work the shower, as he called it, she knew what she had to do next.

THE SOAP smelled of milk and honey, and the water of rich minerals. Edith would've stood under the heated waterfall forever, if Kenzo hadn't warned her of the heater's limits.

She lay beside him that night, her hand on his chest, feeling it rise and fall as he breathed. Innocent enough, it was. Just to see what it was like. Just to know.

When the sun crept above the horizon and long fingers of pale light stretched across the path into the clearing, Kenzo rose and helped her pack the sledge in the cool mist clinging to the yard around the well.

He gave her a wood box filled with soap wrapped in cloth and leather. "For your kin, or for trade, if you have a need."

She took the box and held it against her stomach, cradling it as if it were a child. How could something so small and ordinary feel so precious to her? "Thank you, Kenzo."

"Will you be back?"

If she'd been a meaner woman

sharp as broken glass

she would've left him to wonder. But Edith was not a mean woman. She was not Amaris with her coy words and sly glances. "I'll be back, Gospel man."

"Let me go with you as far as Uptown." He glanced away and down, along the path leading back to Shanty. "Watch over you."

Her mouth twitched into a smile. "Been keeping myself safe these many years. Reckon I can keep on doing it now."

He nodded, as if he'd expected her to say such. "You don't come back, maybe I'll come looking for you. Bring you back whether you want or not."

"So desperate for a woman now, are you?"

"Just the one woman," he said gruffly.

She wanted to ask what she'd done to deserve his regard, but the question died on her tongue before she could speak it. He took the box from her, packed it carefully on the sledge. Helped her slip on the harness and fit it to her smaller back. The horse wandered over and nudged her with its head, and tears sprang into her eyes.

A horse. Soap. Hot water and a settlement and men to help with the plowing.

It was too much. She pushed the horse away, gentle, and leaned into the harness, pulling the sledge steadily out of the clearing. Kenzo laid a hand on her arm as she left, let it slide along her skin and fall away. She had no words for him, none that would move beyond the knot tying her throat shut.

There was more to this world than trading and stories, more than words writ on pages or spake into the air. More than woman alone could do, aya, and more than man alone.

Ahead of her, the sun rose full and round, and beyond, the women of her kin waited in Shanty for news of the beyond.

THE JOURNEY to Shanty was long. Kenzo had told her of a way shorter than going back through Big City. A shortcut, he said, less dangerous than the way she'd come.

Fewer Gospel men, she thought. No Elias with his forked tongue and twisted stories, no women burning books until the spines glowed red. No lies for her to walk around.

She puzzled over Kenzo as she skirted the ruins, puzzled over the union he wished to make, or not, as she chose. Puzzled over her own desire and the needs of her kin.

At last, she decided, knew, that she would've wanted him without the soap and hot water.

Which amused her no end.

Gospel man or no, Kenzo had a good heart. How he knew he was fertile, she hadn't asked. There was time for that later, time for them to know one another, if he still wanted her when she returned. If he still thought she was worthy of his heart when she told him of her plans.

She reached Uptown with the box of soap cakes intact, having traded baskets and furs and some meat from a stag she'd taken down along the edge of the forest. No time to dry it. Better to trade than to waste.

From Uptown, she could almost taste the ripa beckoning her home. Her steps were more urgent now, more hurried, and her gut clenched tight under the weight of the sledge. Duchamp was a constant presence in her dreams, his aged voice weaving between visions of monkey and cheetah and elephant and the others. Between mountains and sun, and ripa and fields of tall grass where bison roamed freely around cabins made of wood and stone, bearing the marks of men determined to rebuild the world.

She smelled the smoke before she saw it, and saw it before Shanty came in view.

And when she was close enough, saw the baobab stump sitting empty under the noonday sun.

She shrugged out of the harness, left the sledge where it was

hurry, now, hurry, what's wrong, where is he

and cried out to the fabler as she stumbled into a run, her voice strangled and small around the worry clogging her throat.

"Duchamp," she said. "Grandfather!"

Hamisi ducked out of her cardboard and rusted tin home

no more, mother, there's something better waiting for you

her shoulders sagging, her tunic ragged. She wailed when she glimpsed Edith and held her arms up and wide. Edith ran to her and gripped her arms and breathed Duchamp's name.

Hamisi shook her head and turned her gaze to the healer's hut. Edith saw him then, stretched out flat on his back atop a blanket laid across the dirt courtyard.

"No," Edith said, and ran to him, dropping to her knees beside him. His skin was ashen, more ghost than man. Lines of dried blood closed around deep, bruised cuts in his face and head. The other women gathered round, forming a wide circle, all save one.

Hamisi sank to the ground beside her, planting her knees in the yellow dirt. "Daughter, my daughter. Where have you been?"

"Trading. Learning." Edith shook her head. "What happened?"

As one, the women turned and parted, like the Red Sea before Moses, and in the gap they left stood Amaris's hovel.

Rage flooded Edith

ripa overflowing, water rolling along the dried earth

and she stood and staggered toward it, pushing women out of the way

flooding through Shanty, consuming their homes

and her throat opened up, letting loose her anger in long, hoarse yells. She reached Amaris's tiny home and yanked the tattered cloth door aside, leaving it to flutter in the wind

swirling around the women's ankles as they fled the ripa's pull

and reached inside and yanked Amaris off the mat where she'd been resting *the waters receding, claiming years of labor as its own*

and dragged her into the courtyard. Pushed the younger woman down next to Duchamp and grabbed her hair, yanking her head back so Amaris was forced to look at the damage she'd done.

"This," Edith screamed, unaware of the tears rolling down her cheeks through a layer of dust and grime. "Why?"

Amaris's eyes glittered defiantly. "He carries knowledge, evil, evil knowledge, just like them books."

Edith's hand drew back and lashed out without a second thought, and she slapped Amaris hard across the cheek, drawing a line of red blood. Hands slid along her arms and caught, tugging her back, and the women's murmurs rose around them, like the wind.

No, careful now, she's with child, mind the babe.

Edith froze, her face twisted into an unrecognizable expression. "Elias?"

Hamisi whispered, "Ya-ya, the Gospel man. He come along after you left..."

But Edith was no longer listening. She'd heard what she needed to hear, heard it and in the hearing, her anger had died.

She'd known this would happen, known it in some part of her mind she'd refused to examine too closely. If Kenzo was fertile, it stood to reason that the other Gospel men were, too. She should've questioned him more deeply. She should've spent more time listening.

No, she thought as her gaze drifted to where Duchamp lay dying. If she'd taken more time with him, she would've gotten here too late.

"If not for the babe," she said slowly, "I would have you staked out on the edge of the ripa, on your back where the water would cover you during the tides."

No one spoke or moved, not even Amaris, though her eyes were round with horror.

"You murdered this man," Edith continued. "Murdered an innocent who nurtured and protected you. A man who fed you from his own hand, hunted for you, clothed you. For what? The false Gospel?"

She turned to the women and looked each of them in the eye, one by one, as she had done many times before. This time, she was the fabler, the one they would look to for justice and guidance, for the stories that had always given them the truth of life and death and everything they'd ever needed.

"I've been to Big City, to the mountains beyond." Edith stretched her hand out, pointing to the sledge where it lay abandoned on the edge of Shanty, near the baobab throne. "I've seen the old machines, the rubble left by the bomb, and I've seen the edge of the settlement the Gospel men are building at the base of the mountains.

"We were good once, a good people. Good hearts, here in Shanty. That didn't change when the men left, and it won't change now that they've come back carrying the lies of another age."

"Lies," Amaris said, spitting the word out. "What know you of lies? Their words are just as good as the ones you speak."

"No," Edith said, gentle now. "I know why the bombs fell. I've read the papers carrying news of such things, and I know what the before times were like. What they were really like, not what Elias has said."

The women were silent for three slow beats of Edith's heart, then Hamisi squared her shoulders and stepped forward, her chin held high. "Tell us of the before times, daughter. Tell us of the bombs falling and of men and women and Big City."

So Edith did, spreading out a tale of discord and envy, but also of the beauty of that world. The books filling row upon row of shelves, the machines that wrought magic, the buildings so sturdy, even a bomb couldn't knock them down.

And she told them of her plans, of bringing the machines back to life, of printing books and teaching others to read. She told them of Kenzo's house and the horse and well, and of soap so fine and lovely, it melted on your skin.

When her words ran dry, the women bent their heads together like wheat ripening under the sun, and whispered of the wonders Edith had carried down dingus path.

A dry, croaking voice, thin and unsteady, drifted to them. Edith glanced down and met Duchamp's wavering gaze, and knelt beside him once more.

"Granddaughter," he said.

She took his frail hand between her own. "You should rest. Gather your strength."

"No strength. The sun will take me soon."

"Hush now," she said, but his hand fluttered in hers, halting her admonishment.

"My son...not deserve you."

"Your son," she murmured. "My father?"

"Ya-ya. Stupid...boy."

Hamisi's hand fell to Edith's shoulder and squeezed. "Enough of that, Duchamp."

Duchamp wheezed out a rusty laugh, coughed, and blood spattered his lips in tiny droplets. "You found the...library."

"I did," Edith said. "It was glorious, fabler. You should see it."

"Did, once. Long...time." His voice petered out, rose again. "Men...fell asleep, then. Forgot to wake."

A laugh sputtered out of her, though her brows furrowed. "Another story, fabler?"

"Always a story, girl. Always a..." He choked and coughed, and the healer bent and rolled him onto his side.

Too late. Duchamp's coughing died out on a long exhale. His body stiffened and his spirit fled, searching stories in the beyond.

Edith rose slowly, her vision blurred by tears. "Goodbye, old man. May you journey where the sun always shines and the ripa never floods."

There was no wailing for his passing, only quiet tears and remembered stories. Edith dug the grave herself, leaving the other women to sort through their meager belongings for the ones they would need on the journey to the Gospel men's settlement.

Not all Gospel men, she was sure, and of those that were, she hoped only a handful clung to those mistruths so steadfastly they could never know the truth. For it was truth she intended to spread, once she'd laid her grandfather to rest.

Her grandfather in truth, though she had always afforded him the honor out of respect.

Amaris would bear the babe and the babe would be given to a new mother, then Amaris would be banished to the wilderness where her tongue could do no more harm. And if she died, Edith would not miss or mourn her, for even a good heart has its limits.

The women would find men, even Hamisi, and the library would lend its wisdom to their growing village. And in the spring, they would plow new fields and sow new seed, and tend to their gardens, and winter would never find them again, so long as they loved and laughed and remembered.

Silver Birds

The last working airplanes were shot down five months ago over Missouri. Well, the last planes that a pilot dared to take up anyhow. My birds worked just fine, thank you very much, and would as long as the parts held out. I tinkered with them every day to make sure they were ready when we needed them.

When, not if. My mind shied away from the thought of never taking to the air again.

Lem stood beside me, his gaze drifting over the makeshift cemetery where we were laying what was left of Bobbi Turnbull to rest. He wore polarized aviator glasses and had his thinning carrot-colored hair slicked back in a bouffant do that'd make Elvis proud. For today's solemn occasion, Lem had pulled out his cleanest bowling shirt. It was red with black sleeves and collar, and had a fancy emblem sewn into the back that read, "Benson's Bowlers."

The shirt was his grandfather's. The rest was all Lem.

"Dearly beloved," he said, casting his voice into the breeze dancing around the airfield. "We're gathered here today—"

"That's for weddings, Lem," I said.

His pale, freckled skin reddened, almost matching the color of his shirt. "I know that, Iz. Can't you see I'm doing my best here?"

I stuck a tongue in my cheek and tried not to smile. He *was* doing his best. It wasn't that Lem was slow, just that he was brilliant in a specific way and the rest of him was never going to catch up. I would've suggested digging a Bible out of the Cap'n's office, God rest him, but that would've sent Lem off on a tangent and we had work to do.

For one, a hole the size of a '72 Riviera had opened up on our one and only runway last night and it needed mending.

Lem picked up where he'd left off, intoning a solemn speech intended to guide Bobbi's soul into the afterlife. Outside the fence, a flock of griggs darted among the marsh weed. They were about the size of a Labrador retriever, but looked more like birds in their blue and green plumage, with their narrow orange beaks snapping closed on thin air.

Nasty little critters. After the rift opened off the coast of Florida and kaiju poured through and decimated the local human and large game population, the scavengers came through and picked at the bones. Gone were the spoonbills and the herons, the 'gators and the terrapins. We'd managed to catch some marsh rabbits before they were gone and raised them in cages in one of the hangars, but the rest of the animals in this area were extinct.

And everybody'd always thought humans were bad.

Lem sniffed and swiped the back of a hand across his nose, bringing me back to the present. "She shoulda never gone outside the fence."

I laid a hand on his bony shoulder and squeezed. "We needed to eat, Lem."

"That don't make it right."

He sniffed again and rubbed at his eyes, and I let my hand fall away, giving him what time I could to pull himself together. It was just him and me now, a snot-nosed kid who'd just lost his best friend and a middle-aged woman with arthritis in one hip.

Overhead, the sun burned down on us, and the roar of the Atlantic Ocean drifted across the island, not quite drowning out the triumphant squawks of the griggs as they pecked at the pieces of Bobbi we hadn't been able to find.

LEM AND I drifted away from the makeshift cemetery on the leeward side of the airfield, well away from the fence so as not to tempt the predators nosing around outside. Bobbi was the fifth of us to pass on, the fourth to be buried in the loamy sand, but I didn't like dwelling on it. The past was there whenever we needed it, and otherwise a distraction from the dangers surrounding us.

I jogged to Cap'n's office, mindful of my hip, and marked Bobbi's burial date on the whiteboard, to the right of the day she'd died. The office was largely untouched, a memorial to the one member of our ragtag band of survivors whose body we'd never found. What did we need with navigational maps and whatnot now? Couldn't fly no more, could we? And the rest was just stuff.

My own space was part office, part bedroom, part library. I'd commandeered it when the rift opened and I'd been grounded out of necessity. God knows, I'd wanted to try for home. Cap'n had talked me out of it, then risked his own fool neck in a desperate flight for help when an amphibious kaiju flopped inland past the beach and ground half our main runway into chunks.

Crazy bastard. He'd been a pilot during Vietnam. Got shot down and captured. Spent a coupla years in a Viet Cong prisoner of war camp and came out the other side with a bad limp and a spine pared down to steel. Maybe that's where the gumption came from. It sure hadn't come from running a tiny airport in the Golden

Islands.

I shimmied out of my good shorts, pulled on worn coveralls over a t-shirt and panties, then shoved my feet into work boots and tromped off toward the runway with the laces flopping against the ground.

It happened like this: Long ago, in a land far away, I did the smartest dumb thing a kid could do and enlisted in the Air Force. Airplanes had always fascinated me and...

No, you don't want it from the very beginning, so let's do the long story short.

Long story short, I went from working on cargo planes in the Air Force to learning how to fly the birds I worked on. It wasn't such a huge jump from hauling soldiers to hauling parts, especially if you were willing to start small, and I was. I hitched on with a hot shot company out of Atlanta, delivering cargo that *just had to be somewhere* in a hurry.

And that somewhere something had to be on the Day of the Rift was here, in St. Simons.

We felt it open up. Thought it was an earthquake shaking us around inside the terminal. To this day, I've never heard how it happened. What force was big enough to open up a hole in the Earth large enough to let a beast the equivalent of Godzilla step through?

A pretty big one, I figured.

Maybe somebody'd worked out the logistics. If so, we hadn't heard about it. That was Lem's end of things. The brilliant part of him knew communications inside and out, just like I knew my birds inside and out. He'd spent the better part of the past five months since Bessie knocked down the tower trying to fix the comm.

Bessie didn't eat the Cap'n. She's a pescatarian, far as we can tell, an oversized cross between a whale and a walrus, a monstrous beast with a snout full of whiskers, thick gray-brown skin, and a thicker layer of blubber. Thankfully, she only comes ashore once a month or so. I think she gets lonely. I sure do.

I tapped the picture of me and Cap'n pinned to the wall above my bed for luck, then walked out of my office slash bedroom slash whatever. We'd been friends, before. More than drinking buddies, less than lovers. You make enough runs to the same landing strip and you're bound to wind up with friends. Friends good enough to face the apocalypse together. Good enough for him to risk winding up as sushi over. Good enough for me to watch over his grandson, now that Cap'n had flown into the Great Beyond.

My heart jittered and shrank in my chest and tears threatened to well over. God, I missed that old coot.

We'd had contact with the outside world just once since then. That's how we learned about the Missouri fiasco. It happened a coupla weeks after Cap'n went down. Some fool decided to make a last stand and sent up half a dozen fighter jets to take out a monstrous armored beast we'd nicknamed Porc for the missile-like quills quivering along its spine.

The parallels in evolution would've been funny if the kaiju weren't so damn big.

Anyhow, those quills are deadly. We'd seen a Porc in action on the Day of the Rift. Kaiju on kaiju, a Porc versus a Rex. Rex won and took up residence on a neighboring island where it'd been nibbling on the remains of Porc ever since.

As for those pilots, I hope they ejected before their jets were skewered by a giant quill missile.

THE THING about Lem is, he's a good kid. Not a kid in age, but a kid at heart.

Which makes us a matched pair, by my reckoning.

Even a good kid has bad days. I figured this was going to be a bad one.

The airport was built in the thirties on the site of an old antebellum plantation. Over the years, the island had grown around it, filling the land with houses, businesses, and tourist attractions. Resorts, hotels, and the like. The Seaside Golf Course lay between one end of the main runway and the Atlantic. Or used to, anyhow. Bessie had taken it out on her first inland adventure, the day Cap'n decided to be a hero and fly for help.

Sheer luck had kept the other airport buildings intact. God above knew Bessie had the aim of a half-blind pilot drunk on Jamaican rum. Bless her, but she always aimed for that one patch of land where the main runway once lay, maybe because there weren't any buildings between there and the ocean.

We'd gotten the fence up afterward, both times, which was a small blessing. It kept the griggs out, and the griggs held the other scavengers at bay.

I found Lem in his hangar, still wearing Cap'n's lucky bowling shirt. He was staring glumly at what we'd managed to salvage of the comms from the ruined control tower after Bessie flopped her way back into the ocean on her second visit. He'd already fed the rabbits and was treating them to Elvis courtesy of his turntable. Bluesy rock drifted through the air, tempting my own legs to jitter into a dance.

"Ready to move fill dirt?" I said.

Lem's gaze didn't so much as flicker away from the mess of wires and rods and busted electronics spread out in front of him. "Why'd she have to go and sit on the tower anyhow?"

I sighed and squatted beside him, mindful of my creaky hip. "Bessie's just an animal like any other, Lem. She didn't know any better."

"She shouldn'ta done it. She shoulda just stayed in the ocean with the fishies."

Just like Bobbi should've stayed on this side of the fence. He didn't have to say it again for me to hear it in his voice. "Any luck with the ham?"

"No."

"Wireless?"

His gaze snapped around to me. "You know I ain't got no control over that fool internet. Dang telephone lines is down, Iz. What'm I supposed to do about that, huh? You tell me what I'm supposed to do about that!"

I laid a hand on his scrawny shoulder and rubbed gently, soothing him. "I know, Lem. I'm just asking in case you figured something out."

And to try to distract him from Bobbi's death. We needed communications the same way we needed food and water. It's not like the post office had any mail carriers running routes between here and wherever people had managed to create toeholds against the kaiju, assuming we could figure out where that was.

Shoot. At this point, I would've settled for UPS, especially if the driver was cute and wore those sexy shorts.

Lem turned his gaze back to the broken whatnots, still frowning. "I need parts, Iz. Parts and tools and...and..."

I squeezed, forestalling his panic attack. Lem intuitively knew what he needed, electronics wise. That's what made him so brilliant at it. Didn't mean he could always articulate his needs. When he couldn't, it frustrated him to the point of him curling up in a ball and yanking at his hair. It took hours, sometimes days, for him to calm down. I'd learned early on not to let him walk too far down that path, if at all possible.

"C'mon, buddy," I said, pitching my voice low and gentle. "You can run the backhoe today. How's that?"

I'd hoped that would jog him out of his bad mood. No such luck. But at least it got him on his feet and working.

Now, I'd always prided myself on being a self-learner.

Schooling could only take you so far, you know?

But the Day of the Rift had been an eye-opening experience for all of us. You wanted to survive, you had to be a quick thinker, light on your feet, and ready to take advantage of the smallest sliver of an opportunity at a moment's notice.

Take the heavy equipment. When the first kaiju showed up off the coast, Cap'n had taken one look at it and said, "I'm of a mind to do a little shopping, Iz. How about you lend a hand?"

Me, I was all for hopping in a plane and flying as far away from the rift as it was possible to go.

But Cap'n was a practical bird. While everybody else was busy running around like chickens with their heads cut off, Cap'n rounded up a crew, guided us on foot to a nearby construction site, and helped us thieve anything we could drive. It's like he knew we were going to need a bulldozer not far down the road.

Same thing with supplies. While Porc and Rex were duking it out next door, Cap'n grabbed me and Bobbi, and we did a kamikaze run to Harris Teeters in our newly acquired dump truck, dodging kaiju and humans alike. That was before the scavengers popped their ugly heads out of the rift, so it was a little easier then, even though there were more people.

If he'd had the foresight to store extra doodads to repair the comms, I would've thought he was an angel sent by God.

Lem took the backhoe and I manned the dump truck, or womanned it, if you wanted to get particular. Filling that sinkhole would take some finessing. We'd have to pack the earth, hope for the right amount of rain to help settle it (but not too much, mind, or it'd flood the dirt out). Then we'd hope even harder that it really was just a sinkhole. It would take time to get it right, since we'd have to pack it level with the tarmac.

And it had to hold a moving airplane.

I could've fretted about it, but the truth was that we were

working with limited supplies and knowledge. No need to fret over things that were out of your control.

We started digging off the taxiway of our remaining runway, between the fence and the woods. Lem filled the dump truck by reaching the backhoe's scoop over the chain link fence and carefully scooping up dirt.

Sand, really, but there's no quibbling in the apocalypse. He couldn't dig deep. The airport sat at about nineteen feet above sea level, give or take a few inches, and we didn't want to risk the fence. So he'd scoop a little, clumsily dump his haul into the truck, scoop some a few feet down, and so on until we got a quarter of a load of good island loam.

That's the way it was supposed to work.

Today, we'd barely got two half-assed scoops of dirt when we heard Rex making a ruckus next door. And when I say next door, what I really mean is that it sounded like he'd found a way off Sea Island across the inlet into St. Simons proper.

I killed the dump truck's engine and hopped out. Lem had already done the same for the backhoe. We'd run into this problem before and knew exactly what to do: Head for the nearest shelter in the hopes that we got there before Rex spotted us.

If you're thinking that Rex is an oversized tyrannosaurus rex like Godzilla, think again. Rex is a kaijin, a weird bipedal reptile that looks human. Kind of like a merman, but air-breathing.

We thought. Who really knew about these creatures? It's not like we're xenobiologists. Lem swears he spotted gills on the side of Rex's neck, but since Lem dresses like a refugee from an Elvis convention, I'm never sure whether to believe him.

Rex does have one thing in common with his namesake. He doesn't really see you if you don't move, but he does have a propensity for setting his flipper-like feet down right on top of anything shorter than his knees, which the heavy equipment was.

I didn't particularly feel like being squashed flatter than a pancake. Judging by the way Lem hotfooted it toward the terminal, neither did he. Youth being what it was, he easily outpaced me. I hobbled along behind him, moving in a shuffling run meant to save some wear and tear on my aging joints while getting my saggy ass under shelter before Rex reached us.

His steps shook the ground beneath our feet, vibrating right through the soles of our boots. I glanced over my shoulder, glimpsed his iridescent head and shoulders sparkling in the sunlight, and cursed. Not only was Rex on the island, he was headed this way.

The griggs knew he was coming, too. They were squawking up a storm outside the fence, running for bear. Griggs were low down on the food chain, right around where humans were now that bigger, badder predators had appeared on the scene. Their natural instinct was to flee, and flee they did, right into the fence.

I slowed down long enough to watch half a dozen run headlong into the chain, making sure it held. Wham! The fence shook. Wham! Wham! One of the posts tilted inward. My heart leapt into overdrive. If the fence went down, we were doomed. The griggs would overrun us long before we could lock ourselves into a hangar.

Another wham, then the island fell silent except for the booming thuds of Rex wandering seaward, looming ever higher above the town. No more griggs appeared. The fence stayed where it was, nominally protecting us from the smaller beasts. I heaved a sigh of relief and turned into a slogging jog

My arthritic hip chose that moment to seize up.

I cringed as my foot caught on a clump of grass and I went down face first. Dust puffed up around me through the grass's sharp blades. I inhaled and choked, inwardly cursing my own clumsiness. I was graceless on land, had only ever felt at home in the air flying free and easy as a bird.

The muscles around my hip cramped, ratcheting up the ache

in the joint itself, and I cursed again. Hadn't even made it to smooth hobbling on the taxiway.

I twisted around on the ground, searching for Lem. He was already halfway home, but he'd never make it if he didn't hurry. Rex was too close.

I wasn't going to make it at all. No time to get up, sure as hell no time for me to haul my rickety bones down the taxiway to the closest safe building. Rex was gonna get me like he'd gotten the Cap'n, only I was going to die on terra firma, while Cap'n had had the good grace to die doing what he loved best.

Ah, well. It'd been a good run.

Maybe if I just stayed still...

I rolled onto my back so I'd at least have a good view. It was humid and hot, par for the course down here. The air was filled with the salty tang of ocean and the peculiar rotting fish stench of the griggs. The sky above me was nearly cloudless and so blue, it brought tears to my eyes.

'Course, that might've been the dust.

The ground shook beneath me, kickstarting my heart every time Rex set down a flipper-foot. I turned my head toward the last place I'd seen him and nearly choked again. He was right on top of me, towering above the airfield like a statue, facing the ocean. His foot lifted, and I knew, just knew, that his next step would be right on top of me.

I closed my eyes and started praying, not for myself, but for Lem. With me gone, there was nobody else to look after him. Maybe he'd get the comms up and radio for help. Hopefully he had the sense to stay put. We hadn't stored back a lot of food, mostly because there wasn't a lot of food to store, but he had a steady supply of water and the marsh rabbits if he got desperate enough.

A low, booming moan filled the air and Rex froze with his foot lifted for the next step.

I nearly laughed. Bessie had great timing. Maybe Rex would go after her instead, saving my sorry hide so I'd live to see another day.

He didn't go after her. He did, however, turn and walk back the way he'd come. Strange, but I didn't worry much about it. I was too busy being thankful I hadn't been squashed into a blob of blood and muscle.

LEM CAME BACK for me as soon as he hit the terminal and realized I wasn't behind him. Good thing, too, since my bum hip made it nearly impossible for me to get up. It'd need rest and a good soak. Medicine would've been nice, but we were long past that point.

Bessie hallooed again and a thud reverberated through the earth. Lord help us, she was headed this way.

Lem wrangled me off the ground, slung one of my arms around his shoulders, and half dragged me toward safety. "I thought you were a goner for sure this time, Iz."

"Gonna take more than ol' Rexie the Merman to do me in, Lem."

He snorted out a giggling laugh. "Izzat what your last date looked like?"

"Naw," I said. "He had a droopy mustache and his boobs were bigger than mine."

That earned a guffaw. The reprieve wouldn't last long. Lem was bound to remember Bobbi any second now, but at least I'd got him to forget long enough to laugh.

Still just a kid, I thought, then a huge splash drifted to us, probably Bessie heading back to sea, and I knew we'd made it through another day.

***

IT TOOK a week for my hip to stop hurting long enough to risk patching that hole in the runway. Meantime, I hobbled around the planes, updating my to-do list for maintenance, opting for shade whenever I could, which wasn't often. We'd been hit at a slow time for the airport, in the dead of winter when sensible tourists stayed home and locals did what they could to make ends meet until the busy months. Not many aircraft had been on the ground on the Day of the Rift, so it wasn't like I had a lot of work to keep me busy now that summer was upon us.

All the more reason to do it right.

I didn't have a favorite. I really didn't. The plane I'd piloted down was a Cessna 172, a reliable standard. My boss had just picked it up used and wanted a shakedown run, and I'd only had a single package to deliver for a friend of his here on the coast. Seemed like an easy thing. Fly down, drop off the package, cajole Cap'n into buying me supper, fly back to Atlanta. Easy peasy.

Shows what I know.

At any rate, the planes now under my command ranged from personal aircraft like the Cessna to small passenger jets, including a Bombardier Challenger 300 abandoned by a wealthy businessman.

By abandoned, I meant eaten by the griggs during the first scavenger melee.

Cap'n's personal bird was an '81 Piper Seminole he'd picked up for a song from a guy who knew a guy who, well. Cap'n had connections. Let's just leave it at that.

The 'Nole was a real beaut for all its age. Streamlined and polished to a shine so bright, she glinted silver from a distance. Immaculate engines, and I should know as I'd examined 'em up one side and down the other for Cap'n before he bought her. I'd never taken her up myself, but he'd told me I could anytime I wanted, just to get a feel for her.

I never had. Now that he was gone, it just didn't seem right, especially since he'd opted to leave her here when he'd flown for help. Or tried to.

Plus there was Rex, who was batting one thousand where aircraft were concerned.

When I was feeling really down, I'd take a bottle of Four Roses and climb into the cockpit, remember what it felt like to soar through the air. My heart ached like I'd lost a lover, I missed flying so much. About as much as I missed the cap'n. Liquid gold in a bottle. The stuff was so precious, I only allowed myself a single sip, but that single sip smoothed over the jagged spots, made the ache a little easier to bear. I could still smell him there, in his sanctum sanctorum, more so than I ever had in his office. I guess that's why I sat there, week after week, trying to hold things together, wishing it was him in charge instead of me.

Cap'n'd know what to do. Cap'n always knew what to do.

AT NIGHT, Lem entertained me with drawings he'd made of the kaiju and scavengers.

Picasso he was not, but he had a fair hand with his set of colored pencils.

He drew sketches of Rex and Porc, of Bessie and a centaur-like kaiju Lem called Marty. The griggs, of course, which were the most populous of the local scavengers by far, but also the pterodactyls nesting farther inland. We spotted them occasionally, flying seaward in search of fish, or dipping down into the maritime forests if closer game was at hand, which it wasn't much anymore, thanks to the griggs.

There were others. Lem knew them all by sight. I hadn't bothered. We had enough to worry about near the airfield.

It was a shame Rex had done in the only kaiju mean enough to challenge him.

On the other hand, he was the devil we knew. There was a lot to be said for that.

At supper each night, we made the most of what we had. That was a tradition Bobbi started when we realized we weren't getting off the island. We used a tablecloth and real silverware she'd scrounged up from God knew where, and candles and cheap china from Walmart, because that's all we had.

Bobbi had been our cook until she went out searching for fresh food to supplement our dwindling supplies. Before that, she'd handled the airport's finances. Still a baby by my standards, not much older than Lem, but had a heart of gold. A bright, shining star, was our Bobbi.

I cut off those thoughts and tried to concentrated on the conversation with Lem. He was rambling about the parts he needed to fix the comms. Mostly, he was filling dead air. The sun was close to setting. We were holed up in the kitchen in the fixed-base operator building. It was just the two of us, alone on the island with only the griggs and the distant crash of waves against the shore for company.

I'll admit it up front: I drifted a little while Lem was talking. Had my feet propped on the seat of another chair, trying to ease the strain on my hips while my mind calculated how long I could drive the dump truck the next day so we could finish patching the runway. I wasn't paying a bit of mind to him, so imagine my surprise when the part of my brain that was still working cottoned on to the direction he'd taken the conversation.

"And I think," he was saying, "we could take the Piper and make it to BQK, and they'd have parts—"

My boots hit the floor with a thud to rival Bessie's. "We're not flying to Brunswick, Lem. That'd be suicide."

He scowled at me, his face more freckles than skin. "I thought that was why we was fixing the runway in the first place, so we could go get help."

"We're fixing the runway," I said, enunciating carefully so he wouldn't misunderstand, "so if we have a chance to leave, we can."

"Cap'n'd let me try it."

"Well, Cap'n's not here, is he?"

I bit my words off before I said something one of us would regret.

Too late. Lem's face crumpled into misery and tears. "You're a mean heifer, Iz. Just a mean ol' heifer."

He scooted back his chair and walked away, leaving his plate on the table still half filled with fried spam and sautéed dandelion leaves.

"Lem," I said.

He waved a hand at me over his shoulder without turning around, and I sighed and put my feet up in the chair again. I'd talk to him tomorrow, sort things out when we'd both gotten some rest.

EARLY THE NEXT MORNING, while the sun was still pushing through the island mist, I rolled out of my cot groaning. Long day ahead of us. Better to get it out of the way before Lem decided to hijack one of the planes.

I'd seen the way Lem drove. No way was I letting him sit in the pilot's seat.

I figured on trying his hangar first, but the minute I stepped outside, I heard the rumble of heavy machinery. A few minutes and a lot of limping later, I found him working the backhoe, steadily dumping half scoops of dirt into the bed of the dump truck.

Which suited me just fine.

I waved to let Lem know I was there, then climbed behind the dump truck's wheel. We worked the morning away, filling that hole, tamping down the dirt, layering more on top. Worked right through lunch, my stomach grumbling the whole time. What the hell. I could always feed it later.

Long about mid-afternoon, we finally got enough dirt in to call it even. I stood looking down the runway, measuring the distance from each end to the hole. Damn thing had opened up near the middle, rendering the entire runway useless no matter which way you were going.

But if we could get this dirt tamped down and the land didn't sink any farther, there was a good chance we could use the runway again. *When* we needed it, not if.

I clapped Lem on the shoulder. "Good job on the backhoe."

He blushed and ducked his head. "Aw, Iz. I just didn't want you to be mad at me no more."

"I was never mad," I said, and that was the truth. "What's say we open up that pack of bacon in the freezer, have us a real treat."

"We was saving that for..." Lem's gaze drifted to the ruined runway, set at an acute angle to the one we'd just fixed. "You reckon he'd mind us eating it without him?"

How could I tell him his grandpa wasn't coming back, ever?

I shoved aside the memory of Rex casually batting Cap'n out of the sky with a webbed hand, of the plane twisting out of control, of the crash and the smoke and the knowledge that Cap'n couldn't have gotten out even if he'd had a 'chute with him.

"He wouldn't mind a bit," I finally said.

Lem nodded and grinned easily, his expression wide open and so guileless, my heart ached for him. "Ok, then. Last one in has to cook."

I laughed and let him run ahead. Lem was a lousy cook anyway, and I didn't mind getting splattered by bacon grease if it meant seeing him smile again.

* * *

IT RAINED that evening, a long blow of water driven by the wind. I watched it from the lone window in my room, wondered idly if Bessie was enjoying it. Wondered less idly when it would let up.

Thought about checking on the hole we'd just filled and decided to stay put. The damp made my hip ache. After twisting it last week, I wasn't ready to test it again.

Instead, I cracked the window and listened to Lem playing Elvis to the marsh rabbits. I couldn't see his hangar from where I was standing, but I knew he was gyrating like the king himself. Probably singing, too. Those poor rabbits probably didn't know what had hit them.

The rain didn't let up that night, or the next, or the next. When the sun finally popped out again, I'd run through my regular indoor chores and started rummaging through buildings we never used, looking for something to do. Lem knew them all by heart. He'd as good as grown up on the airfield. These rooms were memories to him. To me, they were just something to fill the time.

The hole seemed steady and stable, which was such a relief I didn't blink an eye when Lem broke out into song and dance on the runway, Elvis style. I was happy, too, and I said so, which prodded him into taking my hands and dancing with me.

"Lem!" I said, squealing, and he threw back his head and laughed and said, "We're gonna make it outta here, I just know it!"

I swear, it was like God heard us having fun and wanted to nip that in the bud lickety-split. Next thing I knew, the ground was shaking. Lem stopped dancing on the spot and his grin dropped away.

"Oh, no," he said. "Not again."

I looked around, wildly searching for Rex or another kaiju, but no, it was the big merman himself, the king of the kaiju, walking toward us in long, determined strides. His scales glistened in the sunlight, glinting blue and green and silver, except around his eyes, which seemed oddly human. Water dripped off him, as if he'd just walked out of the water.

Bad for us. We weren't that far from the shoreline.

"Run," I whispered. "Get inside."

Lem's expression set in a determined stubbornness that looked eerily like the Cap'n's. "Not without you, I ain't."

He caught me around the waist and hauled me along with him in a wobbling gait straight toward the nearest building. Lem's a slight thing, as scrawny as a sapling, but he was young and he was strong, and I was no match for him. I looped my arm around his shoulders and tried to keep up, and Rex kept marching on, coming closer with every step.

There was a great, big splash. Bessie, probably, and I was almost relieved. Better the devil you know, and Bessie wasn't such a bad devil. At least she'd never tried to eat us.

We hadn't quite made the nearest building when Rex reached the airfield. I thought for sure we were goners, I really did. He was a sucker for movement, and we were as spastic as a couple running a three-legged race with potato sacks over our heads, blinding us.

I looked up, just to check. He hadn't noticed us, probably because he was half-turned toward the ocean, watching it instead. There was another thud, heavier than his footsteps, and a screeching moan. Sounded like Bessie on steroids, but we made the building then, Lem's hangar, and I was almost afraid to peek out again.

Which is how I noticed the Cap'n's Piper. It was sitting smack dab in the middle of the hangar, so I would've noticed it sooner or later, but it was out of place. The 'Nole was usually parked outside. When had Lem brought it in?

Why had Lem brought it in?

But I already had a notion of the whys, so I let that go even as he dropped my arm and scurried toward the Piper.

Rex's footsteps veered around the airfield, thank God, but we weren't out of trouble yet. Bessie wasn't far behind him, though what could've driven her out of the water was beyond me.

"Iz!" Lem hollered. "C'mon! This is our chance!"

I hobbled toward him, cursing my aching hip. "What in tarnation are you going on about, Lem?"

"Rex and Bessie." He yanked the wheel chocks out of the way and stuffed them inside, behind the front seats. "Wouldja hurry the heck up, Iz? We don't got all day."

I was almost at the 'Nole by then, close enough to wince when one of the chocks scraped over the paint. "Careful there, Lem."

He shot me a wide-eyed look. "We're gearing up to get outta this place and you're yelling at me to be careful?"

I stopped dead in my tracks, still a good ten feet from the airplane. "We can't get out of here. Have you forgotten about the giant merman currently tromping around outside?"

"That's what I was saying. Gee whiz, Iz. You're usually quicker'n that."

I raised my eyebrows, lifted my hands in a *what are you talking about* shrug.

"Rex and Bessie," he said slowly. "Ain't you the one always going on and on about how Bessie is a fish eater?"

"A pescatarian, sure. What's that got to do—"

"And how Rex is a merman?"

"Rex is a…ooooh."

I nearly smacked my forehead. How could one woman be so dumb, when the obvious had been staring me in the face the whole time? Rex was a kind of fish, and Bessie, well. She was wild about her fish. I'd sure seen her fill her great moon of a belly with them enough, before the scavengers popped up and we were pinned down inside the airfield's fenced-off perimeter.

"Take the co-pilot's seat," I said, and pushed myself into a painful jog, then up into the cockpit. Lem was right. This was our chance to hightail it out of here, while Rex was too busy fighting off a hungry Bessie to swat us out of the sky.

Lem was already climbing in and reaching for the headset. "I done packed us some supplies, in case it come to this."

Like grandfather, like grandson. "Bless you and all your forefathers."

"Set the rabbits loose, too," he said. "Weren't right keeping 'em caged like that."

Like we'd been caged, albeit in a bigger cage. Bobbi wasn't the only one of us with a heart of gold.

I slipped my own headset on and ran through the quickest pre-flight check I'd ever done. Wished for half a second that I'd been able to plan our flight, file a flight plan, but who was left to file one with now? It would've been nice to push the 'Nole outside first, too, but that was a luxury we couldn't afford. I was fine with it, once the engines roared to life and vibrated into my hands through the controls, and my heart filled with anticipation.

I was fine with anything when I was behind the controls.

We rolled out of the hangar down the ramp onto the taxiway. Lem swung his head around, searching for Rex and Bessie, and I concentrated on getting us off the ground. The runway loomed ahead, like she'd been waiting for a chance to send us off. Rex's roar filled the air, drowning out the engines even through the headset.

I lined the Piper's nose up with the markings, let out a soft prayer. Then we were off and running, steadily pushing the plane's limits in a bid for airtime and freedom.

"Get 'im, Bess," Lem hollered.

I didn't bother looking around. Bessie could take care of her own, and me? I was taking care of my own, too, doing what I'd always done best, in the air, where I belonged.

ACKNOWLEDGMENTS

Many thanks and much appreciation to the following, without whom (or what) I could not have completed this collection.

It's no secret that I spend a great deal of time at airports. As mentioned in the introduction, many of these stories were written while I was parked near the Greenville-Spartanburg International Airport in Greer, South Carolina, watching airplanes land and take off. It's one of my happy places and being there usually results in a very productive writing session. Plus, it makes a pretty handy social distancing spot.

I visited two other airports during the writing of this collection, the McKinnon St. Simons Island Airport in St. Simons, Georgia, and the McGhee Tyson Airport in Alcoa, Tennessee, just outside Knoxville. Both were heavy inspirations for post-apocalyptic stories, though only one of those stories made it into *Apocalypse Weird*.

Subscribers of my old Dreaming If newsletter read and commented on several of these stories as I finished them and willingly provided feedback and support. Their input was invaluable. A very special thank you to reader Elizabeth Pruett, who never fails to offer encouragement.

Dave Boyd let me pester him on innumerable occasions about the details of air travel. His comments provided some of the groundwork for the setting of "The Infinite Bright." Any errors in interpretation are my own.

Stan Pressley read an early draft of "The Wandering Man" and encouraged me to finish it. When the zombie apocalypse gets here, Stan, you know where I'll be.

Jim Matthews helped me identify potential markets as well as serving as a sounding board for the details behind a couple of the survival situations in various stories. Again, any errors in interpretation are my own.

Richard E. Hopkins, Jr., has tirelessly served as my editor for the past seven years. I usually give him more lead time, but with *Apocalypse Weird*, the timeline was so tight, I'm not sure how he managed to edit the stories in time. That's what makes a great editor: He came through for me in a huge way, and I am deeply grateful.

Amy Ledford, Richard's girlfriend, threw her support behind me from the beginning, when she and Richard first started dating. She listens when I'm stuck, gives hugs as needed, and opens her home to me when I need inspiration. I owe her some mega pumpkin products for this one.

And finally, my family, who tolerates my creative process, doubly so when I provide desserts. This short story collection could not have come about without their support as individuals and as a family. Special thanks go to my father, who let me borrow his loaner truck when I hit a deer and wrecked my own vehicle (several stories were conceived, written, and polished in that truck); my son Caleb, who is my continual inspiration and foundation; my sister DeeDee and my niece Bailey, who helped me brainstorm apocalyptic scenarios; and my nephew Bryce, who served as a sounding board for the ramblings that eventually became some of the stories contained herein. "Silver Birds" in particular benefitted from his listening ear during the long drive back from a lockdown vacation in St. Simons.

Thank you all for your love, support, and inspiration. I couldn't have done it without you.

C.D. Watson
September 2020

ABOUT THE AUTHOR

C.D. Watson lives in Cashiers, NC, where she weaves dreams for a living, in between knitting badly, road tripping often, and rounding up her pet alien, aka her son. She writes under multiple pen names, including Lucy Varna and Celia Roman. Her fiction has been selected as finalists in the Maggie Award for Excellence (Lucy Varna) and the Rash Award for Fiction. Find her online at:

www.cdwatsonauthor.com
www.dreamingif.com

Also by C.D. Watson
Dreaming of a Dark Christmas
Darla the Redneck Zombie Slayer
Romancing the Weird

Did you enjoy the short stories in *Apocalypse Weird?* Get another story, for free, at:
cdwatsonauthor.com/newsletter/

www.ingramcontent.com/pod-product-compliance
Lightning Source LLC
Chambersburg PA
CBHW010348170726
48284CB00011B/2840